PENGUIN BOOKS
SKIN DEEP

Nergis Dalal has been writing for over fifty years. She is the author of four novels, a collection of short stories, a book for children, a cookery book, a best-selling book on yoga and, under the pseudonym Aries, a collection of middles that appeared over three decades in the *Times of India*, the *Statesman*, the *Hindustan Times* and other national newspapers. Several of her short stories have been broadcast over the BBC and published in anthologies in India, UK and Australia.

Nergis Dalal has three children and three grandchildren. She lives in Dehra Dun.

nergis dalal
skin deep

a novel

PENGUIN BOOKS

An imprint of Penguin Random House

PENGUIN BOOKS

USA | Canada | UK | Ireland | Australia
New Zealand | India | South Africa | China | Singapore

Penguin Books is part of the Penguin Random House group of companies
whose addresses can be found at global.penguinrandomhouse.com

Published by Penguin Random House India Pvt. Ltd
4th Floor, Capital Tower 1, MG Road,
Gurugram 122 002, Haryana, India

Penguin
Random House
India

First published by Penguin Books India 2005

ISBN 9780144000326

Typeset in Perpetua by Mantra Virtual Services, New Delhi

Printed at Repro India Limited

www.penguin.co.in

This is a legitimate digitally printed version of the book and therefore might not
have certain extra finishing on the cover.

For Roshen,
without whose help and encouragement this book
might never have been finished.

one

It is a perfect day in February, bright sunshine with a hint of winter coolness still in the air. The mountains, wreathed in mist, seem as elusive as the light that shimmers over them. The hills in the distance glitter with snow, and in this diffused light the trees look suspended, their leaves floating, winged, like butterflies.

I am waiting for Yasmin, waiting for her in this beautiful house, built for me by Ramesh. I don't know why she is coming after all this time. Yasmin—my sister, my twin, my enemy.

Even as a child she was beautiful, and as she grew, everything about her just seemed to get better. Shining nut-brown hair the colour of ginger biscuits, skin of creamy pallor and darkly fringed eyes of a peculiar shade of grey. Strangers looking at the two of us would exclaim, 'Are they really twins? They don't look at all alike,' and Sophie, my English mother, would look at me with a long-suffering expression on her face, as though my dark skin, plumpness and rough curly hair were specifically designed to slight her. Sophie had not yet acquired the stoical attitude of my Parsi grandmother.

Yasmin, so effortlessly graceful and beautiful, made me look, by comparison, both lumpish and plain (even after all these years I am careful not to use the word 'ugly').

The house is beautiful, gleaming with polish and filled with flowers. My house—something that Yasmin, for all her beauty, has never had. My house—far from the over-populated, noisy and dusty city—tucked away in a forest of trees, on the road to Mussoorie.

The air here is clear as spring water, the winds mountain-fresh. The house is hidden behind high walls and tall trees, and is invisible from the road. Noisy, dusty and over-crowded, the town does not penetrate here.

There are only four months in the year which are truly pleasant in Dehra—March, April, October and November. The rest are too hot, too cold, or too wet. Winters are freezing, summers hot and sticky and the monsoons provide one hundred inches of rain in three months.

Nevertheless, these four months are so extremely pleasant that Dehra has an unfounded reputation for being the ideal place for children and retired people.

Yasmin's room is ready, and from the window I look out at the flower-filled garden and the trees forming a green barrier against the world. On the table beside her bed I have placed a bowl of yellow roses, and inevitably I am drawn back in time into the inescapable centre of my haunted mind.

I am a child again, wandering aimlessly in the garden of our house in Hyderabad. It is an old house, eccentrically built, with porches, balconies and terraces jutting out in all directions. It was built by my grandfather when Banjara Hills was still an undiscovered, rocky, sandy area, not the expensive and elite part of town that it eventually became. Hyderabad can be very, very hot in the summer, and the house had been specially built with thick walls.

The garden was Sophie's special domain. Father had brought her here to this house as a bride, and she had spent many euphoric hours among the roses, which reminded her of England: clipping, pruning, spraying and mulching. No one was permitted to touch a single flower without her express permission.

I cannot now recall what small thing had induced my black mood, but I clearly remember the rage I felt as I wandered alone, banished from Sophie's rooms for some minor infringement of her rules.

Although most of the garden was shadowed under the trees, the rose garden was in full sunshine, with the colours of the blooms reflected in undefined splashes. The gleam of the silver secateurs caught my eye as they lay abandoned on the path. They felt cold and heavy in my childishly plump hands. Adjusting the blades with some difficulty and holding them in both hands, I began to deliberately snip off the heads of the roses. It was, I think, early March, and the roses were at their best, great heads of scarlet, pink, orange, white and creamy yellow. There was also a new single plant with exquisite silvery lavender-coloured flowers.

I worked steadily and with total concentration, progressing from bush to bush, adjusting the blades from time to time, so that the roses fell behind me like a brilliant Persian carpet, whose design was none the less beautiful for being unplanned. As I approached the very last bush, I paused briefly to inspect a small, furry green caterpillar inching its way slowly along a petal, and heard at the same time a high, stricken scream. Quickly, I raised the secateurs, intent on finishing my self-appointed task of destruction.

A hand struck me violently on the side of my head. I was flung down and the secateurs torn from my hands. Through the tears (which were not mine), the screams and angry cries, I was taken to my room and locked in.

'Wicked! She is just wicked,' I heard Sophie cry, still hysterical from shock and disbelief at seeing all her cherished roses lying prettily on the ground.

That Father should have chosen to marry an Englishwoman was a great blow to the family and especially to my grandmother, who believed, however mistakenly, in the racial purity of the Parsis in India. She was also an unflinching believer in *khandan*, a pedigreed background which could be traced through the ages back to Persia, from where we had fled nearly fourteen hundred years ago. She also disliked and opposed inter-marriages between Parsis and others; now here was her only son, married to a foreign female.

But Grandma was pragmatic, and had decided to make the best of what she considered a very bad bargain indeed. Sophie had met and fallen hopelessly in love with Father when he was on one of his visits to London to inspect the family's furniture-design department in Knightsbridge. Father was very tall and handsome, and Sophie was intrigued by the fact that his skin was fairer than her own.

Because the Parsi Zoroastrians in India refused to accept converts to their religion, their numbers were steadily diminishing. In a strongly patriarchal system, children of mixed marriages were only accepted into the religion if their fathers were Parsis; in rigidly orthodox areas, even this concession was denied. But young Parsis were not inhibited by this, and inter-marriages had become more and more common.

'There are simply not enough Parsis to choose from,' said one indignant young cousin to Grandma. Although Grandma would have loved to reverse this trend without violating her religious beliefs in tolerance and reasonableness, more and more young people were marrying outside the community. In India they married

Hindus, Sikhs, Jews and Muslims, and from abroad they brought back English, American, German, French, Brazilian and a liberal sprinkling of Middle Eastern spouses. At this rate, Grandma felt, Parsis would cease to exist.

Like the great majority of Parsis of his generation, Father was staunchly pro-British. He believed firmly that the British had been good for India, and would have liked them to stay forever. Grandma too was pro-British, but that did not mean that she wanted an English daughter-in-law when there were dozens of pretty little Parsi cousins who would have been more than happy to marry her son.

If Sophie had expected to be received into the family with effusive delight, she was disappointed. Grandma's reception was correct but noticeably chilly, even as she went through all the proper ceremonies.

The front verandah, porch and stairs had been decorated with fishes, flowers, birds and geometrical designs stamped from perforated tin moulds, and filled with chalk powder. Every doorway was strung with *torans* of flowers and leaves, mostly roses and jasmine. The family were there in full force to welcome the new bride, all of them glittering with jewels and wearing their best silks and crepe-de-chine saris.

Sophie, too, had been dressed in a pink brocade sari pinned securely around her. As she descended from the car and came up the stairs, Grandma was waiting to do the *achoo meecho* ceremony to welcome the bride. A large, flat silver tray was filled with symbols of good luck and prosperity—rice grains, sugar crystals, dried dates and rose water in a *gulabus* made of silver, reminders of our Persian heritage.

Sophie was garlanded, kumkum applied to her forehead and then the silver tray was circled six times around her head. Since Sophie was tall and Grandma tiny, it was necessary for Sophie to more or less crouch on a lower step. Grandma then took a raw egg from the tray and broke it near the doorway to keep away the evil eye. The coconut was circled in the same way over Sophie's head and banged down near the egg. There were cheers as it cracked neatly into two; it is considered very lucky if the coconut breaks at the very first try. Sugar was placed in Sophie's mouth and rose petals and grains of uncooked rice in her cupped hands before she was asked to step into the house with her right foot.

Another larger tray had been prepared with clothes, jewellery and gifts for the bride. Father had already given Sophie a wedding ring, but now Grandma presented her with a huge emerald set in white gold, surrounded by diamonds. Sophie seemed dazzled by all the jewels. There were three-strand necklaces of Burma rubies, lapis lazuli from Afghanistan, and jade from Burma. There were earrings to match, and bracelets of twisted gold set with tiny rubies and pearls.

The bracelets had been made for fine-boned, narrow Indian wrists, and they simply would not slip over Sophie's wrists no matter how hard everyone tried. It is not only that Indians have smaller bones and more delicate hands and feet, but from a very young age little girls are taken to the bangle seller, who chooses bangles which are slightly smaller than needed, and then squeezes and moulds the hand, pressing and massaging the knuckles expertly till the glass circles slip on to rest triumphantly on a narrow wrist. Sophie had large bones with large hands and feet.

We heard all this later, both from Grandma and from Sophie herself. She said it was extremely mortifying to find that the same bracelets slipped so easily on the girl cousins' wrists, while they stuck so stubbornly over her own.

Sophie was not unaware of the correct but chilly welcome she had been given. Like so many people she had expected that Father's family would be overjoyed to find that he had married an English girl. Most white people have this feeling of superiority in connection with coloured people, and Sophie was no different. She had no idea that the Parsis considered themselves the chosen ones—people who accepted no converts to their religion, and who allowed no outsiders into their Fire Temples.

Since Father was the only son, and Grandma old and widowed, he considered it only natural that he should choose to live in the huge ancestral house rather than move to another place.

Father, or JJ as he was known (because his name was Jehangir Jamshed Jussawalla), was by temperament very

8

easy-going and relaxed, but when Sophie suggested that they move out and acquire a house of their own, he was adamant. As long as his mother lived it was only right and proper that they should live with her. It was his duty, as the only child, to take care of her.

We lived in Hyderabad when it was still a princely state, barely affected by the 'Quit India' movement against the British. Like all the other rajas, princes and nawabs who had flourished under British rule, Nawab Osman Ali Khan too felt safer with the British in charge, even though they behaved with the princes like a strict nanny with recalcitrant children; as long as they were prepared to abide by the rules laid down by their British masters, everything was fine, but even a small infringement brought a sharp slap or even worse. They were allowed their palaces, their enormous wealth, their harems and pretty boys as long as they obeyed absolutely the dictates of the Raj.

Hyderabad in those days was a wonderful place to live in—an Arabian Nights' dream of a city, filled with marble palaces, mosques with domes and minarets, and Mughal-inspired buildings flanked by broad avenues and flower-filled gardens; there was enough colour and pageantry here to delight the heart of the most pleasure-loving people. Muslims and Hindus lived together amicably, and the nobles of both communities followed the same elaborate code of manners. A man's honour and his word—izzat and *zaban*—were of paramount importance. I recall the time when a

9

Muslim friend brought Father the gift of a special *attar*. Father stood up and salaamed six times before accepting it.

Parsis had a special niche in the social fabric of the city. We were neither Hindu nor Muslim, but all our names were Persian and therefore Muslim. They too had their Jehangirs.

The Nizam was entitled to a twenty-one-gun salute, and was known to be the richest man in the world. The announcement of the birth of a new prince in the palace would mean the boom of a cannon and holidays in schools and colleges. Since the Nizam's zenana was not inconsiderable, this happened with pleasing frequency. We woke each morning to the sound of the long-drawn *azaan* calling the faithful to prayer. I have always considered this to be one of the most hauntingly romantic sounds in the world.

On the rosewood writing table in Yasmin's room I have placed a silver-framed photograph of two little girls in frilly, starched frocks, white kid shoes and lacy socks, the ribbons in their hair matching the pink and blue sashes tied in huge bows around their waists. I stare at the photograph, trying to see further into its depths, and little by little that hot summer day in June returns.

At first glance it appears a charmingly sentimental picture of long ago—a happy picture of two little girls with skirts riffled by the breeze, smiling into the camera. Only I know that it was not like that at all, and it puzzles me that I should have unearthed this picture from some drawer where it had lain buried for many years.

We were six years old that day. A great deal of fuss was made on birthdays, and one of Sophie's eccentricities was to order all our party-frocks from Harrods. The dresses were identical—fluffy concoctions of lace and organdie, with frills edging the sleeves and neck, and layers of frills on the skirts. The dresses were worn over stiffly starched petticoats and tied at the waist with broad satin ribbons. Yasmin's was pink, mine blue.

For days the two of us had stood in front of the huge Victorian cupboard in Sophie's room, admiring the dresses as they hung on padded hangers, the frills moving languidly under the fan.

Birthday breakfasts were always the same—Parsi rava made from semolina sautéed in butter, and then slowly simmered in milk, flavoured with sugar and sprinkled with slivered almonds and nutmeg. It was then poured into glass dishes and served ceremoniously by Moti, who brought the confection down from Grandma's rooms, where it had been made.

Whenever I make this dish from Grandma's special recipe, it tastes of love, and I never fail to feel that she is watching over me and smiling tolerantly, no matter what I do.

After breakfast we went to Sophie's room and stood in

our starched petticoats, waiting for the frocks to be slipped over our heads and the satin bows tied securely at the back. My mother looked at Yasmin and my eyes turned with hers. Yasmin was a spun-sugar fairy, poised for flight. Her cheeks were tinged very faintly with pink, and her hair flowed down to her waist, polished and shining, like strands of silk.

Sophie said, 'Oh darling, you look beautiful.' Her eyes, and mine too (as though our eyes were controlled with the same set of muscles), turned now to my reflection in the mirror. A faint frown appeared between her thin, arched eyebrows. She bent over and began to tug at a flounce here, a frill there, and then stood up biting her lips.

'Honestly, if you don't look pretty in this, I don't know how you ever can.'

I fought back the tears that sprang to my eyes and put on my stubborn face; I would not show how hurt I felt. All the foolish pleasure I had taken in my appearance vanished. The dress was absurd on me. I was fat, and the frills and flounces made me look like nothing so much as a small, stuffed pig.

Taking our hands in hers and sighing ostentatiously as though defeated, Sophie led us out to the terrace where the photographer waited. Father was there with Grandma and Moti and most of the other servants, waiting for a glimpse of the birthday girls. By this time I was hanging back and doing my best to disappear behind Sophie so that as we came in, everybody saw only Yasmin, who was greeted with murmurs of admiration and delight. I was then dragged out into the light. The silence that greeted my appearance was slight before Grandma came forward and kissed us both, 'How very nice you both look,' she said warmly, kissing us, and Father added, 'Yes, pretty as a picture.'

Two chairs with black satin cushions had been placed against the trellised, rose-covered wall. On these we were arranged, Yasmin sitting as though she had been posing all her life for a succession of photographers, while I was prodded and pulled into place. Photographs were taken from all angles before I could escape, but not before hearing the photographer say, 'I'd like to take some more pictures of this little lady.'

I saw Yasmin preen and giggle and toss her head so that her hair glittered in the sun. No one noticed as I slunk away.

The true heart of darkness has no real physical location, and even after all these years I can find myself there. I wandered slowly down the steps and into the garden. No one saw me go—all eyes were on Yasmin, whom I hated at that moment with a deep, all-consuming hatred; I knew, I was absolutely certain that the only reason that she was more loved was because she was beautiful. I wandered aimlessly in that radiant garden, putting as much distance as was possible between myself and the others. At the bottom of the garden, almost touching the boundary wall at the back, was a small shallow pool, hidden behind tall trees.

This was the more neglected part of the garden. Narrow steps led down to the pool, green with the detritus of decaying vegetation and the bleached leaves of the silver-oak trees drifting down into the pool and surrounding grass.

Here I sat, unconcerned about the dampness or the smell. I was thankfully alone and hidden from the house and the sunlit veranda. I began to idly pluck at the hated dress. To my astonishment the frills came away easily as I tugged, and I began slowly and methodically to rip off the flounces which seemed to be held with only the lightest, most delicate of stitches. Soon I had a pile of glimmering stuff piled near me. I then turned my attention to the sleeves and neck. These were more difficult to pull off, but I persisted till I could add these frills and flounces to my pile. I removed the blue sash from around my waist and yanked the ribbon from my hair. Piling everything together, I waded into the pool. My white shoes and lacy socks were covered almost at once in green, clinging slime, and several frogs leapt out in alarm. I pressed the small pile of frills and ribbons into the water, but they kept floating up, and it took a long time before they became saturated enough to sink satisfyingly to the bottom. After all this exertion I climbed out of the pool, collapsed on the grass, and fell asleep. For many years afterwards I would wake in the night with the same recurring nightmare, except it was not the frills but I who lay there at the bottom of the green, slimy pool as water poured into my open mouth.

The search for me only started when it was time for lunch, and the consequences for me were even worse than the reaction to my snipping off all of Sophie's roses. It was some time before they thought about looking at the bottom of the garden near the moss-covered pool, and it seems that Sophie stared at my strange-looking dress, stripped of all its frills and flounces and resembling nothing so much as a petticoat, before realizing what had happened.

She had hysterics as I was led away to be washed and shampooed, and the frills were pulled out in a bedraggled, wet mess. Scrubbed clean and put into my room, I sat on my bed, stubbornly refusing to cry or say I was sorry.

This memory was to remain one of my most vivid recollections of an unhappy childhood. I did not feel sorry for what I had done, I felt aggrieved and resentful.

I was fortunate that I was not altogether the outsider; for me, there was always Grandma. She saved me from a feeling of emptiness, of being unloved. She gave me the precious gift of love that never alters. I knew that no matter what I did, I was always the one she loved most. There is this widespread notion that children are open and confiding, but no one is more secretive than a child, and no one has greater cause to be so.

two

The train was late. This was not unusual, but today it was more than two hours late. I wondered what had happened. I decided to wait on the verandah with a cup of coffee and Maxi at my feet. When the car finally drew into the porch, Yasmin sprang out and ran up the stairs.

She said, 'Do you know why the train was delayed? Of all things, we ran into an elephant on the track—a baby elephant, which was killed.'

'Oh God! Not again,' I said.

'When the train stopped, the whole herd arrived, trumpeting and blocking the track. We had to wait till the forest people arrived and fired into the air to move the herd, but even then the mother refused to move.'

'This is always happening. The railway line runs right through the reserve forest, and the authorities refuse to slow down the train for the crucial eighteen kilometres.

16

They claim it is an Express train, and that the tourist trade will suffer if they slow it down. For them, tourists are obviously more important than our endangered wildlife.'

Yasmin was wearing black silk pants and a pink roll-neck top. Maxi growled, and she turned to look at him.

'A dog! I never imagined you with a dog—and a mongrel at that. He certainly does not match the house.'

'He is a very special dog, and is the boys' pride and joy. He doesn't likes what you said; that's why he is growling.'

'He looks like a moth-eaten fur rug,' said Yasmin.

'Why on earth have you called it "The Wilderness"?' she said, turning to look at the formally planted beds, the neatly clipped hedges and the green, green lawns.

'When we decided to build here, this place was a tangle of lantana bushes, creepers and trees—the area seemed almost impenetrable. We left most of the trees because Ramesh believed that the only way to build a house was to follow the Buddhist Tantric method. First you allow the site to select you and then the power in the site influences the type of house you build. He believed that there was an invisible psychic energy which could be tapped into to produce harmony.'

Yasmin shrugged as if this was just something esoteric and totally unintelligible to her, and in no way important. I took her upstairs to her room where Ahmed had already put her bags. She exclaimed with delight at the view of hills and forest and at the room itself, with its delicately

tinted walls, its silk curtains and bedspread in shades of
pink and brown. She opened the wardrobe doors, peered
into the bathroom and then flung herself crossly on the
bed.

'Such luxury!' she said, 'I see you even have Grandma's
fabulous carved rosewood cupboards. She left everything
to you.' Suddenly, she caught sight of the photograph. She
snatched it up and stared at it for a long time, sighing as
she put it down.

'Those were such happy days. How loved we were, and
cherished. Who would have thought that fat little you would
end up with all this, and I—I, with nothing.' Her mouth
curved down in a bitter smile.

I ignored her remarks, which for me at least, were
totally without substance. Those were not happy days, at
least not for me. I have learnt with some distress that the
present is often heavily influenced by the past; the past,
present and future interfere and interface eternally with
each other.

Yasmin said, 'The house looks enormous . . . Why do
you need such a big place?'

'Ramesh built it for a family—the boys and the two of
us. Who could have predicted his death—so sudden and so
inexplicable—from a heart attack? And now that the boys
are in school, only I am left here with Maxi.'

Maxi wagged his tail on hearing his name. All the
bedrooms upstairs had views of the hills, and the cloud-

diffused light fell on Grandma's beautiful Persian and Turkestan rugs, glowing like jewels on the polished floors.

Yasmin followed me from room to room, and I watched her eyeing herself in every mirror we passed. Although it was still sunny down here, the hills of Mussoorie had withdrawn almost imperceptibly in a blue haze.

The house fitted snugly into the dense background of trees and hills, sitting back like a large and somnolent animal, at ease in its own protected forest. Sometimes when the mist floated down, the rooms turned into bowers of blue-green light.

My room occupied the whole of the north-west side of the house, and two huge windows faced the forest and hills. From here I could step right out on to the covered verandah and look down on the trees, the flowers, and Maxi gambolling on the lawn. In winter I would sit here to catch the last rays of the sun before retreating inside.

Sipping a cup of chicken soup, I could watch the snows and feel safe and happy.

Dehra Dun can be very cold in the winter, but most houses are built to ward off the summer heat, and cold, snow-laden winds insinuate themselves through badly fitted doors and windows, and through old-fashioned skylights which never seem to fasten tightly enough. My house had been designed by Ramesh to allow summer breezes to cool the rooms, but to keep out the oppressive heat; in winter it was warm inside; in the summer, cool. Living alone, my days and nights were precisely planned for my own convenience. There was no one to tell me what to do or what not to do. I could sleep early or late, spend my day in the garden or inside, reading books, listening to music or birdwatching, which was a new and fascinating hobby.

With Yasmin here I felt the old sense of insecurity, never quite knowing what the day would bring. They say the past is a different country, but my past and my memories seemed to me like the remains of an ancient city in which every stage of development had been preserved in careful layers, and if the layers were peeled back who knew what they might expose?

Yasmin came down the next morning long after my breakfast was over. She was wearing what I supposed could be called a kaftan—a long loose shift, slit up the sides and lavishly embroidered at the neck and sleeves. It was in deep purple, with the embroidered flowers worked in shocking pink. On any one else it might have appeared garish, but on Yasmin it looked stunning.

'What would you like for breakfast?' I asked.

'I never eat breakfast. Just a glass of orange juice and black coffee.'

I shrugged and rang the bell. But Sher Singh intuitively guessed what she wanted and came out with a pot of hot coffee. Yasmin smiled her thanks.

'I suppose you woke up early and tucked into an enormous breakfast,' she said.

'I always eat a good breakfast. It sets me up for the day.'

'So what did you have today?'

'An omelette with herbs from the garden, home-made butter and marmalade, and some coffee with sugar and cream.'

She made a face. 'You always did like to eat. No wonder you we so fat as a child. You are still fat, but somehow it is not so noticeable.'

'I see no reason to starve myself so that I resemble a refugee from a famine area.'

'You mean that's what I look like?'

I laughed. She looked much the same as before, but a little more tired, a little more strained. I had not yet discovered the reason for her visit and she had, so far, said nothing. But she too was thinking of the past. She said, 'Do you remember how Gran used to bring trays of food to your room when Sophie had sent you there without lunch or dinner? I have never forgiven her about the pearls. Never. They should have been mine; Sophie said so. She said they matched my skin.'

It was the day I had been sent to my room for ruining that hated birthday dress, tearing off all the frills and flounces and drowning them in the pool.

'I simply don't understand the child. Only a monster would deliberately destroy something so exquisite and expensive. She does it deliberately to wound me. I can't bear it. I tell you, I can't bear it,' Sophie wailed.

In the background Father tried to make soothing noises. He was a man who valued peace at all times, but I suppose even he found me baffling. He was always kind and he certainly did not approve of Sophie losing her temper or hitting me.

'Well, even though it is her birthday, she can't come down for the party now. She must be punished.' This was Sophie recovering somewhat and turning spiteful. 'Spoiling poor little Yasmin's day.'

Poor little Yasmin, of course, was gloating over the fact that now she could have the stage all to herself. The party was well under way, as I could hear from the shrieks and giggles and the sounds of bursting balloons, when Grandma came into my room followed by Moti, her personal maid.

Grandma was at that time about seventy—small, round, neat and always dressed in black. Her saris, although plain and unadorned, were made from the finest silks, soft and supple. Since grandfather's death she had worn nothing else and no jewellery except her wedding ring. Her hair, sparse and grey, was usually covered. She had a smooth, very fair, unwrinkled skin and she looked mild and totally innocuous until you saw her eyes, which were very bright, sharp and observant.

Her centre was pure Parsi-Zoroastrian—unchanged, untouched—but outside and around her was the modern, cosmopolitan world to which she had adjusted admirably.

22

Zoroastrianism is above all a tolerant religion which does not seek to impose its beliefs and rituals on anyone. Indeed, Zoroastrians refuse to allow any converts into their religion, and in the thirteen hundred or so years since they had arrived in India as refugees from Persia, they had managed to keep their religion and its rituals and temples closed and secret from *pardesis*, or those who belonged to other faiths. No one other than a Parsi was admitted to their temples, nor permitted to take part in the secret rites performed at births, deaths and funerals.

I had never considered whether Grandma was ugly or good looking, she was just Grandma—enormously rich, head of a thriving business and the owner of many houses and properties in Hyderabad including the old and very beautiful house we then lived in.

She entered my room now, followed by Moti, who trailed Grandma like a faithful dog, making sure she did not slip and fall or come to any harm. Moti was carrying a tray covered with a fine linen napkin, as well as a very long cardboard box. She put the tray on the table while still continuing to hold the box. Grandma sat on the edge of my bed and regarded me sternly.

'You have been a very, very naughty child. What on earth did you do to your birthday frock? Sophie will never get over it.'

For some reason we never called Sophie 'mother'. I have no recollection of how this came about, whether as

23

very small children we simply imitated Father, or if it was at her request. It was just something that happened through the years, scandalizing many of our family and friends.

Although Grandma's voice was stern, she had a twinkle in her eye. All day I had been sullen and defiant, refusing to apologize and stubbornly resisting breaking into tears, but now everything came pouring out. I sobbed and sobbed all over Grandma's sari, making it quite damp. No one loved me, I cried, because I was not pretty like Yasmin, and Sophie deliberately dressed me in clothes that made me look ridiculous. I hated those horrible dresses she forced me to wear.

'I looked like a pig,' I blurted out. 'A fat pig.'

Grandma laughed and cuddled me, rocking me in her arms as though I were a baby. She then produced one of her large handkerchiefs, smelling as always of 4711 eau de cologne, and wiped my face thoroughly.

'Now stop crying. See what I have brought for you.' She whipped the napkin off the tray, displaying a large slice of fruit cake, almost black and smelling richly of brandy. There were lots of small, flaky chicken patties and a generous pile of assorted sandwiches. I gobbled up everything except the cake, which I was reserving for later. Perhaps I would only get soup and toast for dinner; you never knew with Sophie.

Food always has a calming, soothing effect on me and I was feeling considerably better when Grandma said, 'Now

24

we have to do some very serious talking. Yasmin is pretty and you are not. That is the way it is and that's the way it will always be. No fairy godmother is going to wave a magic wand over you and give you silky hair and a perfect profile. You can't go through life tearing up things to prove that you are as good as she is. You have to make the most of everything you can do and Yasmin can't—you are clever and can work hard to do better, not only better than Yasmin but better than everyone in your class. Don't try to compete with Yasmin. Be different, make people look up to you because of your exceptional abilities and focussed work ethic.'

There was silence while I, only six years old, pondered her words. I leaned my head against her softness, only half understanding what she had said.

At last I said, 'But you love me best. You love me more than you love Yasmin.' She sighed and rested her chin on my head.

'Now see what I have brought for you in that box. A birthday present.'

I looked suspiciously at the long cardboard box. It looked remarkably like the boxes in which Yasmin's dolls were packed. She had a huge collection of dolls, many of them from other countries. Most of them came from England and I especially hated these dolls, with their wide blue eyes, silky blond hair and pink, pouting lips. I hated them. Insipid, vacuous things with staring eyes and perfect complexions. Everyone knew I hated dolls. Instead I was given books, puzzles, jigsaws of the greatest intricacy, and, of course, chocolates.

Now Grandma took the box from Moti and handed it to me with a mischievous smile. I looked at it with misgiving; if it wasn't a doll, there was something very like one in this long box. Hesitantly I took off the lid and gasped. Inside lay a bear. No one could have called him a teddy bear, he was too large and fierce-looking. I eased him out of the box and clasped him tightly in my arms. His fur was dark and silky, and his black, slanting eyes stared straight into mine. He had round furry ears, like the ears of a lion cub. He was gorgeous and he was mine.

Grandma and Moti were both laughing as I clutched him close to me. 'How did you know that this is what I wanted? Where did you get him from?' I hugged Grandma with one arm while still holding on tightly to my new acquisition.

'Mr Ross brought him from Hong Kong on his last trip. I told him exactly what to look for. I knew you didn't want a Pooh bear!'

Mr Ross was one of the half-dozen or so men of varying ages who came and went on their own mysterious businesses with Grandma. Some were connected with the furniture business, others with investments and still others with her vast properties. All of them appeared to be anything between forty and fifty years of age, all wore business suits, and all were suave and exceedingly polite. To know that the elegant Mr Ross had gone to Hong Kong specially to look for a bear for me was gratifying.

'What will you call him?' Grandma asked.

From the moment I had seen him I knew that I would name him Attila, thanks to Father who liked to read aloud to us children every night to counter, as he put it, the vast amount of whimsical children's fare that we were imbibing in the way of fairy tales and stories of animals that talked and humans who grew wings.

His choice of reading material was eccentric in the extreme, but most small children love being read to. We sat on either side of him on the divan in our room as he read us stories of Alexander's conquests in India, and of the first Afghan war in which the British sent an army of 15,000 men and 35,000 camp followers to replace the ruling Dost Mohammed with their own choice, and from which only one man returned from Kabul to tell the story. I often pictured that lonely figure riding back when 50,000 of his comrades lay dead on the battlefield.

A story I was particularly fond of and which I forced Father to read to us again and again was about Attila the Hun and his hordes, who swept through much of Europe and Russia, forcing the aristocracy of Russia to act as slaves to their Mongol master. 'The blood of the Russians today reveals the story of their subjugation,' ran a sentence which I loved.

There was a colour picture of Attila astride a sturdy pony, wearing what looked like a felt hat, a long coat and high boots. He had slanting, enigmatic eyes and an arrogant expression; perhaps Nijinsky and other Russian ballet dancers got their eyes from him. The picture fascinated me and I returned again and again to stare at that proud, fierce face.

Yasmin too enjoyed being read to but she invariably fell asleep, leaning her head against Father's arm, looking peaceful and happy.

Grandma said, 'Attila seems a good name for him. Now see, I have another present for you. Today I gave Yasmin the Chinese bracelets for her birthday.'

The bracelets were famous, and Hyderabad's jewellers would have given anything to get their hands on them. Made from 22-carat gold in a filigree pattern, the bracelets had dragon-head clasps with tiny ruby eyes. Although they looked so fragile, they weighed fifty grams each and were heavy and solid, perfect for small-boned Indian hands.

Great-grandfather had traded extensively with China and helped the British in their opium wars. Opium exports proved to be extremely profitable, and many of the aristocratic, rich Parsi families had made enormous fortunes in this trade. For the most part, the Parsi traders owned their own ships and maintained very large fleets, but they were careful that the ships were always captained by Europeans. Many of the old Parsi families brought back a lot of jewellery from China, including pink, white and green jade.

Now Grandma extracted from a small velvet pouch the pink Basra pearls—three long strings of perfectly matched huge pearls, lustrous and tinged with pink. Sophie had once been allowed to wear them for some important reception at the Nizam's palace and according to Father, she had wandered around with a look of dream-like seduction on her face. Everyone wondered what had caused the transformation. They seemed to lend some of their soft glow to the wearer's skin, and had a magical effect. Sophie would have given anything to keep them, but after the reception, they went straight back into the safe.

Now Grandma opened the clasp and fastened the pearls around my neck. I was wearing a cotton nightie with a round neck, and the pearls gleamed and shimmered as though lit from within.

'They are yours, Naaz. Now they belong to you. I will leave them with you tonight and tomorrow I will put them back in the safe.'

I threw my arms around her and hugged her tight. No matter what had happened before, my birthday had been totally transformed by Grandma into something very, very special. I knew how valuable the pearls were, how special.

Left alone I padded over to the mirror and stared at

myself. It was my first experience of the magic that jewels could create.

I was sitting on my bed, Attila clutched under one arm and the pearls still around my neck, when Sophie and Father came into the room. Sophie was now probably full of guilty feelings which she had about me anyway; she had probably decided, with a little nudging from Father, that it was time to forgive the naughty girl who had perhaps been punished too severely on her birthday.

She saw the pearls at once. Her eyes narrowed and her mouth tightened into a thin line. Since my own mouth was full of fruit cake, there was nothing I could say.

'What on earth are you doing with those pearls? How did you get them?' Meanwhile, Father had caught sight of Attila. 'I say, what a splendid bear! Did Mother give him to you? Can I hold him?'

I put Attila into his outstretched hands. 'His name is Attila,' I said, swallowing the last of the cake.

'Is it indeed? Very appropriate with those slanting eyes and fierce look.'

Turning to Sophie, I said, 'The pearls are Grandma's birthday present for me. Attila and the pearls.'

Sophie was so angry she could hardly speak. She whispered, 'How dare she. She undermines everything I do.'

Father said placatingly, 'Yasmin got the Chinese bracelets, it is only fair that Naaz too should be given

30

something equally valuable; it is her birthday too you know. And she has been punished enough.'

Sophie sulked for days. She knew she could never have worn the bracelets, but she remembered how she had looked when she had worn the pearls.

three

Until the day Yasmin got married, I had led a more or less invisible existence. We could both be standing in the same room, within touching distance of each other, but no one saw me. All eyes were riveted on her, and if it happened to be the first time, there were gasps of astonished delight. I couldn't help wondering what infernal power had created twins so grotesquely different.

I recall the time we both wore saris for the first time. It was a family wedding and Grandma thought this was as good a time as any for us to make our first appearances in saris. We had been allowed to choose from Grandma's huge collection. Yasmin had selected a pink silk with gold embroidery, my choice was a family heirloom—a hundred year old *gara*—a wine-red Chinese silk, hand-embroidered all over with flowers, vines and exotic birds. Although most of the embroidery was done in white, there were touches of brilliant colour in the heraldic plumage of a bird, the scarlet petals of a flower, and the parrot-green of vines and leaves. The embroidery was so close and fine that very little of the background silk showed. Each sari had taken six months to complete.

Foreigners seem to think that every Indian girl knows how to wear a sari from the day she is born, as though some esoteric knowledge had been implanted in our genes. The reality is very different. To wind six yards of silk, cotton or satin around the body in a particular manner, without the help of a single stitch is very, very tricky. While, predictably, I clutched frantically at trailing ends and pleats that kept unravelling, Yasmin moved with effortless ease, the sari as though glued in place and flowing prettily around her feet.

In spite of the exquisite sari I was wearing, no one had eyes for me; if they stopped to stare, it was at the sari. They would gaze in astonished admiration, finger the silk and marvel at the closeness of the stitches. 'It's like a painting,' they would say, forgetting I was in the sari. 'Did you ever see such tiny, exquisite stitches? It should really be in a museum—it is so gorgeous.'

Most Indian households are conservative about their daughters going out alone with young men, but lots of suitable young men from well-known, rich Parsi families were invited to the house— ostensibly for both of us— but who would look at me when Yasmin was around?

That evening, a very special young man had been invited to the house to accompany us to the wedding. He was handsome and dashing, wearing that patina of confidence that comes from being extremely rich. Son of old man Mehta, who had made his millions from bathroom fittings, Bobby Mehta was every young girl's dream come true. When he entered the room, Yasmin and I were standing within touching distance of each other, but he never even saw me.

He stared in astonishment at her. 'Jesus!' he said inappropriately. Yasmin held out her hand, smiling, and he took it in his, as though he would never let it go. It was not the first time that I had been so completely ignored, but I was still not inured to the pain, the feeling of panic that overcame me, as though I simply did not exist.

There is no use telling me that beauty is only skin deep, and that the qualities of head and heart are what endure. It is the outer shell that makes an impression and often it is the only thing that is seen. At that particular moment, I would willingly have sold myself to the devil if he could have given me the sort of beauty that Yasmin possessed. There were other young girls who were as plain, but they did not have to compete with someone like Yasmin.

Yasmin had married her romantic prince within a year, on her eighteenth birthday, and I had started college in Hyderabad. I planned to go to Delhi the following year.

Who was to know that old man Mehta would shoot himself instead of declaring bankruptcy, and the golden fortune would no longer exist? Bobby Mehta became just another bitter young man who had never been trained to do anything, and who found that life was no longer a playground that provided him with all that he needed. There were no more fast cars, vacations abroad and houses with enormous staffs to run them. Now nothing remained but debts, and neither he nor Yasmin had been brought up to compromise or find solutions. They both had bitter grievances against a world that could treat them so shabbily. They lived by selling Yasmin's jewellery and by flitting, like unwelcome birds, from one friend to another, until they had very few friends left.

Not too long after, Bobby's death in a car accident came as something of a relief to Yasmin, who was tired of the recriminations, betrayals and the scrimping that went on every day. She went home to Sophie, who was living comfortably enough in the old house in Hyderabad.

At that time Ramesh and I were still living in Delhi and after some years, we would move with the boys to a bigger flat in Golf Links. The boys were almost nine years old then, and still in day school. Identical twins, they adored each other. They were handsome boys with fair skin and light eyes. Sturdily built, they had excellent appetites, and seemed to enjoy life as though the world had been designed just for their happiness. I loved to watch them tucking into hearty breakfasts, piling butter and jam on to endless quantities of toast.

I frowned when I recognized Yasmin's spidery handwriting on the envelope which had just arrived in the mail. I read the letter twice and then passed it to Ramesh. Yasmin had written that after Bobby's death in a car accident in Belgrade, she was left with nothing put debts. She was presently in Bombay, staying in a two-bedroom flat lent to her by a friend. Since she had been trained for nothing, looking for a job was proving difficult in the extreme. She had managed to get a temporary job as a receptionist at the Taj Hotel.

Ramesh finished reading the letter. He said, 'This must be very hard on your sister. Don't you think we should invite her to stay with us for a while?'

He knew something of how I felt about Yasmin, and knew that whatever it was I felt for her, it was certainly not love. I had very little desire to see her again, and after all that had happened, I certainly did not want her staying with us. The past years of my life had been happy and fulfilling. What had I to fear? I was happily married, with a wonderful husband and two incredible sons; surely all this was sufficient armour against Yasmin?

'All right,' I said. 'I'll ask her to come for a while.' Ramesh insisted that we go to the station to meet her and there she was, getting down from the train, perfumed and still startlingly beautiful.

Ramesh appeared to be quite unprepared for the way she looked. It was true that I had described her, but the reality was somehow different.

There were new hollows below her cheekbones, and her eyes had lost something of their sparkle, but she still had that spun-sugar delicacy about her. I suppressed a stab of fear; surely her acquisitive fingers would not be able to peel off the layers of contentment and sense of security in which I now lived? My life with Ramesh and the boys was too solidly constructed for even Yasmin to make a difference.

The boys were fascinated with her and she treated them as she treated all males, with a mixture of flattery and flirtatious charm, to which they responded with giggles.

They were playing on the tiny lawn outside our flat one morning while Ramesh, Yasmin and I sipped coffee and watched them indulgently.

Suddenly, Ramesh turned and looked at me in absolute astonishment. He had always been intrigued by the boys' looks. 'They look just like Yasmin,' he said to me in wonder. 'They could be her children.'

My heart skipped a beat as Yasmin smiled at me with something else in her eyes. Of course it was true, by some quirk of genetics they did resemble her—they had inherited her looks. But they had not inherited her nasty, scheming temperament.

They were good-natured children, capable, it seemed,

of loving everyone and everything. The servants adored them and spoiled them terribly, but nothing seemed to affect their gentleness and concern for others. Comically alike, they shared everything.

After all these years, that scene still brings a stab of pain to my heart. Yasmin was wearing a silk of some bright colour—purple or perhaps royal blue. Her hair, cut short, fell in smooth, shining wings on either side of her face. Her eyes glittered in the sun and one delicate, ringed hand rested lightly on Zubin's shoulder.

Ramesh, Yasmin and the boys form a small intimate group together; only I remain outside, and in Yasmin's eyes there is not only triumph, but also a threat. A threat of what might happen in the future.

A few days after Yasmin's arrival Ramesh said to me, 'Yasmin's affairs are in a proper mess. There are still debts to pay off and she is living in a small flat in Bombay lent to her by a friend who has gone to New York for six months. Her salary is a mere pittance. Don't you think it would be better for her to move in with us, for some time at least? It would give her a break, and in the meantime I could look around for something better for her; perhaps in my office.'

I wanted to scream and leap at him and tear his hair and scratch his face, but I recalled Grandma and her soft voice.

'I don't think that would suit Yasmin at all,' I said. 'She

is convinced that the Taj job will lead to better things eventually. In fact, she is leaving on Saturday.'

He looked astonished, as well he might. After dinner I went to find Yasmin in her room. I had her plane ticket to Bombay in my hand. She was sitting in front of the mirror, wearing a red chiffon nightie and brushing her hair. She met my eyes in the mirror and smiled. She looked as smug as a cat that has found a whole carton of double cream.

I said, 'This is your plane ticket to Bombay. You are leaving on Saturday.'

'Oh, I don't think so at all. Ramesh has invited me to stay as long as I want, and that is exactly what I plan to do.'

I sat down on the bed and looked at her smiling face in the mirror. My voice was neither menacing nor angry. I said, 'I believe you are receiving Rs 45,000 from the bank every three months. This will stop immediately if you continue to stay on here.'

'But this money has absolutely nothing to do with you. Sophie arranged for me to get it.'

'Sophie spoke to me after your visit to her. She said she knew it was all your fault, and that no one in their senses would have run up such huge debts, but perhaps, in spite of all this, I might be able to help in some way. I arranged for this money to be paid into your account every three months. I think another instalment is due next month. If you don't take this flight to Bombay on Saturday, I will give instructions to have it stopped.'

39

She sat staring at herself in the mirror, her face pale, her mouth set in an ugly line. 'How you hate me. You always did hate me. You even tried to drown me when we were children.'

'Don't be absurd, it was all your fault. You always act on impulse without thinking of the consequences. If you hadn't thrown Attilla into the pool, nothing would have happened.'

We were just six years old, and the birthday and all that had occurred was over. I still remember—it was a cloudy day, and rain dripped softly on the trees and bushes in the garden. We had been sent to the playroom, and I, at least, had gone eagerly. A new jigsaw of some complexity—with a picture of a game reserve in Africa—had just arrived, and I was eager to get started on it. It was so large that it covered the entire wooden table on which we often painted, constructed elaborate houses with bricks, or made collages from old Christmas cards.

The glossy picture showed brightly coloured birds in the trees, and hippos, lions and giraffes, as well as deer of every description, with fearsome crocodiles in the pool. The sky was varied shades of blue, and the trees and lake incredibly green or silvery blue. I was good at solving jigsaw puzzles but this was a real tricky one, and what I thought was sky often turned out to be the water instead. I began by fitting together the outline and was working diligently at it when Yasmin said, 'I can't do it. It is too jumbled up.'

I shrugged and continued with my painstaking piecing together of the puzzle while Yasmin went back to dressing and undressing her dolls. I had by now completed—successfully—the entire right hand corner of the puzzle, when Yasmin wandered over to take a look. Seeing the neatly finished portion, she put out her hand and deliberately dislodged the pieces, scattering them all over the floor. Laughing uproariously, she ran out of the room. The rain stopped. I picked up the scattered pieces, and dumping everything into the box, ran after her muttering, 'I'm going to kill you.'

No sooner had I reached the top of the stairs, than I saw why she was running so fast, half screaming and half laughing. She had Attila in her arms and was running as fast as she could towards the dirty green pool at the bottom of the garden. It was due to be cleaned soon. Thick with green slime and rotted leaves, it almost did not look like water at all.

I tore after her, but already it was too late. I saw Attila soar through the air and fall with a whoosh into the pool. He disappeared slowly into the murky depths, sucked into the soupy, green water. I did not waste a single moment, wading in shoes and all. Yasmin seemed to have gone mad. She was jumping about on the bank and screaming, 'Attila the Hun, sank like a ton! What fun, what fun!'

The water came up to my knees but I could see nothing,

since rotting leaves and slime formed a kind of soupy mesh.

Plunging my hands into the stuff, I could feel all sorts of slithery things—things that moved, as well as roots, rotting leaves and even a startled frog. I was now covered in green slime—my frock, my arms and legs and even my face, but still no Attila.

Yasmin continued her mad song and dance, but I had no time for her now. I had nearly traversed the whole pool when my groping hands discovered Attila, completely smothered in clinging, green, smelly stuff. Clutching him tightly to my chest, I began to negotiate my way out of the pool. This was far from easy as I kept slipping, or being sucked into strange hollows and puddles.

At last I managed to pull myself out on to dry land. Yasmin's demented screaming seemed to have drawn quite a lot of people from the house—all bewildered about what was happening—until I emerged from the pool, streaming with water and covered in green slime. Sophie and Father and some of the servants began to make their way towards me. I probably looked a sight, but I paid no attention to anyone. I had a different goal.

I walked, or rather squelched my way towards Yasmin, who was still standing at the edge of the pool. She saw my face and turned to run, but I caught her dress from behind, bunching the material up in my hand. I turned and ran her down to the edge. There was no way she could escape. One strong push, and she was face down in the water. She did not sink as Atilla had done. She choked and struggled up, her hair and face streaming with green muck; sticks, leaves and slime clung to her just as they had on Atilla. When she could open her mouth she began to scream, 'She tried to drown me. Naaz tried to drown me.'

They pulled her out, still screaming, but I was not interested. I started slowly to make for the house, Attila clutched to my chest.

Moti stopped me. 'What happened, child?' Wordlessly, I held out Attila for her to see. She gasped, 'Yasmin?' I nodded. I could hear questions from Father and Sophie but I continued along. Moti said, 'Never mind, I will clean him up for you.'

I heard Father saying, 'I have no idea what has happened, but the first thing to do is to get the children out of those clothes and into hot baths. Questions can wait.'

Sophie said, 'All right. Come on, the two of you. I can't imagine what they have been doing.'

Moti said, 'I'll take Naaz upstairs and you can see to Yasmin. It will be quicker that way.'

I plodded slowly upstairs, squelching at every step. Grandma was waiting at the top. She said not a word. Taking Attila from me, she laid him down carefully on a folded newspaper. My clothes were stripped off and discarded. Moti was waiting in the bathroom. I was soaped, scrubbed and shampooed, and while Moti went downstairs to get me some clothes, Grandma wrapped me in a huge towel.

Still without saying a word, she dried and powdered me, and rubbed my hair dry with a towel. Moti brought up a pair of pyjamas and I was buttoned into them. I had begun to feel really ill by now, alternately shivering and burning hot.

Moti said, 'They are waiting downstairs for Naaz.'

Grandma held out her hand and we went downstairs together.

Yasmin was already there. She too had changed into pyjamas and was alternately sneezing and whimpering. Father said, 'All right. Which of you is going to tell me what happened?'

'Naaz tried to drown me,' Yasmin wailed. 'She wanted me to drown.'

Grandma said, 'Naaz?'

'Yasmin stole Attila from my room, then ran down to the pond and deliberately threw him in. While I was searching for him she started dancing and singing, "Attila the Hun, sank like a ton; what fun, what fun."

'When I found Attila he was covered in slime and clingy green stuff. Even his eyes.' My voice wavered. 'After I brought him out, I caught Yasmin's frock and pushed her in.'

Yasmin began to wail again. 'She tried to drown me. She wanted me to die. Ask her.'

Father said, 'Stop being so silly, Yasmin. You have both been very naughty and silly. Both of you.'

Grandma intervened. 'I agree, but both children are shivering and sneezing, and I think Naaz, who was in the pool much longer, has a touch of fever. What they now need is to be in bed, and given some warm milk with brandy.'

Sophie said, 'I suppose they had both better come into my room.'

Grandma intervened. 'I think Naaz will be better off in her own room. I will send Moti to stay with her. Yasmin—next time, remember that you might have drowned, even in three feet of water. It was you who caused this to happen. If you hadn't stolen the bear and thrown him into that dirty pool, none of this would have happened.'

Yasmin began to wail again and was led away by Sophie.

I was brought back into the present by Yasmin saying, 'You did try to drown me, didn't you?'

I laughed. 'In three feet of water? I just wanted you to experience what you had done to Attila.'

'That wretched bear. What happened to him?'

'I still have him. He sits on the top of the bookcase in my room.'

Yasmin and Ramesh had three days together, but that was enough.

four

There was no precise moment in time when I made up my mind to excel in ways that Yasmin never could. If she had beauty, I had brains, a quick intelligence and the knowledge that money meant power. Grandma—old, small and fragile—controlled everything and everyone in the family.

Sometimes, with the chocolate still melting in my mouth, Grandma would give me the keys which were pinned at her waist and ask me to open the big wall safe.

This was a big, old fashioned Chubb—black and solid looking, but the door swung open easily at a touch on well-oiled hinges. The first time, I was astonished to see huge piles of bank notes spilling out as the door opened. Grandma laughed at my astonishment. She said, 'I always like to have plenty of cash available for emergencies. I am going to the bank today. Would you like to come with me?' I nodded eagerly.

Sophie and Yasmin were engaged in a hairdressing session which would take all morning. They waved to us happily as we left.

We drove to the bank in the old brown Daimler, polished to a high gloss by Ahmed. Since Grandma absolutely hated to go fast, Ahmed drove at a slow, regal pace, as though we were royalty drifting down from Banjara Hills to the main shopping centre, without a single bump or pause.

Although Hyderabad was now part of independent India, change came slowly, and it still remained very feudal, a centre of Islamic culture and learning. Its long heritage of Mughal, Qutub Shahi, Iranian and Central Asian influences could not be erased in a hurry. Extravagantly formal manners and a very distinctive language, music and cuisine, as well as the magnificent palaces and mosques made it very different from the rest of India. All would be lost in the next decade, but for now it was still the Hyderabad that Grandma knew and loved.

The bank on Abid Road had once been a nawab's palace, and it still remained an imposing building, with its marble pillars and great cusped gateway. At the door the Nubian guard stood with a bandolier strapped across his massive chest.

I was fascinated by him, but Grandma went straight past, up the carpeted stairs and into the bank manager's room. There were still many Englishmen around at this

47

time, some in the army, or heading various government institutions and other departments. They were there to make the transition easier, but most would have liked to stay forever. They had been so many years in India that the thought of returning to England—small, damp and cold—frightened them.

The process of complete Indianization would take many, many more years, and they were glad for it; here they were lords of all they surveyed—treated with exaggerated respect, living in huge, sprawling bungalows, cared for by armies of devoted servants—white men in a country of dark skins. Many of them truly loved India; they were enamoured by a country so different from theirs, so vast, unexplored and undecipherable. A country alive and teeming with colour—there were flamboyant birds in the trees, and groves of coconut, mango, tamarind and banana spread around. The atmosphere and culture was friendly and informal, and everybody dropped in on everybody else without the formality of appointments.

From Father we had learnt all about the British as explorers par excellence, their ventures into distant and unexplored places to draw their maps—writing up careful despatches, enduring the heat, the cholera, dysentery and typhoid, the mosquitoes, dust, noise and a culture of excess—which enfeebled them and drained the blood from their veins, and very often killed them; nothing deterred or discouraged them.

It was as if they were immersed in the inked fibres of their maps, painstakingly drawn, forever charmed by the discovery of an unknown tribe, or a new and unexplored river or forest. 'They crisscrossed the country, travelling between land and chart, between reality and legend, between the true and the invented, collecting and collating valuable information on mountains and valleys, forests and rivers, deserts and plains.'

Cunningham, Everest, Rennell, Smythe, Thornton, Hamilton, Falconer, Ross—their names still mean something in the new India. Some of them went native, discarding suits and ties for saffron robes, retreating into ashrams; often starting ashrams of their own.

Their despatches made fascinating reading. The risks were great—when it was impossible to map the secret interior of Tibet because of their white skin, they recruited and trained the legendary pandits, who mapped a million square miles of Tibet disguised as Buddhist pilgrims, counting off their paces on specially adapted prayer beads, with compasses in their prayer wheels and thermometers in their staffs.

The people of the mountainous regions were, quite naturally, very suspicious of intruders, and more especially of white intruders. The British surveyors decided to train hill people in the elements of survey—the measurement of distance by pacing, and the fixing of bearings and positions by star observation. They explored the uplands of Tibet, Mongolia and Central Asia, traced the course of great rivers, mountains, lakes and roads, and also wrote of the customs and manners of the people they came across. Venturing into wild and unexplored territories, death stalking their every step, these native explorers and spies worked for almost nothing, and were rewarded with gold watches and meagre pensions. The British inspired loyalty.

The bank manager turned out to be a very tall, thin Englishman called Andrew Holt. He towered over Grandma, whom he treated with the greatest deference and respect, bending over her hand, pulling out and holding a chair for her, before settling himself on the opposite side of his cherry-wood table.

Grandma introduced me, 'This is my granddaughter, Naaz. I would like to open an account for her today.'

Mr Holt beamed at me. 'And how old are you, my dear?'

'Eight years old.'

His eyebrows went up slightly, but only slightly. 'Naaz,' he said. 'What a pretty name——the beloved.' He smiled kindly at me.

Grandma began to discuss money matters with him while I wandered around the room. It was a large, cool room with many green plants in large containers, their leaves riffling gently under the circling fan. There were lots of pictures on the walls, but there was one I particularly liked. A young woman in a pink silk ruffled dress was playing with a dog, her hair and clothes streaming behind her; the dog's bright, slightly protruding eyes fixed on her, his paws raised in appeal. I stared at the picture for a long time. It was a happy picture, and I imprinted it on my mind.

Mr Holt said, 'Ah! You are admiring George Romney's picture of Lady Hamilton as *Bacchante*. You like it?'

I nodded. I had no idea who Lady Hamilton was. I said, 'I like it because the dog looks so happy.'

Mr Holt said, 'Good gracious, yes. He does look happy, as though he really adores his mistress.'

Years later I discovered who Lady Hamilton was, and admired other pictures by George Romney.

A servant brought in a tray which held three small glasses of iced coffee so cold that the outside of the glasses were frosted, and the cream floating on top was lightly misted.

Mr Holt leaned his considerable length in my direction and said, 'Naaz, would you rather have a lemonade or orange juice instead of iced coffee?'

I loved the way he said my name. Na-a-az—making it sound quite exotic.

'No thank you,' I said. 'I love cold coffee.' Grandma looked amused, but said nothing; she knew I had never tasted cold coffee or in fact any kind of coffee before. Served with the coffee were small plates of very dark brown biscuits studded with slivers of burnt almonds. They were utterly delicious. I sipped the wonderful coffee, nibbled the biscuits, and felt as happy and cherished as Lady Hamilton's little dog.

Grandma opened my account with two thousand rupees and I signed my name carefully in my new blue passbook—Naaz Jussawalla.

Mr Holt beamed at me. 'Splendid,' he said. 'Now you can withdraw money any time you want to buy a new doll or something else your mother won't give you.'

'I hate dolls,' I said coldly.

'Indeed. What is it you like?'

I thought for a moment. 'I like books and jigsaw puzzles,' I paused. 'And these biscuits.'

They both burst out laughing. Grandma said, 'I agree with Naaz. I have never tasted biscuits so delicious. Are they home-made?'

'Yes indeed. They are my wife's speciality and I keep them only for very special people.'

He turned to Grandma. 'Your little granddaughter has excellent manners. I can see that we will get on very well together.'

In the car on the way home Grandma said, 'Now Naaz, this will be our own little secret. You don't need to mention it to anyone else.' I nodded—I understood perfectly—she didn't want Father to know, or even Sophie or Yasmin. It might have been better on the whole if I had mentioned it to someone. It would have prepared them somewhat for Grandma leaving everything to me when she died. Not only the money, but all the properties, the jewellery and the jade. It came as a terrible shock, from which Father never recovered. None of them ever forgave me.

five

We were eight years old when Grandma dropped a bombshell. She came downstairs one morning and announced that it was time for us to prepare for the navjote ceremony.

For Zoroastrians, this is like a First Communion or Bar Mitzvah, a formal initiation which every Parsi child—male or female—must undergo. The sudra, a thin muslin shirt worn next to the skin, and the kusti, the sacred thread, handwoven from white lamb's wool, are formally put on the child by a priest in a ceremony which had great religious significance for all Zorastrians. For Sophie, however, it came as a complete and very unpleasant surprise.

In England, Father had seemed so very westernized—tall, handsome and fair-skinned, wearing his beautifully tailored clothes, and speaking such impeccable English. Sophie and her family did not associate him with the teeming millions, those 'poor black bastards', who spawned so prolifically and who lived in such abject poverty. That he seemed so much like them and yet possessed such an exotic background, made him just that much more exciting and desirable. It would have needed someone far more perceptive than Sophie to untangle his profoundly mixed identity and his emblematic ambivalence towards India and Indians.

Sophie had expected to be greeted with warmth and perhaps even effusiveness when she first arrived. After all she was white, and natives were notoriously enamoured of white skins. She was hurt and astonished by Grandma's chilly welcome.

She was aware, of course, that Father was not a Christian and that he was a Parsi and a Zoroastrian, but she had never known him to go to a Fire Temple, nor had she ever seen him saying his prayers to whatever God he believed in. The navjote, therefore, came as a very unexpected and unpleasant surprise. It was at this time too, that she learned about the vultures.

The playroom we shared had a large rocking horse with a red bridle and red saddle, which was so high that we needed to climb on a stool in order to mount him.

We were both there—Yasmin painting at a large table, and I on the horse, rocking rhythmically to a tune I was singing. When this palled, however, I dismounted and went to see what else I could do. I was in no mood for jigsaws and I had read all the books there many times over. I decided to check on what Yasmin was doing.

She had painted a huge bird which covered the whole sheet of paper. It had outstretched wings and curving talons on its feet. Light from the overhead lamp lit up the orange-tinted water in which Yasmin was dipping her brush.

Glancing over her shoulder I said, 'Painting vultures! They are going to eat you up when you are dead.'

She spun around on her stool at once. 'It is not a vulture. It is an eagle.' She held her paintbrush like a dart, ready to fling it at me. 'They will eat *you* up because you are a bad girl.'

I smiled smugly, secure in my superior knowledge. 'You are just silly,' I said. 'You don't know anything. When Parsis die, they are never buried or cremated. They are taken up into high towers and made naked, and then the vultures first tear their eyes out, and then their hearts, and then their livers.'

I had no idea where I had acquired this piece of esoteric knowledge, but its effect on Yasmin was gratifying. She turned as pale as the paper she was painting on.

'It's not true,' she said, her voice quivering. 'It's not true. It's not true. Sophie won't let them.' She flew at me, pulling my hair and screaming.

I pushed her away easily. I was always so much stronger and heavier than she was.

'It is true, it is true,' I said, dancing around the table

55

and lunging at her with an imaginary hook—'Rrr . . . ip.'

Her screams were so loud and piercing that they seemed to reach every corner of the house, although the purpose of this room was that we could make as much noise as we liked without disrupting the more orderly life of the adults.

Sophie was the first to come running, followed by some of the servants and Grandma, who happened to be on one of her rare visits downstairs. Yasmin flew to Sophie, who held her tight, rocking her in her arms as she knelt beside her.

'Quiet, quiet. It's all right. It's all right.' She glared across at me. 'What on earth did you do to her?'

Yasmin's voice rose hysterically. 'She said, she said, that when I die they will put me in a tower for the vultures to eat.'

Sophie looked at me with utter disgust. 'What a perfectly revolting and disgusting thing to say. You need a jolly good spanking. How dare you make up such horrible stories to frighten your sister?'

Grandma—small, but with a commanding presence, moved into the room.

'Wait a minute, Sophie. I know it is very naughty of Naaz to frighten Yasmin like that, but of course it is true. Didn't you know Parsis don't bury their dead? It is a custom we brought with us from Persia. The dead are carried up to what are known as "Towers of Silence" and exposed so that the vultures can remove the flesh quickly and cleanly from the bodies. The bones roll into a special place and dissolve in lime. In this way neither the earth, the air, nor fire nor water are contaminated. Ecologically it is the best way to dispose of dead bodies. All over India, trees are disappearing to feed hundreds of thousands of funeral pyres. Burials use up land, which is scarce and valuable. This is clean, quick and efficient.'

All this was said in the most matter-of-fact way possible, but Sophie's face was a mask of horror. Her every nerve, rubbed raw by Yasmin's screams, was now laid open and exposed.

'It's not true,' she gasped, echoing Yasmin's cry. 'You are supposed to be civilized people, not barbarians.'

Grandma bridled. 'I don't see what is barbaric about it. What about the worms that crawl in and out of bodies when they are buried under the ground, devouring the body bit by bit? This whole process is finished within hours, quickly and cleanly.'

Sophie's response was to pull Yasmin out of the room—the room where she now felt contaminated—and run to her own room, in which they remained locked until Father returned from work in the evening.

Grandma looked at me severely. 'You are not only very naughty but very silly too.' She looked at Yasmin's drawing which still lay abandoned on the table. 'Even you should know the difference between eagles and vultures.'

I went to my room to get away from everybody. I had

created quite a spectacular upheaval, and I was feeling both frightened and sulky.

When Father came home there was another tremendous row. I could hear him saying, 'It may all be true, mother, but there was no need for Naaz to spring it on Yasmin in such a deliberately brutal way. I really feel there is something seriously wrong with that child. How could she be so mean and vicious? You spoil her.'

Grandma said 'This is what comes of marrying a pardesi. I warned you that the children would grow up neither one thing nor the other. That is why I say it is time to prepare them for the navjote. It will take them quite some time to learn the prayers.'

Sophie hated the whole idea. Long prayers intoned in a dead language needed to be learnt, and it was decided that every evening, after supper, we would go up to Grandma's rooms for instruction. Even Yasmin knew that when Grandma decided on something, there was absolutely no use throwing tantrums.

Sulkily, and with many appeals to an impotent Sophie, she climbed the stairs with me to Grandma's rooms. Grandma often stayed here for days without coming downstairs. She had her own kitchen and a balcony full of green herbs. Moti too had her own rooms here. I loved it and often visited Grandma, but Yasmin came rarely, if at all. As soon as we reached the top of the stairs she wrinkled her nose and sniffed. 'It smells,' she said.

It was true that Grandma's rooms smelt different—of Bayrum, imported for her from London, and the distinctive scent of pickles gently soaking in vinegar and spice, and various fruits—cherries, peaches, plums and qumquats, soaking in brandy or rum. There were also prunes steeped in port wine, which were my favourites.

Grandma came from a long line of gourmet cooks, and many of her recipes came to her from both sides of the family. From the time that the Parsis had migrated to India, their food was a wonderful blend of different cultures and cuisines. From Persia they brought their love of nuts and saffron, which they used lavishly in curries and sweet dishes. Meat-eaters, they had no particular restrictions or taboos. Parsi cuisine borrowed lavishly from everywhere—from the British, from the west coast of India, from Gujarat, Kashmir and Goa. There were no restrictions on the consumption of alcohol, and Grandma swore by the therapeutic value of Hennesey's brandy, which she used as a rub for headaches or backaches, and as a quick and effective remedy for tiredness and insomnia.

As soon as we reached the top of the stairs, we were sent to wash our hands. The soap in her bathroom was always the same—ball soaps made by the house of Pears, and especially ordered for her from London when they were no longer available in India. We stood side by side before Grandma, who was sitting as she always did, on her huge, four-poster bed, propped up by mounds of snowy-white feather pillows.

Embroidered skull caps were produced and jammed on to our heads. We began to repeat after her:

Ashem vohu, Vahishtem asti
Ushta asti, Ushta ahmai
Hyat ashai, Vahishtai ashem.

I liked the sonorous sound of the Avesta, and the old Persian words, but Yasmin got the giggles and when scolded, sulked. After less than a week I could perfectly repeat the prayers we had been taught so far, but Yasmin stumbled over the unfamiliar words which she couldn't seem to remember, and ended up in tears. I heard Grandma tell Father, 'The child may be pretty but she doesn't seem to have a brain in her head.'

Sophie was excluded from all this. She was not a Zoroastrian and therefore an outsider. When the Parsis first arrived in India, they had promised an apprehensive Indian raja that they would practice their religion discreetly and make no converts. This policy is followed even today, although the orthodox priests claim the reason is that converts would dilute Zoroastrianism from its pure Aryan culture. Of all this Sophie knew little and cared even less. All she knew was that she was being excluded from something that affected her children intimately. She would not be able to touch or approach us after the *nahn* or purificatory baths had been given to us before the ceremony.

When we were reasonably proficient in saying the prayers, preparations for the navjote began. Invitations were sent out and masses of pink, scented roses and white tuberoses ordered. Dressed in silk pyjamas, fine white shawls covering the upper portion of our bare bodies and embroidered caps on our heads, we were led to the dais where the ceremony would take place. Four priests dressed completely in white, with gold embroidered cummerbands, were waiting.

There were hundreds of guests, mostly Parsis with a smattering of others. Yasmin and I were supposed to chant the prayers in time with the priests, but Yasmin seemed paralyzed with fright and forgot everything she had been taught. My voice rang out clear and confident, and glancing up I saw Grandma smiling approvingly at me.

The sudras were slipped over our heads as the shawls were removed and the kustis wound three times around our waists. It was only when everything was over that Sophie was allowed to approach us and help us dress in the new clothes that had been laid out in silver trays which also held grains of rice, coconut flowers, dried dates and silver mugs of water.

Sophie took her revenge by encouraging Yasmin to discard the sudra and kusti, something that had long-lasting effects for both of them.

For a whole year after the navjote ceremony we were supposed to go up to Grandma's rooms and say our prayers with her. Yasmin always had some excuse (backed up by Sophie), and it was eventually only I who made my way up the stairs and stood there winding the kusti three times around my waist, tying the knots correctly and intoning the prayers. I enjoyed doing this, and afterwards I would sit on the bed beside Grandma and she would allow me to choose a chocolate from the box as a reward. With the chocolate still in my mouth, I felt warm, happy and safe.

six

Grandma loved Hyderabad, the city in which she was born and in which she ultimately died. She loved it for its Arabian Nights' atmosphere, for its Byzantine ambience, its exquisitely elaborate code of manners and most of all for its wonderful cuisine. Grandfather, although a Parsi, had been elevated to the rank of nawab and was known as Nawab Jamsheed Yar Jung.

In the nineteenth and twentieth centuries, Parsis played a prominent role in the Nizam's court. Most of them knew both Persian and English, as well as Urdu. Trained under the British, they were preferred as higher officials for their administrative abilities and for their indifference to court intrigues.

Unfailing courtesy and an almost overwhelming sense of hospitality distinguished the old Hyderabad from the new. The Nizam, reputed to be the richest man in the world and a direct descendant of the Mughals, ruled over a state situated in the heart of South India. Although eighty per cent of his subjects were Hindus, it was still very much a Muslim dominated state and the manners of the court, whether Hindu or Muslim, were totally influenced by Mughal etiquette.

The Muslim nobles were a mixed lot, descended from Turkish, Arab, Persian and Afghan ancestors. They possessed huge lands, armies of retainers, and great wealth. They paid no taxes and enjoyed so much royal patronage that they never needed to do a day's work. In an atmosphere of such wealthy distractions, pleasures were concentrated for the most part on music, women and food—not necessarily in that order. In Hyderabad, manners were everything.

Most of Grandfather's great wealth came from royal patronage, and the family's Chinese connections. But he was a Parsi and business was in his blood. When he watched his friends the nawabs sell off exquisite old furniture, he decided to buy up as much as possible and start his own furniture shop. He paid fair prices unlike the shops in Char Minar, and soon he had a shop full of carved and inlaid furniture made from the finest woods from all over the world—teak and cedar, sandalwood and sal, cherry and rosewood, all made by great craftsmen and attracting connoisseurs from far and wide. When Father took over, he introduced more modern pieces, made in his own workshop by master craftsmen.

Hyderabad, the largest of India's semi-autonomous states, did not merge easily or gracefully with the new India. When Clement Atlee announced in 1947 that Britain was prepared to hand over power to the Indians, Hyderabad declared its intention of assuming the status of an 'independent, sovereign state'. The British complained that the Nizam continued to be 'the inhabitant of an unreal world', and the viceroy of India, Lord Wavell, said that the prime minister of Hyderabad had 'put forward the extraordinary suggestion that his Majesty's government enter into a separate treaty with Hyderabad as an independent state.'

Wavell departed and the dashing and glamorous Lord Louis Mountbatten became the last viceroy of India. He had expected that his charm and undoubted ability would prove persuasive where others had failed, but the Nizam's advisors continued to be 'obstructive and stubborn'.

The Nizam's government wanted dominion status, if not complete independence, but in the new India there would be no place for these Highnesses, 'pliant tools of the British'. The Nizam's government prepared for war. It was an unequal struggle.

On 18 September 1948 the Nizam's troops surrendered unconditially to the advancing Indian forces. A *Time* magazine reporter, John Luber, who was covering the story and taking photographs of the 'war', listened to the Nizam's speech and asked a friendly Indian soldier what he was saying.

The soldier laughed. 'He says he is sorry. He wants to be friends.'

To appease his dignity, the Nizam was initially made Rajpramukh, the equivalent of a governor, but he retreated to his King Kothi palace and remained there, emerging only to attend namaz. He knew that for him, it was the end. The transition from the old regime to the new was not welcomed by the nawabs and their friends, who mourned the passing of what they considered 'a golden age'—the end of their privileged existence. Many left for the newly created Pakistan. While India was celebrating its freedom from colonial rule, it was not only the nawabs who viewed the future with anxiety and fear. 'In India, and in vast stretches of the British Empire, the ground burns and there is plunder, bloodshed and anarchy. But there is freedom, for whatever it is worth and whatever it may mean to the ordinary man or woman.'

For us it made a difference, but only a very small difference. Grandma's considerable wealth did not depend on royal favours. Her houses, her jewellery and the furniture business would remain untouched by the new changes which would make Hyderabad a radically different place. Most Parsis, however, saw the departure of the British with regret.

Some things would change but the Char Minar area would remain the same for many, many years. As a child I found it absolutely fascinating. Even today I like to wander through the small dark gullies with names such as '*Aine Walli Gulli*', or the street of mirrors, and small shops selling the famous *Nahari*. Here the spirit of old Hyderabad still lingers in the traditional chai khanas, where Hyderabadi tea is served, known as Burqevalli-chai—the tea that wears a veil, the tea that Hyderabadis love—made with thick cream, in which a spoon can stand upright.

Each little gulli had its own speciality—the street of attar, the street where silver was hammered into thin sheets, the street of flowers, and the famous Lad Bazar, where the special Hyderabadi bangles were made from lac, glittering with fake precious stones.

Instead of going to the modern showrooms of Abid Road, Grandma came here for her pearls and other jewellery. Tiny shops faced the main road but opened up at the back into huge courtyards, filled with brilliantly lit glass-fronted rooms containing all the treasures of Araby. And here too were the Nahari shops with names like Rainbow Café, Niagra Café or Rafreeh Café. Nahari is one of Hyderabad's most famous culinary delights, and is made from sheep's tongue and trotters simmered overnight in an unusual gravy which includes such exotic ingredients as powdered sandalwood, dried rose petals, cassia buds and an aromatic bouqet garni, known here as 'potli ka masala'.

Nahari is a breakfast dish, eaten at dawn, just as the sun comes up over the minarets and the air still retains something of the night's coolness. Many Hyderabadis ate this everyday, but for us it was a once-in-a-while, very special treat. If one could take a bite out of the city, this is how it would taste, the pungently sharp flavours of the south mingling with the best of Mughal spices.

Grandma would suddenly announce one day that she had an urge to eat Nahari, and anyone wanting to join her had better be up and ready at the crack of dawn. Even Sophie would join in these early morning excursions, and Father teased her, saying she had become more of a Hyderabadi than he was.

Grandma had her own special Nahari stall, and the early morning drive through deserted streets, with all the shops closed and shuttered and the sky still pearly before the sun rose and drained the colour from everything was an enchantment. There were no beggars or bearded holy men demanding alms in the name of Allah.

As soon as the car drew up outside the shop, the owner, Ali Majid, an old man with greying hair and beard, eyes heavily blackened with *surma*, would come running out, salaaming deeply as he waited for our order.

Nahari was always served in soup bowls accompanied by platters of steaming hot kulchas straight out of the oven.

Although Ali Majid would put a spoon on Sophie's tray because she was a firangi, the proper way to eat Nahari is to break off bits of the kulcha and scoop up the meat and gravy with it. The gravy, in fact, is so thick, and the meat so soft after having simmered all night in its special spices, that there is no real distinction between gravy and meat, the two having melded together to form an utterly delicious, rich and satisfying mixture.

While we sat in the car and guzzled, the driver sat sedately in the shop eating his own bowl of Nahari. Every one had second helpings and offers of more were reluctantly refused. Hot, damp towels were brought to wipe sticky fingers, and with many compliments from Grandma on the excellence of the food, money was handed to Ali Majid, who accepted it with many flowery compliments about how his poor shop was honoured to serve us. He bowed low and salaamed repeatedly as we drove away.

When we returned home. Father was sitting on the verandah in his blue dressing gown with a cup of tea and the morning paper. He regarded us indulgently.

'Naaz, how many kulchas did you consume?' he asked.

'She ate five,' Yasmin said quickly. 'Naaz is always so greedy. I only ate three.'

'Not much point going all that way if you are not going to overeat,' Father said repressively.

Grandma sent for a cup of tea, saying that she drew the line at drinking tea thick with clotted cream. She said to Father, 'Why don't you tell them the story about the kulchas?'

Father smiled. 'Sophie, have you heard the story?'

Sophie shook her head muttering, 'I am not a Hyderabadi.'

This is the story that Father told us:

'The very first Nizam of Hyderabad was one of Aurangzeb's generals. A brilliant young soldier who had been made viceroy of the Deccan at the end of the Qutub Shahi dynasty. Once, during a particularly bloody battle, he lost his way, and while wandering in a forest saw a small flickering light among the trees. It was the hut of a fakir, and the holy man was just about to start his evening meal. The holy man invited the young general to join him. Qamruddin (for that was the general's name) accepted as he was very hungry indeed. Washing his hands, he sat down with the fakir and ate seven kulchas. The fakir urged him to eat more, but Qamruddin politely refused.

The Fakir looked at him intently and said, "You will become king, but because you have eaten only seven kulchas today, you and your dynasty will rule only for seven generations."'

'Was this true?' I asked.

'Yes, it was true. Qamruddin became the first Nizam of Hyderabad, and his dynasty ruled for exactly seven generations, which is why the Hyderabadi coat-of-arms has a kulcha as the centrepiece.'

'I meant is the story of his meeting the fakir in the forest true?' I asked.

Father laughed. 'Let's just say there has to be some very real and valid reason for a piece of bread to be in the centre of the state flag, the velvet despatch boxes of the secretariat and even in a policeman's epaulettes.'

I liked the story. It was just the kind of whimsical thing that appealed to me. It was a pity there was no fakir around to tell me what would happen after eating five kulchas.

seven

I have often wondered who coined that idiotic phrase about childhood being the happiest time of one's life. The process of growing up is, for most of us, an awkward mixture of dependence and a desperate longing for independence. I struggled unsuccessfully to gain the undivided attention of both my parents, without ever succeeding. It led to a strong sense of envy, and an equally strong desire to disrupt other people's lives.

I learnt from watching Yasmin that women become submissive and silly when their one aim in life is to attract men. I also learnt, but only after many long years, that having enough money to meet all one's needs is the basic and necessary ingredient for a contented life. Money may not bring happiness, but it certainly makes it easier to be unhappy in comfort.

I learnt to temper unhappiness with chocolates and books—especially books, which acted for me as powerfully as any drug. I could lose myself in those pages and pages of words, which I devoured with as much eagerness as I devoured the boxes of Belgian and Italian chocolates which Grandma handed me from time to time. Even today I am never without my pile of new books waiting on my bedside table, to distract me from the complexities of real life. Buying new books was for me pure, undiluted pleasure. Good writers, who could draw me into different environments, different worlds, embracing a host of landscapes, cultures and people, with a quality of alert openness, came high on my list of people certain to go straight to heaven. To enable people to live outside of their own frustrated and unhappy lives is surely a gift beyond comparison.

Although I did have a room of my own as a child, when we built the house in Dehra, I planned my room as a refuge, a sanctuary in which everything would be exactly as I wanted it.

Yogis have many different techniques for producing a relaxed state of mind, and one which appealed greatly to me was called 'Creating a Space'. In this technique, one creates an ideal location mentally—a garden wild with trees and flowers, a lonely beach with the sea a silver shimmer, or a thickly forested glade, green and silent.

The space I created, however, was none of these. It was

always a quiet, book-lined room, luxuriously carpeted and with curtains which could shut out the world. When the house was built I achieved what most people never achieve in a hundred lifetimes—my dream, perfectly fulfilled.

Growing up, my most enduring conviction was the importance of physical beauty. Yasmin was always singled out, for no better reason than that she had a pale, creamy skin, masses of shining, flowing hair and a profile to die for. I learnt that the outer shell is what matters to most people; it is all they will ever see. No wonder then that even the World Wildlife Fund has a cuddly panda as its logo, and not an endangered crocodile or reptile.

Herman Hesse speaks of 'the charmed valley of childhood', and for me this was a bitter irony. Inside even the most solitary of human beings lies the need for contact with others. I might have turned into one of those withdrawn, artistic children who find it difficult, if not impossible, to connect with the outside world had it had not been for Grandma.

I found danger everywhere. Although for me school had always been a place of comfort and security, there was one time in the year when again it was Yasmin who held centre stage, and I became invisible.

Each year, our school put on one of their famous Gilbert and Sullivan productions, which were considered to be so good as to be almost professional—and of course Yasmin was the star performer. She had a very charming, light

74

soprano voice. The whole school was passionately involved in these performances, and the children who were acting had a certain glamour about them.

This time the school had chosen '*Iolanthe*'. While we lesser mortals who had not been chosen for even a small part tried to study in our classrooms, the rehearsals would take over from all else, and even as we bent over our books, voices would come floating up to us as Miss Wales, the producer and director, would make some unfortunate child repeat a phrase that she was getting wrong, over and over again.

I remember one couplet particularly which, even now, after so many years, seems indelibly inscribed in my memory. It was—'A plague on this vagary, I'm in a nice quandary, of hasty tone, with dames unknown, I ought to be more chary.'

The song was repeated so often, with such obsessive attention to diction and tune, that invariably there were tears from the children and exasperated shouts from Miss Wales.

This never seemed to happen, however, to Yasmin. She may have stumbled over her words sometimes, but her voice was clear and true. A huge fuss was made over the principal performers—I still recall the Allenbury's Pastilles that Yasmin sucked, the raw eggs she swallowed each morning for her throat and the classes she missed for rehearsals.

And then, finally, the performance. I accompanied

Father and Sophie on the first day of the first show. From the moment that Yasmin appeared, the crowd loved her. She was so charming, so innocently appealing, her voice so sweet and clear. After every song she was applauded, and as though her beauty fed on it, she glowed, her eyes sparkled and the flush on her face spread in a delicate patina over her throat. She was irresistible.

How proud Sophie and Father were. They forgot that I, too, was there, sitting beside them, an invisible, forgotten child. I felt a spasm of jealousy so intense, it was almost physical. My heart thudded, my throat was dry and my hands and feet were wet with sweat. If I could have escaped—just turned and run out of that hall, I would have done so, but the doors were locked and there was nowhere to run.

At last it was over and bouquets were sent up for the principal performers. Yasmin curtsied prettily as she accepted hers, a huge bunch of pink roses tied with trailing ribbons.

We had to walk some distance to the parked car and all the way people reached out to pat her on her head or even pinch her cheeks. It was not long before we were back home and I could run up to Grandma. One look at my face told her everything. She asked no questions. I could smell something wonderful cooking.

'Chicken-almond curry,' said Grandma. 'It's almost

ready. We just have to add the final cup of coconut cream and allow it to simmer on a very slow fire.'

Already I felt comforted, the pain and hurt of the evening dissipating slowly under the comforting words and the fragrance of the curry.

'No one can make this curry the way you do,' I said. 'It never tastes the same when someone else makes it.'

'That is because they don't spend enough time sautéing the ground spices over very low heat. There is neither ginger nor garlic in this recipe, and adding them just spoils the taste. I was looking at a recipe book Sophie has downstairs. Cordon Bleu cooking, it says, and their recipe for chicken curry includes apples, raisins and flour.' She chuckled, 'I must try it out sometime.'

I settled myself on the bed while she pottered around, looking in her cupboard for something. Finally she produced a flat wooden box tied with thin strips of red silk. She settled herself beside me on the bed, untied the silk and opened the box.

'The stones of heaven,' she said, as I peered in at the collection of brilliant green gems, shimmering in their nest of crushed silk.

'What is it?' I asked, picking up a perfectly round stone, cool against my palm and shimmering with light.

'This is jadeite,' Grandma said. 'The more rare and expensive of the two varieties of jade. Traditionally, jade is supposed to have miraculous powers. Your great-grandfather got this from China, and today the price of good quality jadeite can be more than sapphires, rubies and even diamonds.'

I stared, fascinated. Some of the green stones had been carved into figures of gods or emperors, or tiny trees and flowers.

'In the eighteenth century the Chinese emperor Qianlong fell in love with jade and collected as much of it as he could.' Grandma said.

'Where does jade come from?'

'Actually it comes from many places around the world, but the best jade comes from the Kachin hills and jungles in Burma. The Chinese were besotted with it, and called it the "Stone of Heaven".'

'So how did Great-grandfather get these stones? I know he was in China, but what was he doing there?'

'Getting rich on Shanghai real estate and also acquiring, perhaps illegally I'm afraid, stones of jadeite for his collection. They say he also helped the British in the opium wars.'

I laughed and put my hand into the box and came up with several pieces of jade. 'It is cold,' I said. 'Is it meant to be cold?'

'Yes, good jade or jadeite is cool to the touch and has a brilliant shine. Some of the greatest collectors are foreigners—mostly Europeans, but also some Chinese like Madame Chiang Kai-shek, who was supposed to have a fabulous collection. I am going to give you a small piece of jadeite for luck.'

Grandma selected a square from the box, smooth, plump and brilliantly green. It had a tiny hook attached to the top, and through this, she threaded a thin silver chain and slipped it around my neck. The piece of jade felt cool and heavy against my chest, against my heart, and out of sight.

'This is for luck and for good fortune. You can put it under your pillow at night. Now let's go and eat that curry.'

Moti had already dished it out in a large round bowl, accompanied by a dish of fluffy white rice. Thin rings of onions and fine slices of fresh lemon were the only accompaniments needed.

The curry was fiery red in colour and yet not too hot, because the chillies used were the Kashmiri chillies, which provided colour without bite. The ground almonds and coconut cream gave it its thick creamy texture.

I have always found that food—and especially good food—has a very calming and soothing effect on me. With the plump, cool 'stone of heaven' lying against my skin under my dress and the chicken curry in my mouth, it was not too difficult to forget the inevitable trials and tribulations of everyday life.

Grandma said, 'I have given this exact recipe, which was my mother's, to any number of people but they come back to me and say it doesn't taste the same—it is not like yours. I have even parted with the secret of a really good curry. The masala must be very finely ground and it should then be sautéed over a very low fire for as long as fifteen minutes. Good food, like everything else that is worthwhile in life, needs dedication and patience.'

I guzzled as Grandma picked out tender pieces of chicken and added them to my plate. Finally, even I could eat no more.

'You had better go downstairs now,' Grandma said. 'They will be starting dinner soon.' I hugged her tight and made my way slowly down the stairs.

They were already at the dining table. 'There you are,' said Sophie, dishing out the cauliflower-cheese casserole and spooning brown mince into Yasmin's plate.

'Come along Naaz. Hurry up or you won't get any supper.'

'I don't want any. I am not hungry.'

'Now don't sulk. Just because Yasmin was the star of the show and got the biggest bouquet, there is no need for you to sulk.'

'Why should I sulk? I know Yasmin was very good— this year she was specially good. But Grandma has made her famous chicken-almond curry today and I shared it with her, so I am really not at all hungry.'

Father looked at the bland food on the table and said, 'Sophie, why do we always have this sort of food at home?

No one would believe me if I told them we were living in Hyderabad and eating brown mince for dinner.'

Sophie turned pink. The English turn pink very easily. She said, 'If you don't like it, why don't you go and eat that wonderful curry too?'

Father got up from the table. 'You know, I think that is exactly what I will do.'

Sophie watched him go in silence. Then, inevitably, she turned to me. 'You always manage to create trouble. If you are not eating dinner, why don't you go to your room?'

I shrugged. Father was a warm man, conscious of his domestic obligations and generous to his friends. But Sophie was different. Reserved, often remote, she disliked all Father's suffocating Parsi relatives—those garrulous, friendly and numerous cousins, aunts and uncles and their progeny who jabbered in a mixture of English and Gujarati, were effusive, and were forever hugging everyone with such abandon.

Although Father himself had no siblings, both grandparents came from very large families and there were cousins galore. Every festival, every wedding was celebrated with food and liquor and hordes of cousins.

Zoroastrianism is not an ascetic religion. In fact, asceticism is frowned upon. One is enjoined to eat, drink and accumulate wealth; but wealth must be shared for the common good. This accounts for the huge charities sponsored by wealthy Parsi families. Schools, hospitals and housing colonies, as well as excellent working conditions are provided by Parsi industrial magnates for their employees.

In spite of being such a tiny community, no Parsi has ever required job reservations or handouts in any form from the ruling party. Wealth is considered fundamentally positive, but it also carries with it certain social and moral obligations.

This tends to set Zoroastrianism apart from other Indian religions which encourage asceticism and a retreat from the world, preferably to some inhospitable mountain-top. Zoroastrians believe in the affirmation of life and share a conscious desire to shape the world for the better. They believe that the world is a battlefield between the forces of good and evil, and that man is called upon to fight for good. This is neither easy, nor indeed possible, if the world is abandoned.

'Not resignation, asceticism or fasting is the task of man, but the attainment of strength and a courageous advocacy of the principle of good. Whoever fights against lies, misfortune, illness, discord, poverty and immorality in this world, is supporting the good in its cosmic battle.'

Sophie of course knew nothing of all this and cared even less. Although Sophie genuinely loved Father, she was beginning to dislike not only the numerous cousins, aunts and uncles, but in fact, all Parsis.

They were so voluble, so given to hugging and kissing

everyone around them, and so pleased with themselves and confirmed in their feeling of superiority that their very friendliness seemed to her an affront.

She simply could not understand how Father could melt so easily into this noisy, greedy, bustling crowd. It was so unlike his usual demeanour.

An English friend of hers, on a recent visit to India, was fascinated by the Parsis. He was writing a thesis on them based on the premise that since they had no literary tradition of their own, apart from religious literature, it made them adopt and study European literature, which, combined with the intensive use of the English language, made them opt for everything English.

He found them, on the whole, fascinating and also somewhat ludicrous. He grilled Sophie on what sort of life she led in a Parsi household, and was disappointed at her replies.

'They sound,' he said, 'just like a middle class English family.' Sophie was outraged. She said, 'They are different. Totally different. They think, speak and act like themselves and like no one else.' She found it difficult to explain how, but she knew she was right.

eight

Grandma was eighty-four when she died quietly, without fuss and with the same quiet dignity with which she had lived her life. As the sun sank behind the minarets and cupolas of the white buildings, she closed her eyes and passed into oblivion, or into another world. I did not know which. As soon as I heard the news, I flew down from Delhi and was just in time for the funeral—Zoroastrian funerals never take place after sunset.

By the time I arrived, the house was filled with friends and relatives, and the body had been laid out in its funeral shroud. Lying alone as though abandoned on the stone slab, she looked frail, small and defenceless. What would I do without her? She had been guide, mentor, friend and protector, my fortress of safety. It was because of her that I had survived. Intuitively, we equate survival with caring.

Without continuous love and care, the self is diminished, alienated, alone.

Sandalwood and incense scented the air, and the fragrant smoke wrapped us all in a pall of gloom. I was forever to equate the scent of sandalwood with death. There was a deathly silence (I thought how appropriate that expression was), broken only by the continuous intoning of prayers by the priests. Into this silence came the corpse-bearers— the Nassasalars—men who would carry the body into the Tower of Silence, strip the clothes from the corpse and leave it for the vultures to consume. They were dressed completely in white—caps, gloves, socks ands shirts, even their faces were covered with white cloth masks. Because they handled dead bodies, they were considered unclean and could not enter the Fire Temple without first going through a purificatory bath. They covered the corpse with a white sheet, and with an iron nail drew a protective circle around the body—from now on no one but the Nassasalars themselves could enter this circle.

The priests began to recite the *Hunavaiti Gatha*, which was meant to console the bereaved and speed the soul on its way to eternal bliss. The prayers sounded impressive in the old dead language of Avesta, but of course no one could understand a word. Later I was to find an English translation of this which seemed to have nothing to do with death or dying. One verse read:

Oh Ahura, grant Zarathustra and his followers eminence and sovereignty through Truth. May they establish a peaceful and happy existence through the Good Mind. I recognize you, O Mazda, as the Prime giver of this gift.

Perhaps it was just as well that I did not understand the words; they sounded better, seemed more filled with meaning, in the old language. The corpse-bearers now lifted the body on to the bier and secured it firmly with strips of white cloth. As the prayers came to an end the body began its last journey, followed by only male members of the congregation. They walked in pairs behind the body, while the women remained behind. The bier would be placed at the gates of the Tower of Silence. Only the corpse-bearers could go beyond this point. They would take the body inside and strip it for the vultures.

The thought of that small body, so powerful in life, now fit only for the vultures to tear apart, made me feel sick. Death was difficult enough for the living to cope with, and funerals should be so designed as to help and console the mourners. A closed coffin, flowers and valedictory speeches would have helped. But best of all, I would have liked Grandma to have had a royal funeral, her body in a coffin draped with the tricolour, carried on a gun carriage followed by a white horse with stirrups crossed, a band wailing a Scottish dirge. Grandma would have smiled at my strong dose of vintage colonial fantasy. I made a vow that my body would never end up like this. Not vultures; it would be the electric crematorium for me, my body reduced to ashes.

With growing urbanization, high-rise buildings and the extensive use of pesticides, the vulture population was fast disappearing. There were no longer enough vultures to do the job of disposing of dead bodies rapidly and completely. The first Tower of Silence was built on land donated by the British in Bombay in 1673. A really gruesome bit of information which I picked up from one of the daily newspapers made me only more determined to avoid this antiquated method of disposing of dead bodies.

'Over generations we have been brainwashed into believing that the powerful sunrays and the vultures are capable of disposing of a dead human carcass completely and within hours. Nothing could be further from the truth. Vultures, it seems, are selective eaters and only accept parts of the carcass like liver, spleen, lungs etc. If the body has a high concentration of chemotherapeutic drugs, the vultures will not touch it.'

After the funeral I went up to Grandma's rooms, where a candle was burning beside the bed. A lamp stood on the polished table on which her bottles of Bayrum and almond oil stood, just as they always had. Her bed was made up as always, with spotless white sheets and her two feather pillows in which I now buried my head. Moti put a consoling hand on my shoulder. She handed me a letter written in Grandma's distinctive, small, upright script.

Naaz, Beloved child,

When you get this, I will no longer be there. I have never believed either in heaven or hell and the burden of commanded rituals has never been a part of our religion, but I still feel very strongly, that something of me, just the essence perhaps, will remain for ever in the energy that surrounds you—a benevolent energy that will help and console you. You brought much happiness into my life. The money that I have left you will ensure that you will be free to pursue whatever you wish to do and also free you from the very real problems that lack of money can bring. I pray that you will use what I have left you prudently and well, helping others less fortunate, causing no one pain.

She had signed the note with her initials—GSJ. I folded the letter carefully and held it tight, hoping that something of her would come through into my skin and flesh, and I would feel her close to me again. But I felt nothing. She was gone, and once again I was alone. I walked out into the sunny balcony, out of the green-lit rooms and into a leafy bower of ferns, herbs and trailing vines.

'She's dead,' I said. 'She won't be here to clip, prune and tend you any more. She's dead,' I burst into tears. Moti put her arms around me and patted and stroked my head.

'Don't cry, Naaz. She loved you so much that in your heart you will feel her close to you forever.'

But I felt nothing. All that remained of her were memories from a mythic, irretrievable past. I was alone again, searching for paths now forever lost. I wiped my eyes.

'What will you do now?' I asked Moti. 'Would you like to come with me or stay here?'

She shook her head. 'I will return to my village in Garhwal.' I was shocked.

'You know you can always stay here if you don't want to come to Delhi. And what about money?'

'Your grandmother gave me more than enough. She was very generous and looked after me well. I will never know another person like her. She taught me everything and gave me so much. But if you need me, I will stay with you until you return to Delhi and if you ever want me, I will come at once.'

It was at this moment that Jaya, Sophie's maid, came up the stairs to call me.

'They are calling you downstairs. The bank people have come.' I smoothed my hair and scrubbed my face with the towel Moti held out to me. I felt numb and stiff, as though walking down those familiar stairs would be impossible.

Grandma would have said, 'You need a stiff brandy,' and in spite of everything, I smiled. It was her cure for everything. Often, as a child, I would pour the small glass of diluted brandy surreptitiously into a flower pot, since it tasted so nasty.

Why did they want me? What had I to do with lawyers? I found them all in Father's study. Sophie, Father, Mr Sharma, and the new bank manage, Mr Hogan. They stood up as I entered the room, but Father sat there staring at me. He said, 'Sit down Naaz. Did you know what was in Mother's will?'

I looked at the four grave faces staring at me, and shook my head. 'Is something wrong?' I wondered if Grandma had not left a proper will. It was Mr Sharma who replied.

'No, no. The will is admirably clear and concise. It is properly signed and witnessed. In fact, as I have explained to your father, I had drawn it up for your grandmother only six months ago with the help of Mr Hogan, who provided details of investments, monies and properties.'

I still could not fathom why they were all staring at me, especially Father, who looked not so much serious as shell-shocked. I sat and waited. At last Mr Sharma said, 'The bulk of the estate has been left to you in its entirety.'

Mr Hogan added, 'This has come as a shock to your father, who has been left in possession of this house and a generous endowment. The rest of your grandmother's considerable—very considerable—estate including stocks, investments, properties, jewellery and the business has been left to you.'

I let the words sink in. How much was everything? How much was all? The silence in the room was so complete that I could hear Father breathing. He was taking deep, laboured breaths.

Into the silence I said, 'Grandma left me this letter. Moti just gave it to me.' I held out the letter, and Father leaned over and snatched it from my hand. He read it and sat staring at me. Mr Sharma said, 'May I see it?' and took the letter from Father's hand. He read it in silence and then passed it over to Mr Hogan, who also read it in silence and then handed it back to me. Mr Sharma said, 'I think there can be no doubt that Mrs Jussawalla had made up her mind and knew what she was doing.' Mr Hogan nodded, but said nothing. They were all staring at me, waiting for some sort of reaction.

'How much is it?' I asked finally. Mr Sharma put down his cigarette. Except when he was with Grandma, he smoked incessantly, every sentence punctuated by small, gasping breaths as he inhaled, blew out the smoke and inhaled again. He turned now towards Mr Hogan, who explained, 'It is difficult to come to an exact estimate as the price of stocks, shares, property, even jewellery, fluctuate enormously, and of course there is the furniture business as well. All I can say right now is that it is a very considerable sum—very considerable indeed.'

91

I stared at them stunned. I thought of Grandma. I knew why she had done this. Firstly, because she had trained me through the years and knew I would be careful. It was also her way of saying, 'I love you, Naaz.' I felt her small, plump hand reach out for me, her voice saying 'Money is very important, perhaps one of the most important things in life. When there is money, it is possible to pursue a good life, by helping others. When there is not enough money, one's mind is constantly engaged with trying to make ends meet. There is little room for anything else.'

They were still staring at me and suddenly I felt confident, my mind sharp and clear. Father put down the pen with which he had been stabbing the pad in front of him. He looked at me.

'This has come as a complete shock to me. I simply cannot understand why Mother did not leave everything to me, her only son. Her only child, in fact. Ultimately, of course, the money would have come to you and Yasmin.'

I kept silent for so long that it was Sophie who said sharply, 'Don't just sit there staring at us. For God's sake, say something.'

My silence had not been deliberate. I was thinking. I have never believed in divine providence and I was not going to start now. This was Grandma's doing and I just knew she expected me to be strong and to handle whatever difficulties cropped up. Of course she had known that there would be difficulties.

Mr Sharma raised his head from his notes and said, 'We will have the formal reading of the will tomorrow. There is a generous bequest for your father, but the bulk will be yours. We thought it proper to inform your father first.'

I had trained myself to listen to voices. Often they gave away more than faces, which can be schooled to reveal nothing. But voices and eyes—these are not easy to camouflage. Father's voice had a hint of desperation in it, and anger. Or was it hatred?

He said, 'I have been discussing the matter with these two gentlemen, and we have agreed that the best and most suitable solution would be for you to entrust everything to me. You are too young and too inexperienced to deal with something like this. I will look after your interests; that goes without saying.'

I made my voice soft and placating. 'I will always come to you for advice, Father, but I think Grandma would have expected me to manage this for myself. I have been doing her accounts since I was thirteen years old, and I visited the bank with her at least once a month. She started an account for me when I was only eight years old. I think she would have wanted me to manage things myself.'

Father looked both astonished and disapproving. Mr Hogan now said, 'I must agree with Naaz about this. Both Sharma and I knew that the old lady was training Naaz for perhaps just such an eventuality.'

After they left we sat down to lunch. It was an

uncomfortable meal. So far Sophie had said nothing and I thought perhaps she felt she had no right, as an outsider, to intervene. Father stared at his plate, but Sophie kept her eyes on me as though she had suddenly encountered a snake in her bedroom, or a two-headed monster. I went to my room, for the last time, perhaps.

I had already made up my mind to return to Delhi and live there permanently, or at least till I had finished my studies. I would wait for the reading of the will and then speak to Mr Sharma about my plans. I would buy myself a small flat.

It was not long after this that Sophie knocked and entered my room. It had been some time since Sophie had visited me here and she looked around with astonishment. My room was now furnished with many of the things Grandma had given me through the years. A blue Shirazi carpet which had hung on Grandma's bedroom wall, was now covering the floor near my bed. There was also the rosewood writing table and the bronze bust of the Buddha that Grandma had kept to give me on my birthday.

Sophie looked around, but said not a word. Instead she pulled up a chair, threw the cushion off and confronted me. 'Your father is absolutely outraged by this will. It is inconceivable that he should be left with nothing except the house. One house! Do you know how many houses your grandmother owned? And did you know that all these years your father spent his own money to run this house—

the money that he made from the furniture business? He paid for everything—the cars, the servants; everything. He never doubted for a single moment that everything would be left to him. He was the only son, we could never even imagine that something like this could happen. If you had not wormed your way into the old woman's heart and persuaded her to leave everything to you, she would have done what was right and proper. You can make amends. Speak to the lawyers and sign over everything to your father. After we die the money can be shared equally between you and Yasmin. And that is another thing—she has left nothing at all to Yasmin.'

I had been sitting quietly listening to this tirade. At last I said, 'Sophie, you know perfectly well that when Yasmin was married Grandma gave her a very substantial sum of money, and an incredible amount of jewellery, some of it specially made for her.'

In fact I remember thinking that I had never seen so much jewellery at one time. Sophie said uneasily, 'We have heard rather disquieting rumours about Bobby's father. There has been talk of financial difficulties and irregularities—perhaps even bankruptcy. Of course, this may only be talk, and we have heard nothing from Yasmin. We have no idea where they are at the moment—in India or Europe. She probably hasn't even heard of your grandmother's death. Anyway, there is no reason why Yasmin should not have her share of the family money.'

'Except that when Grandma was alive, Yasmin would have nothing to do with her. She disliked and despised Grandma. And all because of you. It was you who encouraged her to get rid of the sudra and kusti. You encouraged her to stop saying her prayers. Do you remember the time you cut up Father's kusti, which you found in his sock drawer, to tie up your roses?'

Sophie turned a deep red. That little episode had caused a huge row.

Moti was wandering in the garden one morning, looking for fresh green garlic for Grandma's soup, when she discovered the roses, tied back on supporting canes with bits of snipped up kusti. She rushed to tell Grandma.

After Grandma had come downstairs, inspected the roses and settled herself in a chair, she summoned everyone. We assembled before her, feeling for some reason like guilty children who are not sure what they have done this time.

Grandma held up a bit of snipped off kusti, encrusted with mud. 'Sophie, do you usually tie up your rose bushes with the thread which we Parsis consider sacred, and with which both your children have just been consecrated?'

She said this quietly, without raising her voice at all. 'Whose idea was it?' She looked at all of us in turn. 'Sophie?'

Father was totally bewildered. 'Sophie, how could you? Mother, I'm sure she didn't do it deliberately. No one would do such a thing. She probably mistook it for a bit of string.'

Grandma said nothing. When the silence continued she said, 'Come here Yasmin.' Yasmin came reluctantly. 'You at least know what a kusti is don't you, even if you refuse to say the prayers, and have stopped wearing one.' Yasmin nodded, tongue-tied. She was as pale as wax. 'Did Sophie think it was a joke? Something to laugh about?' Yasmin appeared on the verge of getting hysterics, when Sophie intervened.

'Don't blame Yasmin. It was my idea. I needed something to tie up my roses, and I just picked this up from JJ's drawer.'

Father was looking at her in absolute horror. She turned on him. 'Don't you start getting all pious on me. You have never worn either the sudra or the kusti as long as I have known you. You don't believe in it. You said so yourself.'

'Whether I believe in it or not is immaterial. I don't believe in your rosary either, but I wouldn't cut it up and tie plants with it.' There was silence that lasted so long that I wondered if someone would disrupt it with a scream of hysteria.

Finally Grandma said, 'Yasmin, go into the garden and bring me every bit of the kusti which your mother has cut up. I want every bit, understand?'

Yasmin looked at Sophie with a terrified expression and both of them went out together. We sat in a kind of petrified silence until they returned, their hands full of muddy, wet, dirty bits and pieces, some small, some bigger, but all of them stained and caked with mud.

Grandma directed them to lay the pieces down on the long dining table. With infinite care, she began to piece them together. At last she raised her head. She said, 'One of the tassels is missing. Yasmin, go back and see if you can find it.'

Yasmin let out a loud wail, which turned into a full-fledged attack of hysterics. She screamed, flung herself on the floor, kicking her legs and banging her head on the carpet. Sophie went to lift her up, and was hit with a flailing arm. Grandma sat like a stone, without moving.

Eventually Yasmin's hysterics subsided and she sat up, coughing and sniffling, her face streaming with tears. Grandma looked at Sophie. She did not utter a word but Sophie went out into the garden and returned after some time, empty-handed.

'I can't find it.'

Grandma stared at her for a brief moment. Then she produced a very large white handkerchief and began to put each piece of the chopped-up, dirty kusti into it. When all the pieces had been laid safely on the white material, she gathered up the corners and tied them together securely. Then, without another glance at anyone, she turned her back, walked across the room and very, very slowly up the stairs. We followed her with our eyes till she finally disappeared from view.

In retrospect, I suppose the whole thing was hilariously funny. The old woman, so powerful in her outrage, controlling every one in the room. There was no shouting, no swearing. Without raising her voice once, she totally dominated us. Sophie, white-faced and guilty, Father, baffled and annoyed, and Yasmin frightened into hysterics.

Sophie said, 'What will she do with the pieces?'

'God only knows. Bury them, I suppose, or throw them into a river or stream,' Father said. 'Sophie, you have done more harm today than you could ever have ever imagined.' He was right. It was an incident which had long-lasting effects.

I said now to Sophie, 'You did your utmost to alienate Yasmin and destroy any relationship she might have forged with Grandma.'

'That is no reason to leave her entire fortune to you.'

I shrugged. 'Grandma did what she thought was best for all of us. She knew Father has suffered two heart attacks, and perhaps felt it would not be fair to burden him with managing the estate. I will be leaving for Delhi the moment the lawyers have finished with me. You should look at it this way, Sophie—the house is yours, and there is more than enough money to live as comfortably as before. I will see Father before I leave.'

nine

Women sleep with men for many reasons—for security, from a desire to give pleasure, for money and sometimes, but only sometimes, for love.

I, of course, slept with Ramesh because we were married, but I was not sure if I was in love with him, or even if he was in love with me. I would lie awake beside him and watch him sleep and remember the things he said.

'Naaz, you are beautiful without your clothes. Such soft, smooth skin, tinged with gold. And your back is so pretty— rounded, without shoulder bones sticking out like chicken wings. If I were an artist I would be tempted to use your back as a very special, smooth and tightly stretched canvas. And you have dimples in the most unexpected places. Men who marry skinny women have no idea what they are missing.'

He never seemed to tire of exploring my body with his hands and lips—my body, so clumsy in clothes, was so satisfying, it seemed, without. I developed an appetite for sexual pleasure.

In sexual union we are forced, however briefly, into the present moment. We no longer stand apart from life or from each other. The Buddhist saying 'Present moment, only moment', becomes a reality. For this brief moment of ecstatic communion with another, the essential loneliness of every human soul is assuaged.

I think I knew from the very first moment I saw him that this was someone I could be married to. He was standing in the university library, a pile of books precariously balanced in his arms. He was thin and tall, with a pleasantly bony face and gentle brown eyes. He looked as if he could never hurt anyone or anything. His teeth were very white and he had the high cheekbones that sometimes occur among the people of north India.

I stretched out my hand for a book high up on the shelf, and as he turned, the pile of books he was holding toppled over, landing with a heavy thud on my foot. 'Ow!' I exclaimed.

He was abjectly apologetic. 'I am so sorry. Are you hurt?' I shook my head. He bent over to pick up the books which were, as far as I could make out, on architecture and design. He introduced himself. 'I am Ramesh Verma. I know who you are of course. They call you "the brain".'

He said, 'You frowned. You don't like being called "the brain"?' I did not reply, and he searched desperately for something more to say. At last he said, 'I was just going to the canteen for a coffee. Will you join me?'

I allowed myself to be escorted to the canteen, where we found an unoccupied table in a corner. We sipped watery, lukewarm coffee while he told me about himself. He was twenty-six, a Punjabi from Ludhiana whose family had settled in Delhi. His father had retired from the railways and his mother looked after the house and his teenaged, retarded sister. He found my name romantic. 'Naaz. What does it mean?'

'In Persian it means "beloved". I'm a Parsi, and although we fled Persia thirteen hundred years ago, all our names are still Persian.'

'You are the first Parsi I have ever really met or spoken to. The Parsis are so reclusive that neither I, nor any of my friends, know much about them, except that you are fire-worshippers.'

'That is not strictly true. We consider fire to be the symbol of God, or Ahura Mazda. It is an essential part of all our ceremonies and is kept burning day and night in our Fire Temples.'

There are so few Parsis in India, and they lead such low-key lives, that except in Bombay and Pune they are relatively unknown.

Ramesh managed to tell me quite a bit about himself,

and soon I had a reasonably accurate picture of his life and that of his parents, and their hopes for their only son. He was wearing well-washed jeans, a clean, open-necked shirt and leather sandals on his feet. He had very thick, black hair which fell over his forehead and which he pushed back from time to time without it making much of a difference.

It was the first of many meetings, and from the very beginning I knew that he was the one I wanted to marry. He, of course, had not the slightest suspicion of what was in my mind. To him, I was just a new and rather intriguing friend.

I was determined to marry him, although I was a Parsi and he, a Punjabi, and no one would approve. Parsis think of themselves as very special people; a pure Aryan race, not to be corrupted or contaminated by marriage with outsiders. I was only half-Parsi, but since Father was a full-blooded Parsi, Yasmin and I had been inducted into the Zorastrian religion. It was a very patriarchal religion.

Like many Parsis of my generation whose parents and grandparents had grown up under British rule, I had received an essentially European education. In a home filled with books, I had studied in convent schools, read the British classical authors, and in college my doctoral dissertation was on James Princep, a nineteenth-century British orientalist whose work I admired. Yasmin and I had been given what Father always referred to as a 'Winnie-the-Pooh' background, compared with Ramesh's background, which was grounded in the great Hindu epics, the Ramayana and the Mahabharata.

It took some months before Ramesh began to think of me as anything more than an interesting friend. In the beginning he was just enormously intrigued by everything about me. I was not a Hindu, nor a Muslim. I lived alone, in my own flat, with servants to look after me and with my own car. I seemed a free spirit.

He was especially astonished and charmed by my small flat. I had bought it soon after Grandma died, and some of her exquisite carpets were on the floors and the rosewood furniture gleamed like silk against the beige walls. He was fascinated with the bathrooms with their coloured tiles and flowered curtains.

I would order tea and biscuits and he would sit by the hour and tell me about his dreams for the future. I listened and stored away every little bit of information that I could use. He was a passionate admirer of the American architect Joseph Allen Stein, who had become an icon of modern Indian architecture. Stein had made India his home and dedicated his life to building wonderful projects all over India, through the integration of buildings with vertical gardens. His concern for the environment influenced everything he created, and he believed that when 'sustainable ecology' in an urban context was achieved, life for everyone would be considerably better.

Ramesh too wanted to build climate-responsive

structures which would fit snugly and elegantly into the landscape. He believed that the congestion of modern Indian cities was directly responsible for the deterioration in modern living standards and the stressed-out lifestyles of city dwellers.

He told me about his sister, whom his mother was hoping to get married in spite of the fact that she was retarded.

'Her mind is at the level of a six-year-old's, but otherwise she is a big girl. She can cook simple dishes, wash and clean, and generally make herself useful in the house. She has a pretty singing voice and my parents feel that her only security lies in marriage. But who will marry her, even with a good dowry? And how will they treat her when they find out she is not normal? How safe will she be in a strange household? She is gentle and good-tempered, and Ma has brought her up as though she is a precious, easily-bruised flower. I suppose there are men who might appreciate someone like her—someone who will do as she is told, work hard, and remain pliable.'

There was something in his voice that made me look at him and say, 'You don't like her, do you?'

He shuddered slightly and bent his head. The words came out muffled. 'She repels me. I cannot bear to be alone in a room with her. Those shallow eyes, that smiling face. She sings about the house, and her voice makes me shiver.

I have never told anyone how I feel. Not my parents—especially not my parents—I am ashamed of this feeling.'

He looked up at me and continued in a voice that was carefully without inflexion. 'They expect me to marry well, so that the dowry my wife brings can be used to get her married.'

I had bought a flat in Nizamuddin East, one of the more pleasant residential areas in New Delhi, where lots of young professionals and a fair number of artists stayed. It was a tree-lined neighbourhood, and there were birds and squirrels and pampered dogs with their doting owners instead of pathetic, starving strays.

I sat staring out of the window for some time without saying anything. When I turned I said quietly, 'You could marry me.'

For a moment he doubted that he had heard correctly. He lifted his head slowly and stared at me with bewildered eyes. A flush covered his face and spread over his neck and ears. He laughed nervously.

'That's not very funny.'

'It was not meant to be funny.'

He left the chair he had been sitting in and came over to the window, where I continued to look out. I was able to think a thousand thoughts before he spoke.

'Naaz, are you serious? What will your family say?'

'My family have nothing to do with it. My father is dead, and there is only my mother who lives in the old house in Hyderabad. She is English, and will probably not care one way or the other.'

He looked at me in utter astonishment, 'I know so little about you. How can your marriage not matter to anyone?'

'When my grandmother died she left nearly all her money and property to me. I do not need to consult anyone. You don't have to reply at once. You can think over it. After all, arranged marriages are familiar to both of us.'

He knelt down beside my chair and took both my hands in his. Such warm, strong hands. I still did not look at him, but kept my face averted. What could he know of the dark and hidden jungles of my lonely heart and mind? I suddenly felt a consuming passion to have him all to myself, to possess him, devour him so there would be no one else in the world for us. I was young, rich, clever—surely it was enough?

A silence fell, which seemed to last forever. At last he said, 'I don't know what to say. Even if I were tempted to say yes, my marriage does not concern only me. I cannot get married to anyone without the consent of my parents. I must think of my sister, and the need for a dowry from my bride.'

'I understand.'

'Do you? Do you really understand? You, who come from such a very different world?'

An enormous, numbing loneliness engulfed me. If he said 'no', what would happen to me? I would be alone forever. I had never felt this way before, that happiness

107

with someone could actually be mine. Now all I could do was wait.

It was ten days before he called—I counted the days, so I knew. I was at my desk working, when the telephone rang.

He did not waste any time on preliminaries. 'I have spoken to my parents. They don't know what to make of the whole thing, but they would like to meet you tomorrow. When can you come? How about five in the evening? Would that suit you?'

I kept my voice casual, although my heart was hammering loudly and I thought if I held the receiver against my chest, he would hear it beating. Instead I said, 'Yes, five will be fine.'

'I'll pick you up a little before five, then.'

'Yes, all right.'

The memory of that day which was to change my life forever is still vivid, as if it happened yesterday. I had no idea what to expect. If Ramesh knew no Parsis, I, too, had no Punjabi friends. The girls I knew in college were a different species. The ones who came from very traditional families wore their hair in long braids and smelled strongly of stale perspiration because they had never heard of deodorants. The others were from rich families—poised, pretty, expensively dressed. We said 'hello' to each other, but that was the extent of our involvement.

I dressed as I always did—expensively but

conservatively. I was not pretty, but Indians do not look for prettiness in their daughters-in-law. They want fair skin, or what they like to call 'a wheatish complexion', good strong bones and a general air of wishing to please. For luck I wore Grandma's pink pearls around my neck. Nothing else, not even a gold bangle on my wrist.

Ramesh arrived dead on time, tense with nervousness and worry. I suggested he drive my small Fiat, and we shot off without another word. Perhaps it was better this way, since there really was nothing to say.

I recalled Grandma's advice about the advisability of marrying someone of one's own kind. 'You are not simply marrying a man—you are marrying a whole culture, a religion, a family, a way of life. When these are similar to your own, then you have a fair chance of being happily married.'

Ramesh's background, culture, religion and family could hardly have been more different from mine. But it is also true that each of us show different aspects of ourselves to different people. If I were surrounded now by the people who mattered most in my life—Father, Sophie, Grandma, Yasmin and now Ramesh, each would see me differently from the others. I would reflect their views, their impressions and, of course, their own innate prejudices.

The Vermas lived in a small two-bedroom flat on the second floor of a block of rather dingy DDA flats. The front door opened into a small anteroom which appeared to be crammed with grey steel cupboards, all securely locked.

Ramesh's mother met us at the door and led us into a small, dark sitting room. She kept her eyes fixed on me, and I wondered briefly if she expected me to stoop down and touch her feet in respect—a custom almost universally prevalent in India, but not amongst the Parsis. I thought it well to start as I intended to continue.

The room was shabby and not very clean. It smelt of drains and stale food. Brightly coloured calendars with pictures of various Hindu gods and goddesses decorated the walls, some with strings of artificial flowers looped over them. There were also pictures of the controversial Sai Baba, with his fuzzy hair.

Ramesh's mother ushered me to a dingy divan covered with a faded bedspread. Every small table was covered with hand-embroidered cloths, and in three corners of the room stood plastic dolls on tall stools, dressed in frilly, handmade dresses. I sat on the edge of the divan and looked around.

Ramesh's mother studied me, not surreptitiously but openly, running her eyes over my face and clothes as though she were making an inventory. Ramesh's father now entered the room, and I stood up to greet him. He was in total contrast to his wife. Where she was plump, with fat, brown arms and a thick middle, he was thin, almost emaciated, stooped and prematurely grey. He was wearing a shirt hanging loose over pyjamas, and had a lined and defeated face. Ramesh had told me about him. He was honest, hard-working and gentle. He had received nothing from fate that was good, and he no longer expected anything more from life. He too kept his eyes on me, staring, fascinated, as though I were some unusual bird which had unexpectedly alighted in his sitting room.

A girl entered the room, carefully carrying a tray laid with cups and saucers and a large teapot. No milk or sugar. I winced; I hated tea made the Indian way—tea leaves, milk and sugar all boiled up together into a strong, sweet brew. The girl put the tray down and stood with her hands together, looking at me. It was difficult to tell how old she was. She had an unlined, pleasant face, eyes as shallow as a cat's, and a smile which seemed to be there permanently.

'This is Sunita, Ramesh's sister,' his mother said. I stretched out my hand and drew her towards me. She came at once, smiling. Ramesh avoided looking at me as I picked up my cup, hesitating before sipping the tea, but there was a glimmer of a smile on his face. He had taken tea or coffee in my flat often enough to know what I liked—pale amber tea, with little milk and no sugar, served in bone china cups.

Ramesh's mother was still staring at me. What did she see? An alien female, plump and not good-looking, wearing a very expensive silk sari and a fabulous string of pearls around her neck. In traditional Indian style, she, herself, although wearing a rather grubby sari, was wearing two gold chains, several gold and glass bangles on her wrists and thick gold hoops in her ears.

111

Her first words to me were: 'Why do you live alone in your own flat? It seems very strange for a young, unmarried girl to be living on her own in Delhi.'

I kept my voice neutral. 'My father is dead and my mother lives in Hyderabad. I came to Delhi to study, and it is more convenient for me to live in my own flat than to live as a paying guest. I manage very well this way.'

'Ramesh tells me you want to get married. Is this true?'

'Yes, it is true.'

'Why should you wish to marry Ramesh? We are a poor Punjabi family. You are not like us. You are different, and your religion is different. How will you fit in with us?'

I did not reply and she continued, 'And what of your mother. Will she not object?'

'My mother is English, I do not think she will have any objections at all. I think she will like Ramesh.'

She was not appeased. She grumbled, 'It is very difficult to talk to a young girl about such matters. It would be easier to talk to some older relative.'

When I did not reply she said, 'Ramesh, take you sister outside for a while. I would like to speak to Naaz alone.'

Ramesh got up without a word or a backward glance, and led Sunita out. Mrs Verma stared at me for a long time as though trying to make up her mind what to say. She was dressed in a cotton sari that had been washed many times but not ironed. She had the bulgy look of someone who lives an unhealthy life, a look common to many lower-middle-class Indian women, who feel that once a woman gets married, her looks are not important as long as she has produced children and spends her time cooking and cleaning.

At last she spoke. 'I do not know your Parsi customs but among us, we Punjabis expect the girl to bring a good dowry. I know it is not legal but no one bothers much about that. For us a dowry is specially important in order to get my Sunita married. I believe Ramesh mentioned this to you.'

'Yes, he told me and I understand your problem. It is not the custom among Parsis to give dowries, but I am quite willing to do whatever is needed.'

It was then that Ramesh's father, who had been sitting quiet and still all this time said, 'Please forgive me for asking this question, but who manages your money, your financial affairs if you have neither father nor brother?'

'I manage it myself with the help of lawyers and trustees.'

'Lawyers! Trustees? There must be a lot of money?' he said.

'There is a fair amount. My grandmother left almost everything to me.'

'With this background, why do you wish to marry Ramesh? It is strange and most peculiar. Why not someone in your own community?'

I could have replied honestly that I thought I was in

love with Ramesh. That I thought we could be happy together.

Instead I said cautiously, 'We like each other, and we get on well. I think we could live happily together if we got married.'

There was a long silence as they mulled over my answer, which must have struck them as very strange indeed. They stared at me as though I were some exotic plant or creature which they had never seen before, which they found utterly baffling. In the continuing silence I looked around the room, so pathetically shabby. The unpainted doors, the skimpy curtains, the air, which was stale and smelt of mustard oil. How ugly life could be without money.

At last Ramesh's mother said, 'I will be quite frank with you. We were hoping Ramesh would marry a girl from our community. Someone who would be prepared to bring a substantial dowry, and who would stay here with us and take on some of the burden of cooking and washing and cleaning, which is now becoming too much for us. But you have your own flat. You will not live here.'

'It is true that I have my own flat but even if I do not stay with you, I am quite prepared to give you whatever you need to get Sunita married.'

'Ramesh will not talk about this,' the mother said. 'He does not like the idea—but even he realizes that there is no other way we can get Sunita married.'

'It will be easier for all of us if you just tell me what

114

you had in mind. Parsis do not ask for or bring a dowry at the time of marriage, so I really have no idea about this.'

Ramesh's father now intervened. 'Since Ramesh will not wish to discuss such matters, it would be better if we meet somewhere—perhaps at your flat. Ramesh need not be there. Just the three of us.'

I agreed at once, and we fixed a time and a date. In the car on the way back, I informed Ramesh of our decision. He was appalled, and protested violently. I soothed him down. I explained that it was much better this way, but he grumbled all the way back. 'What a way to arrange a marriage. I haven't even asked you properly to marry me.'

'You can ask me as soon as we get back to the flat.' He laughed reluctantly. 'How can you be so calm, so poised?'

My flat, as always, smelt of polish, of flowers, of fresh, clean air. He sniffed appreciatively. 'Why does you place smell so different from ours?'

I did not feel the need to reply. I settled myself in a chair beside the window and folded my hands in my lap. He knelt beside me without touching me and said formally, 'Naaz, will you marry me?'

I laughed, put my arms around him and said, 'Yes, yes, yes.'

'You make everything seem so easy.' His kisses were tentative, gentle; I felt a lightening in my head, my body seemed to dissolve into nothingness, and tears fell which had nothing do with me. I had always been a private person, secretive out of necessity. How would it be to share everything with another person?

He was murmuring into my hair, 'I never told you before, but when I am near you, even if I were blindfolded, I would know it was you. You smell of jasmine and lilies and ginger, and perhaps some other exotic perfumes of which I have never heard.'

We were still holding each other, he still kneeling beside my chair, when he said softly, 'Will we be happy together, Naaz?'

I stroked his head and back, soothing him down. 'We will be happy and together forever.'

'Is that what you want … what you really want?'

I did not reply, because he was not really asking for an answer. Was he marrying me because of his sister? Because of his family? I felt the weight of his head as it pressed against my heart. Whatever the reasons, whatever would happen in the future, as far as I was concerned, the world could stop right now. 'Present moment, only moment', as the Buddhists said. For me, it was all that mattered.

ten

It started off as one of those beautiful days which come at the end of the Delhi winter, before the terrible heat of summer begins. The sky was almost entirely blue and a gentle wind riffled the leaves of the peepal and neem trees, making them shimmer and twist.

I had thought they might come late, but they were dead on time, standing outside the front door and pressing the bell repeatedly, as though they feared the sound would never reach my ears. I ushered them in, smiling as I greeted them with folded hands. They stood there, staring around, bemused. Although it was not a large flat, the rooms were spacious and airy, with picture windows and high ceilings. One wall of the sitting room was lined from floor to ceiling with teak bookshelves crammed with books. The rugs on the floor—Persian, Afghan or Kashmiri—glowed with colour.

They made their way inside and sat stiffly side by side on the sofa, like two children who have been told to behave themselves and be good. Maria brought the tea and they stared at her in amazement. 'You have a maid servant?' The old lady's voice was sharp, as if this was one of those rather decadent practices of which she did not approve. 'Does she live here?'

'Yes. There is a room for her at the back.'

I poured tea, added milk and sugar and passed around the *bhakras* made by Maria. These are small puffy concoctions made from three different flours and mixed with ghee, sugar, eggs and yoghurt. The yellow tinge comes from the addition of saffron.

Papaji, as I learned to call him, said, 'These are very delicious. Did you make them yourself? What are they called?'

'They are called 'bhakras', and Maria made them. She is a good cook and learns very quickly.'

'Can she also make dhansak? I had once eaten this in a restaurant and I found it very interesting and different from all the dals we cook at home.'

I laughed—the one dish that all non-Parsis associate with us is dhansak—a delectable mixture of four or five different dals cooked with vegetables, meat and special spices.

'Yes, she makes very good dhansak; it is my grandmother's recipe, and very special. I will cook it for you one day.'

'Can we look around your flat?' Ramesh's mother asked, putting her cup down. I took them around to the guest room, the two bathrooms, the kitchen, and my small study. 'But where is your bedroom?'

Reluctantly, I took them into my bedroom. One whole wall was windows, shaded now against the sun and harsh light by blinds. The room looked cool, private, serene. A scarlet handwoven Tibetan rug lay on the polished floor, and the bed was covered in a thick, ribbed, blue spread. A small bowl of red and pink roses scented the air. They stared in silence and then Papaji gave a long sigh. 'It must be very restful to sleep in a room such as this.'

They returned in silence to the sitting room. 'My wife had hoped for a daughter-in-law who would help her with the cooking, cleaning and washing up. But you will be living separately—not with us.' He sighed again.

'I am sorry, but that is true. We will live here in this flat until Ramesh decides what he wants to do. I am too independent to live with anyone. It is better this way. How can I help you with Sunita?'

'You said Parsis don't give their daughters dowries?'

'Yes, it is not usual to give a dowry. If the family is well off, they give the girl everything—jewellery, household goods, money—anything and everything she wants, but all this remains in the girl's name. Nothing goes to the in-laws. No Parsi girl has ever been burned alive or killed for her dowry, or lack of it.'

There was a long silence as we thought of all those young women doused with kerosene and burnt alive by rapacious in-laws. I said, 'Just tell me what you need for Sunita.'

Hesitantly they mentioned a sum. It was not inconsiderable, but less than I had expected. I agreed at once and they stared at me in amazement. They had thought, perhaps, that I would prevaricate, bargain, even refuse. They stared at me, and then at each other. Slowly they began to smile. They began to feel that Ramesh had not made such a bad choice after all.

'What about the wedding? Where shall we have it?'

'I would like a registry office marriage and then later, or the following day, we can have a reception in a hotel. But there will be no religious ceremony, no *baraat* with dancing in the streets and no band.' I did not say that I had no wish to see Ramesh come riding up on a poor little mare, his face covered with streamers of artificial flowers. Any attempt to compare cultures and decide which is superior is doomed to failure, but this was something on which I had absolutely no intention of yielding.

They both looked aghast and affronted. 'What will people say? They will think we are ashamed. That we have something to hide. How can our son—our only son—get married without the blessings of the pandit?'

I did not reply, and they stared at me, baffled and angry. But they agreed reluctantly. They wanted this marriage as much as I did now. They had no alternative but to agree.

Finally what we decided on was a registry marriage, after which there would be a reception.

I thought I had better ring up and tell Sophie about the wedding. I added that it would be nice if she would come.

For a long moment there was silence, then Sophie said, 'So you are marrying a Punjabi boy! How ironic. What would your grandmother have said? If she were alive, she would have cut you out of her will.'

'Perhaps, and perhaps not. She always wanted me to be happy.'

Sophie said, 'I never thought you would get married. What's he like?'

'Good-looking. Brilliant. He is going to be a famous architect one day.'

Sophie said nothing, and there was silence for a long time. Finally she said, 'Well I hope you will be very happy with your Punjabi boy. I'm sorry I won't be able to come. I can't leave here. Are you in touch with your father's cousin, Dina Mistry? I think you should contact her. She could be very helpful.'

I had met father's cousin, whom we called Aunt Dina, at some function not too long ago. I liked her. I thought she had a lot of spunk. Married in her teens to a man who spent his life gambling or buying lottery tickets, she did not sit back and moan but decided to do something about it. Uncle Firoze never seemed to win, and there were bills to pay.

She was an excellent cook, and she informed all her friends that she could supply Parsi food for parties or for everyday purposes, at very reasonable prices. The response astonished her—orders poured in so fast that she had to employ two helpers. Within a year her business had grown enormously and she was making huge profits. Abandoning the small rented rooms they were occupying, she bought a flat in one of the new colonies and fitted the large kitchen with every conceivable gadget. She now had four full-time helpers, all of them trained by her.

When I rang her, said I was getting married and explained the situation, she said, 'Come over right away.'

She was very fair and pleasingly plump. Her arms were smooth and round, her cheeks pink and her sari did nothing to hide her generous curves. She hugged me and said how delighted she was to see me. 'Now tell me everything.'

I told her about Ramesh, his family, and the plans for the wedding. She shook her head in dismay. 'You were planning to do all this yourself? Why didn't you come to me?'

I mumbled something. 'Never mind. Now tell me everything. They want a dowry, I suppose?' I nodded. She looked at me shrewdly but said nothing more.

'The wedding is two weeks from now.'

'Good heavens. What have you done about it so far?'

'They want a reception after the ceremony at a five-star hotel.' She smiled. 'Leave everything to me. But first I must meet your young man. The problem with marrying a stranger is that he hasn't read the same books.'

Ramesh came reluctantly to meet her, but they liked each other at once. He was fascinated by the kitchen, and went around peering into dishes and pans, accepting bits of something in a spoon to taste, or trying out some of the almond sweets she was so famous for.

'Have you given Naaz an engagement ring?' He looked petrified at the question. 'Should I have?'

'Of course you should have. What are your parents thinking of? Aren't they going to do the *sagai*?' He nodded.

'Well fix it up quickly and let me know. Ramesh, I hope you don't mind me saying this, but don't let your mother choose the ring. Your Punjabi tastes don't always appeal to us. Buy something delicate, pretty—like this. She held up her hand, plump and very white, on which she was wearing a single ring—a cluster of rubies encircled by small diamonds set in white gold. It looked very pretty on her hand. But she was not finished with him yet.

'And don't forget that Parsis, unlike most Indians, wear plain gold bands as wedding rings. Not something studded with flashy stones.'

He looked at her and blurted out, 'Why don't you come with me when we buy the rings?'

She was delighted. Ramesh claimed that his mother was annoyed, but also relieved that I had managed to produce an elderly relative who would lend an air of respectability to everything. Aunt Dina also insisted that she would not only act as a surrogate mother to me but would also arrange the reception and pay for it.

'You don't have to do that,' I said. 'It is going to be at a five-star hotel and there will probably be hordes of Vermas and their friends.'

'I never had a daughter, and I have always longed to do this. Don't spoil my fun. Have you made out your invitation list? Decided what you are going to wear?' I shook my head. 'You need me. Now lets see—knowing your grandmother, I suppose she gave you trunks full of fabulous sarees and heaps of jewellery.'

I nodded. She stared at me assessingly. 'None of that awful "bridal make-up" for you. Simplicity, sophistication and elegance. I'll come this evening and we'll decide what you will wear.'

Grandma had given me so many saris that I had a pile of them, absolutely new. Aunt Dina chose a heavy plain cream silk with a tiny, old, woven border. We opened the safe—the same heavy Chubb safe I often opened for Grandma. Aunt Dina opened boxes, discarded and shut them, and finally found what she approved of. It was a diamond and emerald necklace with matching earrings.

'You will wear nothing else. Not any of those awful chains on your hair—no nose rings, no jingling bangles. Only a single white gold bracelet on your right wrist and a Patek Phillipe wristwatch on your left. Nothing else.'

It was impossible to explain how I felt. Someone was taking care of me. With love and tenderness. I could leave everything in her capable hands. I could relax and know that everything would be perfect.

'Tell Ramesh to let me know how many people they are inviting. We will have the reception at the Maurya Sheraton. I know the people there. And I will book a room for you too. Instead of returning to your flat, you can go and relax after the reception with a bottle of champagne and caviar sandwiches.'

I laughed. 'I hate caviar, and Ramesh has probably never tasted it, but thanks all the same. Thank you very, very much.' I hugged her and she patted me on the back. 'He's a good boy. You'll be fine together.'

Everything went as planned. The reception was a huge success. Parsi women in their beautiful traditional saris and the men in dark suits mingled with the more flamboyant Punjabis. The menu incorporated some Parsi wedding dishes—fish *Patia*, saffron-scented pulao with chunks of tender meat, and chicken in a thick gravy with potato straws—the famous *sali marghi*. For once in my life I felt, not pretty, but elegant and well-groomed. My hair had been expertly cut to fall smoothly and curve into my neck. I had excellent skin and my make-up was light and clever, emphasizing my dark eyes. There were many admiring stares at my sari and my necklace. I was no longer invisible. For the first time in my life, I was the centre of attention. There was no Yasmin to make me disappear.

At last it was all over and we were thankfully shut inside our suite. Ramesh had never stayed in a five-star hotel before and he went around looking at everything, opening and shutting wardrobe doors and switching lights on and off. The bed had been turned down, and there was a bottle of champagne in a bucket of ice and a covered tray which contained sandwiches and small, hot, chicken patties. Ramesh took his shoes off and flung himself on the bed. He looked at me, 'Let me guess. You are going to take your clothes off and have a shower.' It was an old joke—according to him I was always taking baths.

'Yes, you are right. I won't be long. Why don't you change into something comfortable.'

By the time I came out, smelling of bath salts and scented soap, he was asleep. He had stripped off his sherwani, shirt and trousers. He had crawled under the sheets in his underwear. His clothes were thrown in a pile on the floor, and he was breathing softly. I smiled. It was better this way. Tomorrow we would be in Mussoorie, alone and isolated, in my not-so-little cottage, high up in Landour.

I got into bed beside him and switched off the lights. Suddenly I remembered the champagne, cooling in its bucket. And the sandwiches. They would have to wait for another day.

eleven

I had suggested to Ramesh that we spend a week in my cottage in Mussoorie for a short honeymoon after the wedding. He was amazed. 'You have a cottage in Mussoorie? Your own cottage? Being married to you is full of surprises. Although I have lived in Delhi for so many years, I have never been to Mussoorie, or to any other hill station for that matter. There was never enough money to go anywhere. Did your parents give you the cottage?'

'No, I bought it after Grandma died. It was up for sale in a terribly dilapidated condition, and going for a song. The idea of having a little retreat of my own, away from everything, was very tempting. I put in new doors and windows, changed all the electrical wiring and completely redid the bathrooms. It is perched high on a hilltop, and from the retaining wall, the land falls away steeply to the valley below.'

We slept late, and only awoke when there was a call from the reception desk to tell us the taxi had arrived. I ordered a continental breakfast in our rooms.

'Why continental?' Ramesh enquired as he buttered a roll.

'As opposed to an English breakfast I suppose, of bacon and eggs, sausages, fried tomatoes and buttered toast with marmalade.'

'What a lot of strange things you seem to know,' he said.

I couldn't help laughing. 'We are already late and we still need to go to the flat and pick up our luggage. At this rate we won't be in Mussoorie till late evening. I had expected to be there for lunch.'

We stopped on the way for tea and samosas at a dhaba. The road to Mussoorie climbs steeply and rapidly from 1800 feet to 7000 feet in a series of sharp spirals and hairpin bends. The air became perceptibly cooler and mist-laden as the car picked up speed, leaping into the gathering twilight.

'Don't tell me you are going to do the cooking,' Ramesh said, when I told him we had enough provisions for two days.

'No, there is a chowkidar and his wife who look after the place, and who can make simple food. We can buy food or eat out if you prefer.'

Mussoorie, once so green, wooded and beautiful, was

now sordid, ugly and treeless, overrun by Tibetan refugees selling sweaters and other woollen garments. Ugly hotels and boarding houses had come up everywhere, and a litter of paper and plastic bags dripped down every slope.

'It doesn't look very attractive,' Ramesh said.

'I agree. The town is a real mess, but the cottage is higher up in Landour, past the American school, and relatively free from tourists and Tibetans.

From the Landour market we began the vertiginous climb on narrow, often cobbled roads. Terraced cottages, their red roofs glittering in the sun, clung perilously to the hill sides, dotted here and there by flame-of-the-forest trees, twisted by the wind into surreal shapes. Low stone walls covered with lichen and moss formed a precarious barrier between the relative safety of the road and a precipitous descent into the valley far, far below.

The road deteriorated sharply as the car bumped gently over the steep, boulder-strewn track. But at last we were there at 'Pine Cottage' and Bhim Singh was waiting to swing open the gate, a wide grin on his brown, wrinkled face. There was small enclosed garden; in front, a forest of pine trees, and behind, a covered porch that led straight into a long, glazed veranda which the langurs did their best to penetrate, peering through the glass panes and trying to force the windows open. On an earlier occasion I had discovered three of them inside the cottage, sitting under a table with a bowl of fruit which they had lifted intact, and were now consuming at leisure—peeling bananas, biting into apples and sniffing at the grapes suspiciously. I thought at first that they planned to carry the bowl with them, but after some hesitation they disappeared through the window, their cheeks bulging, their hands full of fruit.

Ramesh looked around with interest, opening and closing windows, trying out the doors and sniffing the air which smelt different—of mountains, of trees and slightly of mildew. Inside, the high-ceilinged rooms were cold, but a fire had been laid and the beds made up with clean sheets and piles of quilts. Bhim Singh's wife, Lakshmi, now appeared. She greeted us with smiles and folded hands. She had very small hands and feet—the kind that aristocrats are supposed to have, black hair braided with a red ribbon, and skin that was almost black. She was one of the best workers I have ever come across. Whatever she did, she did perfectly. Her dishes shone, the floors were spotless and she rolled chapatis and stirred the food on the stove with expert proficiency. Nothing was too much trouble. I loved having her around, and she seemed to glory in the work. She went into the kitchen now to unpack provisions.

Ramesh said, 'You were wise to leave the original structure unchanged. These are thick, solid walls, raftered ceilings and teak wood doors and windows.'

'The bathrooms were terrible, and the wiring and taps in a state. I had to change it all and put in new wiring, and new pipes. Come and look at the bathrooms.'

He laughed, 'For anyone who has as many baths as you do, that would naturally be a priority.'

Except for our bedroom and the adjoining verandah, there was a faint musty smell in the other rooms, but our rooms were bright, sunny and cheerful. The extra-large bed was flanked by small polished tables. Below the window was a plain wooden coffee table, flanked by two wicker chairs with cushions. The little verandah, completely glazed on one side, had a rocking chair, a divan and thick, handloom curtains in a brown-and-green pattern.

'I'm starving,' Ramesh announced. Lakshmi had unpacked the provisions. Instant coffee, tea, milk, sugar, crusty rolls, butter, a roasted chicken with potatoes and bacon curls, salad and fruit. I switched on the oven and put the chicken and rolls in to heat. Everything else went into the small refrigerator. We sat in front of the window to eat our meal, laid out neatly on the table by Lakshmi, who now brought in steaming cups of coffee.

The food tasted wonderful. Ramesh said, 'Why have I never eaten chicken with potatoes and bacon before? It's good.'

I produced a bottle of cognac and poured some into the coffee. 'Everything tastes delicious,' Ramesh said. 'I suppose it has something to do with the altitude. How high are we here?'

'Almost 8000 feet,' I said.

'Was this tea, or lunch, or dinner?' he asked. 'I'm going to be hungry again in an hour or so.'

I laughed. 'There's plenty of food.' I felt warm, happy, relaxed. Outside, the sun began to relinquish much of its brilliance, and as the colours began to fade, the trees and flowers were bathed in a diffused, reflected light. Lakshmi removed the plates and we were left alone.

I thought of a passage from an ancient text, the *True Dharma*: 'Time has the quality of passing, so to speak, from today to tomorrow, from today to yesterday, from yesterday to today, from today to today, from tomorrow to tomorrow.'

That was how it was here.

We made love, and inexperienced as I was, I knew that for Ramesh it was certainly not the first time. How could it be? He was gentle, but there was no fumbling. He knew exactly what to do and how to do it. I wondered briefly about this before being subsumed, unexpectedly, in delight. For the first time I felt the happiness that comes from sharing with another. I never wanted to feel alone again— not physically, not in any other way.

We slept and woke to find that the evening had merged imperceptibly into the twilight. Bhim Singh's discreet knock brought us back to reality. I felt released somehow from the cage into which I had locked myself. I was no longer alone. There was another who was close to me, part of me. He had gently eased me into the love and the happiness I had been scared of accepting.

In the growing dark the sun had receded from the forest,

and the striped bamboos were shade-filled and muted in colour.

'I'm going to have a shower,' I said.

The power supply in Mussoorie was erratic, and I had taken the trouble of switching on the geyser as soon as we entered the cottage. Tea had already been laid out by Bhim Singh on the little verandah as I emerged, wearing the new fluffy wool dressing gown which Sophie had ordered for me from Marks & Spencer. It had a shawl collar which I could turn up around my neck and deep pockets on either side.

An essential element of love is the longing for intimacy, the creation of a two-person universe—more fundamental to happiness than sexual desire.

'Blue suits you,' Ramesh said. 'And you smell good enough to eat. Bhim Singh seems to think it is teatime.'

'In the hills, it is always teatime,' I said. Later we ventured out into the garden, now heavily shrouded in mist. The Doon valley lay spread out below us, pricked with lights like fallen fireflies. Up here, trees, leaves, flowers and branches had lost all colour and form. Directly above us, wedged into the hillside were other cottages, surrounded by flowering bougainvillea and wild dahlia. From one of them a black and white cat emerged, leaping down the hillside and jumping on to the wall on which we were sitting.

'Hello, cat,' Ramesh said. The cat opened its mouth and mewed soundlessly. It had green-yellow eyes and a black face with a white patch under its chin. All four paws were white. It had the sleek, well-fed look of a domestic cat. It wrapped its tail neatly around its paws and looked at us.

Ramesh said, 'It wants something to eat.' He went inside and emerged with a chicken leg and stuffing made from liver and gizzard. He held the food out on his palm. With a quick movement, the cat knocked the stuffing out of his hand, picked up the chicken leg and vanished.

'It shares my tastes,' Ramesh said. 'Can't stand liver and gizzard stuffing.' I laughed. 'It will come back for it later.'

We went inside. It had become chilly, but the rooms were warm. The curtains were drawn and a fire was burning in the grate. Ramesh explored the books and found an old volume on the history of Dehra Dun. He settled himself in the rocking chair. 'Is it time for dinner?' he asked.

'If you stayed for any length of time in Mussoorie you would put on weight and grow fat.'

'I'm not sure if it is the place, or being married,' he said. He opened the book on Dehra Dun, scanned a couple of pages, then put it down. 'History interests me. But Dehra Dun can wait. It is you I want to know more about,' he said. 'You intrigue me—I mean, your community does. Tell me about the Parsis. After more than thirteen hundred years in India, how have you managed to retain a distinct and separate identity? How have you managed to keep from making converts and from allowing others into your Fire

Temples? Even the Muslims allow visitors into the Jama
Masjid. What is it you are trying to preserve and guard
from others?'

'I'll give you a book to read.'

'No, I really need to know. When my mother's relatives
heard I was getting married to a Parsi they refused to believe
it. They said your family would throw me out. That Parsis
hated what they called "outsiders" marrying into their
community. That the marriage was impossible.'

'So, what do you want to know?'

'Anything that will enlighten me about marrying one
of the most endangered and exotic species in the world.'

'You make me sound like the Great Indian Bustard!'

'So come on. Give me a potted history of the Parsis.'

'All right. We are the original boat people. We arrived
in India as refugees from Persia in AD 745 fleeing conversion
by Islamic invaders. The story goes that the raja of Sanjan,
where the refugees landed, was reluctant to admit these
strangers from across the water. He said there was no room
for them and sent the Parsi head priest a full glass of milk
as a symbol. The priest put a pinch of sugar in the milk and
returned it to the raja, intimating that they would assimilate
totally and even sweeten the place with their presence.'

'Is this historically true?'

'No one seems to know. One theory is that the early
Parsis who made certain cultural concessions to their
Indian hosts, justified it in this way. Whatever it was, the

first Fire Temple was built here on Indian soil to shelter their holy fire—the Iran Shah—which they had brought with them.'

'And what about your rather bizarre manner of disposing of corpses?

'One of the essential beliefs of Zorastrianism is that the earth, air, water and fire should not be polluted. And this was one way of doing that. Rites for Parsis are less important than ethical behaviour—good thoughts, good words, good deeds.'

He looked at me a long time in silence, 'So how Parsi do you feel? After all you are only half Parsi. Your mother is English.'

'I certainly don't feel English, so I suppose I must feel Parsi. My mother actually had very little influence over the way we lived and the customs we followed. Our navjotes—the formal initiation into Zoroastrianism—were performed when were children.'

'But you don't wear the sudra and kusti.'

'No, I stopped when Grandma died. I wore them to please her. I don't believe in symbols.

Bhim Singh came in to tell us that dinner was on the table. He had made hot, potato-filled chapatis with buttery dal and a salad. Everything tasted delicious. We finished as usual with coffee and cognac. I looked forward to lying in bed with him—not touching, just needing to know he was there.

Back in Delhi, Ramesh resumed work, but at night, especially when we were lying in bed, he would resume his questioning about the Parsis, as though he were planning to write a dissertation on us.

One night he said, 'Do I look like a Parsi?'

I shrugged. 'I suppose you could be taken for one.'

'Then why don't you smuggle me into your Fire Temple?'

'Don't be ridiculous. I wouldn't dream of doing such a thing, I don't know why you are so obsessed with us. There is nothing, absolutely nothing, to see in the Fire Temple. It is just like a rather large private house with a special place for the sacred fire. In the early days, people kept the fire burning in their own houses to prevent the destruction or interference from other religions.'

'You don't say your prayers?'

'No. Prayers are meant so that we can express our veneration for God. They are quite extensive. I am not sure that I even believe in God.'

For a moment he stared at me in consternation, then he smiled. 'It is very interesting being married to a Parsi. To my friends I am something of a curiosity. No one they know is married to one.'

twelve

The memory of events long past is stronger and more compelling and, in some universal sense, far more important than what is happening in the present. As I pursued my receding memories haunting the corridors of the past, losing myself in a maze of deserted streets and desolate alleys, I recall mostly the unhappiness and the terrible sense of estrangement.

For girls living in India, the compulsion to get married was immense, although this was much less so in Parsi families, where girls were educated in the same way as boys. They studied and worked abroad, lived independently and held responsible positions. Yet to boast of having married a man both rich and handsome was every girl's dream, and no less mine. But when I married Ramesh it was not because I had fallen in love, whatever those words may mean. The entire process of meeting and choosing him was totally haphazard and unplanned. A chance look, a prickling of the skin on arms and thighs and a strong desire to run my hands through his hair was what I felt. Perhaps there are worse ways to select a partner for life.

Women who enter into marriage thinking of it as the traveller's perfect land in which dreams are the only reality are doomed to disillusionment and failure. Most continue to claim happiness simply because they dare not admit failure or defeat.

I, however, had few illusions and fewer dreams. I wanted, and planned on having, my own home and husband, a husband who not only I, but the world could respect and admire, someone whom other girls considered eminently eligible. Brought up on the assumption that for a girl, beauty was important, I decided I would do everything in my power to compensate for the lack of it.

In the early years, Ramesh and I continued to stay in my Delhi flat, and all the comfort and cossetting surprised and delighted him. Accustomed, as he had been, to sleeping on a string charpoy placed in whichever spot was most convenient, with the bedding rolled up and stacked in some corner during the day, the delight of having a special room in which to sleep, with a firm mattress, clean sheets and fat, snowy pillows, all amazed and delighted him. He would fling himself on the bed, bouncing on the mattress, burrowing his head into the pillows, sniffing with delight.

'Everything smells so good. You smell so good, Naaz. Your skin has its own perfume. I suppose it is all those lovely, fat, scented soaps, body lotions and clean, fresh clothes.'

I was amused. His parents' flat smelt of mustard oil, fenugreek seeds and strong cleaning fluid, which did not entirely hide the smell of drains.

He soon got used to the bedroom, the bathroom with its constant hot water and huge, fluffy towels, but his study was for him, something very, very special—a recurring delight. I had converted the second bedroom into his study. It was book-lined, with a huge, polished desk, comfortable chairs, filing cabinets and a divan under the window where he would often lie with his hands under his head, relaxing or thinking.

When he was working, his papers were strewn all over the place, and only I ever entered to dust and clean, careful to disturb nothing. He was working with a protege of the great architect Joseph Allan Stein. This was the school of architecture whose gurus had been pupils of the legendary Frank Lloyd Wright, and whose cool, low-key houses stood out amid the visual overload and physical density of urban Delhi.

The houses Ramesh began to build were oases of refuge in an urban landscape—cool havens of delight, the interiors an extraordinary mixture of light and space, their low-key naturalism mingling delicately with the gardens surrounding them. The gardens were filled with greenery, with leaves and fronds and palms, providing a barrier between the house and the urban chaos outside.

To make my marriage a success, I planned my strategy like a general in the field of battle, and studied my subject as though I were writing a thesis.

Although I had few friends in college, it was still for me an intensely rewarding time. I had discovered the joys, the extraordinary thrill of research into a subject in which I was passionately involved. My doctoral thesis was written on a nineteenth century British orientalist whose work had been reviled by many Indian nationalists.

Anthropology and historical research were never, for the British, 'a Victorian gentleman's hobby'. Rather it was a huge body of knowledge, amassed in order to control their vast colonies and the natives over whom they ruled. Many of the early collectors of linguistic and ethnographic data were not Oxbridgeans, but colonial district officers, senior policemen, rural missionaries and map-makers, whose acute observations, notes, discoveries and records were to provide fascinating information about ancient India. Father always maintained that without this information, there would have been great blanks in India's history.

I set about making my marriage a success in the same way that I had conducted research into my thesis, although this was infinitely more difficult. How does one define a successful marriage? Is it one in which the husband is catered for, pampered and cosseted so that he could work without a single other responsibility, leaving the house and children entirely to his wife? Or was it one in which both partners try to encourage the other to grow, to be happy, to share all responsibilities and enjoy a perfect mental and physical accord?

I studied Ramesh's likes and dislikes in food as in everything else, helped, or perhaps hindered, by his mother, who was convinced that I would never be able to provide the kind of food her son was used to—hearty Punjabi food full of ghee and spices.

In the early days I served only the sort of food his mother cooked—buttery dals and chappaties, vegetables cooked with paneer or in yoghurt and chillies, thick rotis stuffed with potatoes, cauliflower, spinach or even chopped fresh green chillies. One fateful day, however, finding myself tired of this rich and fattening food, I rebelled and served up for lunch a spaghetti dish flavoured with a light cheese sauce scattered with mushrooms and garlic.

Ramesh invariably ate his meals as though his mind was on something else, never once commenting on whether the food was good or bad. This time, however, having helped himself without seeming to notice what he was putting into his plate and into his mouth, he stopped, fork in mid-air, and looked enquiringly at his plate.

'What's this?' he said. 'It tastes good. I like it.'

I smiled with relief. 'It's spaghetti with a cheese sauce

and mushrooms. Have some more. I haven't cooked anything else. Just this and a salad,'

He gave himself a generous second helping. 'Why don't we have food like this everyday? It's light and delicious.'

This was when I sacked the boy my mother-in-law had engaged for me, and found Antony, who turned out to be a genius with a real flair for cooking both plain and unusual dishes. He quickly learnt how to make special Parsi dishes, and we suddenly became very popular with friends and acquaintances who tried hard to cadge invitations to lunch, dinner and even tea, since Antony's patties, scones, tarts, sandwiches and cakes were both unusual and delicious. Antony cooked meat and chicken in toddy (instead of in wine) and simmered soups overnight in huge tureens to produce a thick soup, with lumps of soft, tender meat as well as potatoes, onions, carrots, green beans, celery, parsley and toddy. Toddy was very difficult to obtain, but Antony had his own source, and would come grinning from ear to ear when he had managed to get some.

We were expected to visit the in-laws once a week. In the beginning his mother would make a big fuss over Ramesh, ostentatiously making all the dishes he was particularly fond of and was presumably being deprived of since his marriage to me. For the first few months Ramesh gallantly played up, eating everything served to him with appreciative murmurs, but gradually he got bored with the charade.

'No thanks,' he said brusquely one day, pushing his plate away. 'I'm not hungry, Ma. I really can't possibly eat any more. We come to see Papa and you, not to eat. So don't bother to cook all this food for me.'

There was a silence in which I searched for something mollifying to say, but it was Ramesh's father who saved the day. He laughed, 'Quite right. You will only make Ramesh fat if you keep on feeding him all this rich food. Already he is weighing more, I am thinking.'

Ramesh's mother sulked, no doubt blaming me in some way for her son's inexplicable dislike, suddenly, of rich Punjabi food. As the only son, Ramesh had suffered most from his mother's obsessive love. Everything would be accomplished, all their problems solved, their dreams and hopes fulfilled through her brilliant son. Whatever failure and lack of success had dodged his father's career would be redeemed through her boy. For twenty-six years he had borne this patiently, but now the release, both financial and emotional, was beginning to be felt. Every month we put a substantial sum of money into his parents' account. When I first suggested this, Ramesh was horrified.

'It's your money. You've given them a huge sum as dowry, which you wouldn't have done in the normal way had you married a Parsi, so you don't have to do this.'

'It's *our* money. Think how much of a difference it will make to their lives. No more pinching and saving and doing without things. Just tell them it is your idea and your money. It will make your mother feel happy.'

Of our private lives there is little enough to say. Is it possible for two healthy young adults to live together on terms of the closest physical intimacy, and yet communicate so very little on any other level? Our sex life was more than satisfactory, our attitudes towards each other pleasant and friendly, yet I knew there was something missing.

Ramesh, who seemed perfectly satisfied with the way things were, was happy to have a wife who ran everything with such admirable efficiency. We had a busy social life, I was an excellent hostess and the food we served, thanks to Antony, was legendary. We went out together sometimes to see a play or a film or to attend a musical recital. To the outside world we seemed an ideally happy young couple, but I could not help wondering if all couples were like us, or if there were some with a closeness, a feeling of identity with each other which we didn't have. When we were together, we talked for the most part of Ramesh's work, and my interest in this was almost as great as his.

Marriage, I decided, was like a feather quilt—an effective insulation against the harshness of the outside world, but sometimes a cold wind could penetrate unexpectedly.

Ramesh was absorbed, dedicated to his work, and nothing was allowed to disturb this inner sanctum to which he devoted so much of his life. I sometimes wondered if he would even notice if I were suddenly to disappear, or if it would take him considerable time to realize that I was no longer there.

He had managed to get into an excellent and very prestigious firm, known for their minimalist schemes and responsible for many of the new buildings coming up in posh localities in New Delhi. It had not been difficult for him to get in. Anyone from Stein's school was always interviewed, and he was taken on immediately. In the first few months he won a gold medal for his design for a new university campus in a nationwide contest. Within a short term of ten years, he was recognized as a name to be reckoned with for his modern but unassuming structures, startling in their simplicity and yet elegant, restrained and disciplined in their pure, almost stark format. Soon there was a demand for Ramesh Verma houses, and it was not long before he left the firm to start out on his own.

In spite of what I considered the deficiencies, I was not unsatisfied by my marriage. I was better off than before—much, much better. I had a husband who was both handsome and successful and I had my own home. I had no doubt that I was envied by other women who probably wondered what Ramesh had ever seen in me. Since it was an intercommunity marriage, and therefore obviously a love marriage and not an arranged one, the speculation was even greater. Ramesh, on his part, seemed genuinely uninterested in other women, and if he appeared sometimes not to notice me, he apparently saw them even less.

I recall a dinner given a few years after our marriage by Bharat Kapur, the millionaire jeweller whose house Ramesh had designed and built. It was a very large house, quietly elegant—a cool, low-key design, understated but still striking, with low-slung wings, expanses of glass and spacious courtyards—a house that appeared to float effortlessly from a carefully planned forest of green trees, palms and tall grasses.

That evening Ramesh was looking not only handsome but distinguished in his black button-up *bandgala* and black silk-wool trousers. Although the party had been given in his honour, he delighted everyone by his boyish modesty and charm. The reason, of course, was that he was totally unused to this kind of attention, and not at all sure that he merited it.

As we arrived I felt him stiffen slightly, as though to prepare himself for the ordeal. All eyes were on him, and even I felt slightly intimidated by the lights flickering on silver and crystal and the jewels of the women.

Our host came forward to meet us and drew Ramesh into the room with his arm around his shoulders. All eyes were on the two men—one rich, successful and powerful and the other young, handsome and just beginning to be known.

Kapur himself was good-looking, with shrewd brown

eyes and that patina of assurance that comes from being both wealthy and powerful. He radiated charm and was the kind of man that both sexes would find attractive. Utterly at ease and secure in his own self, he was a man so cosmopolitan that one never thought of him as having any nationality at all.

Mrs Kapur was small, plump and very fair, her skin smooth and almost translucent. She was wearing no make-up except the lightest touch of lipstick, but the diamonds around her neck and the single ring on her finger were probably worth millions. Not too long ago a wealthy industrialist's wife from India had her posh Belgravia flat in London broken into, and the diamond ring on her finger, worth a million pounds, wrenched off roughly. Here, at least, Mrs Kapur was quite safe. The house and the grounds were heavily guarded.

She put her arm around me and drew me into the room, introducing me as Ramesh Verma's wife. There were assessing looks as the women stared at me, smiling in greeting, wondering what to make of me. Two women, however, barely glanced in my direction. Their eyes were fixed on Ramesh. One was dark, thin and beautifully dressed. She turned out to be the editor of a new and very successful women's magazine launched by Bharat Kapoor. Her name was Shelley Rao. The other was a minor film star who also appeared to be fascinated by Ramesh. Shelley Rao was standing next to me, her eyes on Ramesh. 'I want to do a feature on your husband for the new issue of my magazine. Do you think he will agree?'

I was quite sure that Ramesh would not agree, but I smiled and said, 'You will have to ask him. He is really very busy.'

She ignored me and approached Ramesh. The film star was already standing beside him, smiling and tossing her long, impossibly shiny hair. Ramesh seemed not to see her at all. Shelley Rao, however, drew his attention by putting her hand, with its long painted nails, caressingly on his arm. I heard her introducing herself and saw the blank look Ramesh gave her. He had never heard of her or her magazine, but he tried to look attentive.

'You will sit for my photographer and give us an exclusive interview, won't you?' She had a husky voice, sweet and sexy. 'I want your views on everything—love, marriage, women, your work.'

She was as tall as Ramesh and did not need to look up at him. Without in the least seeming to withdraw, Ramesh stiffened, so that Shelley looked as if she were pulling at his arm. Just about everyone seemed to be watching the two of them, not least of all, I.

Ramesh smiled, still trying to be polite. 'I'm so sorry,' he said. 'But I'm afraid I am not interested.'

She laughed, throwing her head back seductively. She was quite aware of all the eyes trained on them, and she was determined not to be defeated.

'Don't tell me you couldn't use a little publicity. Everyone, even Bharat over there, needs publicity to project a successful public image.'

He smiled. 'I'm afraid I don't have any image at all, let alone a public one.'

By now she was holding his wrist, her fingers caressing it gently. Ramesh removed his hand with a jerk that left her hand stranded in mid-air and moved away.

I was standing beside Bharat Kapur, who was watching Ramesh intently, with a curious expression on his face. He glanced at me, smiled and gave a little shrug.

'So, what do you think of this house built by your husband?'

'It is beautiful,' I said with genuine admiration. 'It suits you and Mrs Kapur perfectly. Restrained elegance, using the most expensive materials without ostentation.'

For the first time he really seemed to look at me. He had a very charming smile which made him look much less formidable. Already, he was something of a legend in the business world, not only for knowing how to get around bureaucratic red tape, but also for his philanthropy.

'Ramesh tells me that you help him with the nitty-gritties of his work. He tells me you are invaluable.'

'I try and take care of all the small but necessary details, so that he has enough time for his real, creative work.'

'I think he is a genius. Perhaps one day he will be as well known as the man he takes his concepts from. But I believe he is a true original and one day there will be houses which reflect only Ramesh Verma's ideas—concepts which are original, inspired and belong to no one else.'

It was always a small triumph for me when we left together, followed by the jealous or speculative eyes of every woman in the room. In the car on the way back we exchanged impressions of the evening.

'I like and respect Bharat Kapur,' Ramesh said. 'But I hate these parties he gives in which he wants to show me off like a new, highly pedigreed dog he has acquired from somewhere.'

I looked at him, startled. He went on, 'And I hate these women with their long painted nails, which give me the creeps, and that fashionably thin look which makes them look like refugees from a famine area.' I could not help laughing.

It was two years after we were married that I decided I would like a child. The idea came to me as though in a dream. I had never given it a thought before, but now it seemed thoroughly enticing. A child—a little boy or girl who would belong to both of us, be a part of us, made in our image. Once I had decided, I became pregnant with exemplary despatch. I was strong, healthy and young. I decided to see a doctor before telling Ramesh. I did not need confirmation; I knew, was certain, that I was with child.

I chose my doctor carefully, checking with friends and women who had recently given birth. It was one of my

many second or third cousins who took me to Dr Felix
Mathews. I liked him at once, and felt I could trust him
totally. I believe strongly in first impressions, and felt that
this was someone I could happily believe in and depend
upon. He was a Goan with strange, light eyes and an
attractive burnt-sienna complexion.

His clinic was bright and cheerful and his young nurse,
Jeanie, gentle, helpful and caring. Dr Mathews' first
question was to ask me if I wanted this baby.

'Yes. I want it very much.'

'Good. Pregnancies are easier and babies healthier when
the child is wanted.'

Jeanie helped me out of my clothes and covered me
with a sheet. Dr Mathews chatted while he examined me,
asking me to relax and murmured, 'Beautiful, beautiful;
you should have no trouble at all. Just the kind of patient I
like. How I dread these fashionably thin women coming in
to have babies. Narrow waists, no hips! Now here we have
lots of room for the baby to grow. But you must not put on
too much weight—no eating for two.'

It was a pleasant change to be told that I was beautiful.
I was given a diet sheet and a pamphlet with exercises to
practice. He recommended yoga asanas. 'Even if you have
never done anything like this before, a good instructor will
teach you two very important things— how to breathe
properly and how to relax. Both these will help you to
have an easy, quick and natural birth.'

Ramesh and I had never discussed children, and I had no idea how he would feel about it. Indifferent? Annoyed? I had decided to tell him casually, as we were lying in bed and just before he leaned over to turn off the light.

'I'm going to have a baby,' I said, turning to look into his eyes. His hand arrested itself in mid-air. He stared at me. At last he said, 'Are you pleased? Did you want a baby?'

'Yes, I'm happy, and yes, I want a child. And you? Do you want a child?' Because he was Ramesh, he gave the matter serious thought. The light was still on and he looked at me reflectively. Then he smiled and leaned over to give me a hug. Ramesh had a very sweet smile. 'I definitely like the idea.' He laughed out loud, 'You know who's going to be absolutely thrilled about this? Ma. You'll have to stop her feeding you glasses of milk laced with ghee.' I shuddered.

'Have you seen a doctor? Is everything all right?' It did not strike him as strange that I should have gone to a doctor before telling him.

I said, 'The baby will be born in early October. Everything is fine.' As it happened, it was not one, but two babies. When Dr Mathews told me I was going to have twins, he was dismayed by my reaction. I was, as he had told me often enough, his best patient, getting along fine, following instructions exactly and with no fussy fads.

As soon as I was dressed, he followed me into the consulting room and perched on the table near my chair.

153

'Now then, what's the trouble? Do you feel two babies are too much to cope with?'

I shook my head. 'No, it's not that. I was a twin myself and I had an utterly miserable childhood because of it.' He looked up sharply. 'Identical?'

'No. My twin was beautiful. Staggeringly beautiful. All my life I had to cope with wondering glances at the two of us. My plainness was accentuated a hundred times when we were seen together. Nothing I said or did made any difference.'

I, who never cried, felt two tears trickle down my cheeks. I fumbled for a hanky. Dr Matthews stood over me, patting my shoulder.

'Look at it this way—you can learn from this experience. A happy childhood imprints itself on the rest of one's life. Without this, people do recover, but the scars remain forever. You can make sure that both your children are loved equally, treated the same. I know you can do this.'

I nodded, determined to do what he said, but, as it turned out, my twins is were identical; two little boys looking absurdly alike. They were very fair, with dark blue eyes which would probably change, and light blonde fluff on their heads. I was amused to think that they fulfilled perfectly the traditional wishes of every Parsi grandmother. On the fifth day after the birth of a Parsi child, the guardian angel of newborn babies is supposed to visit the child and, as in the fairy tale, grant it health, abundant wealth and good fortune. The grandmother too visits the child and wishes him or her, among other things, perfect health, respect, honour, cleverness and beauty. In typical Parsi fashion, beauty consists of blue eyes, golden hair and very fair skin. *Ghano khubsurat, belu ankhvalu, ne sunari bal valu.*

If I had expected that the babies would take over my life, leaving me with little time for anything else, this was not so at all. This was largely due to Rosie.

She arrived on the day I returned from hospital, with a letter of recommendation from Dr Mathews. Thin and small as she was, she had an air of competence and self-sufficiency that I liked. She was wearing a black pleated skirt with a white blouse and shoes and stockings. Convent-educated (as I was) and perhaps brought up as an orphan in a convent. Around her neck she wore a small ivory crucifix hanging on a plain ribbon. I took her to see the twins, who, in spite of the change from hospital to home, seemed totally unconcerned. The nursery was ready; the usual ducks and bunnies gambolling around the walls, and, at Dr Mathews' insistence, one large crib for both babies together.

'You can give them individual cribs later on. Right now they need to be together. Each one feels comforted by the other. They will cry and grizzle less when they feel that the other is close by.'

I took Rosie to see them. She stared at them wonderingly.

'Can I hold them?' she asked hesitantly.

155

'Go ahead.'

She scooped them up competently, one on each arm, and held them snug and secure. They stared at her with unfocussed blue eyes.

'They are beautiful,' she said, smiling down at them. I could not help wondering if she would have said they were beautiful had they had dark skin. I had always thought that it was the long years of colonial rule that had given Indians this passion for fair skin. Most coloured people feel strangely vulnerable before big-boned, white-skinned people. These tall giants make even the most fiercely proud and independent feel small, diminished and the wrong colour. But this is not due simply to our colonial masters. Historically white skin has been equated with conquerors and the upper classes, and dark skin with slaves, menials and the lower castes. This makes absolutely no sense today, but in spite of that, everyone in the Third World longs for fair skin. Being white makes one invisible in developed countries.

I said to Rosie, 'When can you come?'

She was to stay with me for years, even after the twins had grown up and gone away. Fiercely loyal, a trusted confidante and friend, she took over efficiently from the first day she moved in.

I find it difficult to understand women who grow so absorbed in their children that they have no time for anything or anyone else. Ramesh was delighted with the twins and I loved them deeply, as indeed who could help but love such sunny-tempered children.

Ramesh said, 'Who do they look like? Neither you nor I.'

'They look like themselves; they are separate individuals with their own individual eyes, hair, skin.'

Although Ramesh was proud to have fathered two bonny sons, his mother was so thrilled and delighted that she would spend hours just sitting beside the crib or pram, staring at them as they slept. I had gone up inestimably in her eyes. Although I was not a Punjabi and therefore to her, a foreigner, I had given her not one, but two grandsons. They were fair, fat and contented. She could hardly keep her hands off them. She tied black threads around their dimpled wrists to keep off the evil eye, which Rosie promptly removed with many mutterings of 'heathen customs'. She wanted to massage them with mustard oil before their baths, blacken their eyes with kajal and drench their sparse hair with oil. It was a constant frustration for her that she was not able to do what she wanted with them. All her visits were now spent with the boys, and it was a running battle between her and Rosie. She considered the playpen an especially inhuman contraption in which the twins were caged like small animals. She also objected strongly, because both the boys had been given Parsi or Persian names, which sounded very Muslim to her.

'You are only half Parsi,' she reminded me constantly.

'And the boys have only one-quarter Parsi blood. Why have you named them like this?' She also objected to the fact that it was Rosie who looked after them.

'My children were always with me, I never went anywhere without them. My whole life was devoted to them. It was I who gave them food, bathed them, put them to sleep. I simply do not understand how you can let this Christian woman do everything for them.'

I let her talk. It never bothered me and gradually she would run out of words. She objected most of all to the twins having a room of their own. Her babies, she told me, had slept not only in her room, but in her bed. If they woke in the night she was right there to comfort and suckle them.

I have always been convinced that this devouring passion Indian women had for their male children was because all their lives they had been controlled and dominated by men—fathers, brothers and husbands. Now at last they had a male whom they could control, dominate and spoil. It is perhaps what accounts for thousands of young men in India who have a terrible complex about their mothers, and who willingly assist in burning their brides, just to please Mama. One Indian film star even publicly announced that he worshipped his mother as a goddess incarnate, and drank the water her feet were washed in.

thirteen

The curious thing was that in spite of the antipathy (or was it hatred?) between us, Yasmin and I were still bound together by memories and recollections of the past.

Sitting together and having elevenses—that typically British tradition—Yasmin said, 'Remember that ghastly school we went to in Hyderabad? That awful grim building and those bloody awful nuns.'

I had just picked up a saffron bun, still warm from the oven, and I paused and stared in astonishment.

'Grim? There was nothing grim about the building. It was beautiful and imposing. Those long corridors, the big, airy classrooms, and the absolute scrubbed cleanliness of everything. How could you say it was grim? And the nuns— they were darling.'

We stared blankly at each other; our memories were

shared but we remembered them differently. For me school had been a haven, a refuge, sheer delight.

Although the school was walking distance from our house, Sophie decided to drive us in the car as it was the first day. We had been dressed in identical blue linen pinafores with white blouses and frilly collars. Yasmin's hair had been carefully curled, and tumbled about her head in glossy ringlets, while mine had been brushed and brushed till it was, for the moment at least, smooth. The school looked enormous—one of those princely estates which had been sold and converted into this convent many years ago. There were acres of gardens and playing fields, and clipped hedges everywhere. Flowers grew in orderly rows, and the lawns were smooth and green. As we climbed the marble stairs to the verandah, a young nun in a white habit with a wooden crucifix on a chain around her neck led us into the parlour to wait for Mother Superior. Sophie appeared slightly intimidated, and held our hands tightly as we were ushered to some chairs. I looked around with interest. Everything gleamed with polish—the red floor tiles, the wooden doors and the furniture. The smell of furniture polish and cleaning fluid hung over everything. There were roses on the tables and on the wall a life-size figure of Christ drooped on the cross, his wounds oozing blood.

Sophie was not a Catholic, and she appeared surprised and irritated by all this. I stared with interest at Christ, pictured as he always was, with golden hair flowing down his shoulders, his half-closed eyes blue and his skin alabaster white. I did not know then that Christ was a Sephardic Jew, dark-skinned and dark-haired, with pronouncedly Semitic features. Like all other religions, Christianity too had built up its own myths around its sacred figures.

Mother Superior came in silently. She was small and round and her hands were tucked into the sleeves of her habit. She surveyed us from shrewd, dark eyes, and then her face changed as she smiled and held out her hands to us. I went up and put my hand into her soft, plump hand and she smiled down at me.

'What is your name, little one?'

'Naaz Jussawalla,' I replied. 'And that is Yasmin. We are twins.'

'And why is Yasmin hiding behind her mother? Perhaps she doesn't want me to see her curls. We do not allow curls in this school. Hair may be short or long, but smooth and tidy and tied back with a black ribbon.'

Sophie had spent hours on Yasmin's curls, of which both she and Yasmin were inordinately proud. To have them dismissed, or even adversely criticized unnerved her.

A young girl—perhaps twelve years old—now entered the room.

'You sent for me, Mother?'

'Yes, Carol. Come right in. I want Mrs Jussawalla and the two little girls to see our uniform.'

Sophie stared at the girl in dismay, but I wanted immediately to look exactly like her. She wore a pleated navy blue skirt which hung well below her knees. The white blouse had a high collar and long sleeves with narrow cuffs. He light brown hair was pulled severely back from her face and tied at the back with a narrow black ribbon. Sensible black shoes with a strap and white socks completed the outfit.

Sophie said, 'Surely they are too small to dress like this?'

Mother Superior's eyes narrowed. 'Too small? For a pleated skirt and blouse? What would you like them to wear?' Sophie was silent. 'Come, I will take you to the kindergarten class. Sister will see that they are measured for their uniforms.'

Yasmin had been hanging on to Sophie's hand as if she would never let go. Mother Superior looked at me and smiled, and I put my hand in hers at once. We went down many shining corridors, passing many classrooms full of children, up a long flight of carpeted stairs, and at last, reached the class we were to join. It was a large and cheerful room, the white walls bright with coloured drawings. Twenty or so children between the ages of four and six were sitting on the floor or at little red tables, engaged in painting, colouring with crayons, sewing on cards with large needles and thick wool, stringing beads or building houses with bricks.

A comfortably fat nun rose with some difficulty from the floor where she had been sitting and came towards us.

'This is Sister Mary Francis. And these two children, Yasmin and Naaz, will be in your class. Please make sure they are measured for their uniforms tomorrow.'

The children were a mixed lot—some foreign, some Indian, some Anglo-Indian. Mother Superior patted me briefly on the head and left. Quite unexpectedly, Yasmin let out a loud wail, burying her head in Sophie's dress.

'I don't want to stay. Don't leave me here. I want to go home. Don't leave me.' She kicked out blindly at anyone who approached.

Sophie was both embarrassed and irritated. 'Come on Yasmin, don't be silly. You'll be home by lunch. See all the nice little girls and boys you can play with. Now be a good girl and stand up straight.'

In vain. Yasmin began to yell in real earnest and kick if anyone tried to draw her away from Sophie. One little girl began to giggle and imitate Yasmin. Sophie glared at her in absolute fury, but now all around the class the children were imitating Yasmin.

'Don't go. Don't leave me,' they shrieked. 'I want to go home.'

Sophie was really angry now. Glaring at the children, she thrust Yasmin at Sister Mary Francis, who held her firmly while Sophie made her escape. With the sound of the car disappearing into the distance, Sister released Yasmin. Left alone in the middle of the room and surrounded by grinning children, Yasmin stopped screaming and began to sniffle.

Sister held out her hand to me. 'Now, Naaz, look around and tell me what you would like to do.' There were so many fascinating things going on around the room that it took me some time to decide between sewing a donkey onto a card with coloured wool or building houses with colourful bricks. Finally I joined a small boy on the floor who had made a stunning bridge from bricks.

Sister said, 'Peter, this is Naaz. Show her how to use the bricks.'

The boy, his black hair standing up on his head in spikes, looked at me without saying a word and pushed over a pile of bricks. I saw that there were little hinged doors and windows available and small men to put inside the house. I sat down and began to build my house. Peter watched, and from time to time pushed over bricks which he thought I might need. When the house was built, I was pleased, and Peter looked up, smiled and uttered a single word— 'Good'. I beamed back at him. When I finally remembered Yasmin I saw that she was sitting sulkily at a small table all by herself and doing nothing.

Ah! Those were blissful days. No one cared or even noticed

whether I was plain or pretty. Through the years I won prizes galore. Each year, at the annual prize distribution ceremony, my name was called over and over again and there would be murmurs of surprise and admiration as the books piled up beside my chair. If home was often hell, here at least was my little bit of heaven.

fourteen

I said to Yasmin, 'I have never understood why you did not return to Hyderabad after Bobby and Father died. You could have stayed with Sophie as long as you wanted—you were always her favourite.'

Yasmin was silent for a long time, then she said, 'Sophie adored me when I was a child, but when I grew up we seemed to have nothing left of the old feeling. Neither she for me, nor I for her. Sophie now had her own life and her own friends, and of course the house, which now belonged to her. She has made a lot of new friends, mostly with other white-skinned foreigners. She has a superb staff and enough money to live a very luxurious life. When I mentioned that I could use a little help, she said, "You squandered all that you had been given when you were married. You are still young. There is no reason why you cannot do something constructive instead of frittering away your time, and your life as well, doing nothing."'

Yasmin's mouth turned down in a bitter line. It was hard to accept that everything was not going to fall into her lap as it always had just because she was beautiful.

I too remembered the visit I had paid Sophie after Father's death. It was the first time I had been home after my marriage to Ramesh, and Sophie had sent the old Daimler to meet me. It was a long drive from the airport, and I looked around with nostalgia. These were the streets Grandma and I had driven on together. Ancient buildings, palaces, mosques and temples—priceless jewels of Indian architectural genius. The gardens and the white domes were still there, but there was a subtle change—the traffic was chaotic, the crowds more dense, and overall, a general air of shabbiness and neglect prevailed.

My visit to Sophie's was more successful than I had ever hoped it would be. She was waiting for me in the porch, and as I climbed the stairs, somewhat warily, I must admit, she smiled and hugged me warmly. She was looking well. Her hair had turned white but it was beautifully cut and styled. She had put on some weight, but it seemed to suit her. I remarked on the wonderful show of flowers in the garden and she said casually, 'Yes, the head mali is very good. He really has green fingers.'

My eyebrows went up at the words 'head mali', but I said nothing. Inside, too, everything had changed—new raw-silk curtains in the doors and windows, new carpets on the floors and lots of pale furniture. I glanced up at what had once been Grandma's rooms. Sophie saw my look.

'I use those rooms now for my business. There is no longer any trace left of the old woman. Thank goodness, too.'

'Business?' I asked with considerable surprise. She laughed.

'I suppose you can hardly believe it. But yes, I have a very successful business which I run from the house. I'll show you later. Let's have some coffee—I'm sure you are starving as usual.'

A young Tibetan, immaculately dressed in white trousers and a coat, appeared. Sophie said, 'This is Jurmi. He works for me.'

Jurmi smiled widely, his slanting, enigmatic eyes disappearing into slits. He was good looking, with thick, straight black hair and a fresh, scrubbed look.

'Coffee please,' Sophie said. 'And something to eat.' Jurmi nodded and disappeared.

'And where did Jurmi appear from?' I asked.

'There is a small Tibetan settlement here—rather like a concentration camp because the inmates are not encouraged to mix with Indians, or work with them, or marry them. This is, according to the official statement, in order to preserve the Tibetan language, religion and culture and prevent the diaspora from mixing too much with the locals. It is, in my opinion, a very short-sighted and unintelligent policy. It keeps the Tibetans strangers, and therefore suspect, in the eyes of the local population. Jurmi had no desire to spend the rest of his life cooped up in a Tibetan settlement. He was looking for a job and I was happy to give him one. He is now, more or less, a junior partner in the business. I really could not manage without him.'

I was now absolutely dying of curiosity. Sophie said, 'You are looking well and happy. Marriage obviously suits you. When are you going to bring your husband to meet me?'

'I was not at all sure that you would want to meet him, but I will bring him next time. He is always so busy.'

She laughed. 'So you married a Punjabi! You grandmother would be turning in her grave, if she had one! Do you realize that your children will only be one-quarter Parsi? And all that Parsi money is yours. Ironic, isn't it?'

I was determined not to react to her little barbs. 'The house looks very nice. I like the colour scheme of blues, violets and dusty pink. Did you do it all yourself?'

'More or less.'

Sophie was sitting with her hands arranged neatly on her lap, and on her face was an expression closely resembling a Cheshire cat's. Grandma had left Sophie and Father the house and enough money to run it, but certainly not in this style. Now that I looked more closely I could see many more changes—all the old family portraits had disappeared, to be replaced by excellent reproductions of modern Indian artists and, I guessed, one or two originals. Everything gleamed with polish.

Coffee came in a Wedgewood pot—strong, hot and aromatic. Sophie poured, taking hers black and adding cream and sugar to mine. It was delicious. I helped myself to imported chocolate biscuits.

'So tell me about this business. It must be very lucrative.'

'Oh it is! Very lucrative indeed.'

I was both irritated and intrigued.

Sophie looked at my face and laughed. 'I buy and sell all sorts of antiques—statues, pictures, Tibetan tankhas, old jewellery—whatever I can lay my hands on, and whatever brings in a good price. Ever since Hyderabad joined the Indian union, most of the nawabs are in a bad way. Having lost both their special status and their incomes, they have resorted to selling anything and everything to make ends meet. They have no business sense and the shops in Char Minar are full of valuable old paintings, china, crystal, chandeliers and even old jewellery. Whatever brings in quick money. Many of these things are going absurdly cheap. After your Father died I fell into a real state of depression; nothing seemed to matter any more. I did not want to return to England—it was no longer my home. But what was there for me here either? The house still reeked of the old woman, your beloved grandmother. How I loathed and detested her. I could smell her everywhere—that awful smell of Bayrum and sandalwood which seemed to permeate every curtain and cushion in the house. I kept thinking of all the money that should rightly have been left to your father. All left to you. Every bit of it. It killed him you know. He just could not believe it.'

She stirred her coffee, her eyes staring into the dark, fragrant brew. 'I loved him. We loved each other. But now I was alone. I lay in bed for days and stared at the walls and the overgrown garden outside.'

I looked at a Sophie I did not know. I said, 'So how did you get out of this depression?'

'I had nothing better to do one day, and decided to drive down to the Char Minar area to try and sell that hideous pink chandelier, so beloved to your grandmother, that dominated the sitting-room. In the shop an American was engaged in buying all sorts of things—little figurines made from ivory, wood and brass, crystal scent bottles, old paintings, carved swords and ornamental daggers. He was paying ridiculously inflated prices, and it gave me an idea. The house was full of stuff which I could sell and get rid of as well.' She looked at me challengingly, but I kept quiet.

'Jurmi had just come to work for me. I had found him loitering aimlessly in the bazar. He helped carry my bags to the car, and I asked him if he needed a job. He smiled and nodded his head. I brought him home in the car with me, and he has been with me ever since. It was the best thing I could have done. It was he who suggested that I buy up some antiques and sell them. He could procure for me an unlimited supply of Tibetan tankhas, brass and metal statues and handwoven carpets, which I could buy cheap and sell at huge profits. He assured me that some of the statues would sell at very high prices as they were *Yab-Yum* and much in demand. I had absolutely no idea what he was talking about until he showed me. These are small, erotic figures in sexual union—three-headed deities, carved in wood, stone, metal, ivory and even jade. They sell so fast, mostly to foreigners, that I can't get enough of them. I even sold an eight-inch Shiva Lingam, studded with semi-precious stones and mounted on its own bronze pedestal.'

'But where do all these things come from?'

'Jurmi has his own sources. Some are actually from Tibet. Others from Nepal or the many settlements where Tibetan refugees have been given asylum after the Chinese invasion. They are prepared to sell anything to make a little extra money.'

She began walking toward the staircase and I followed. 'Come, I will show you my display cases.'

Grandma's rooms were unrecognizable. The largest room was lined with glass-fronted cupboards, the shelves lined with velvet and lit from within, holding dozens of figures carved in wood, or moulded from brass, bronze or silver. Many were inlaid with precious stones—Lapis lazuli, turquoise, coral, red garnet and amethyst. One entire shelf was given over to erotic statues, figures entwined together in sexual union. Many were fearsome to look at but some were truly beautiful. I admired a statue of Shiva —half male, half female—on one side was a voluptuous breast and hip and a jewelled arm, on the other side the torso of a young and beautiful male; the face serene, compassionate, detached.

I said, 'Many of these must be national treasures. You could get into a lot of trouble if they are sold and taken out of the country.'

She shrugged. 'It is a risk I must take. The Tibetan stuff can be sold and taken out of the country with impunity, but it is the other things I have to be careful about. The fact that it is slightly dangerous only adds a frisson of excitement to the entire business. In fact I am expecting an old and very valued customer today. You'll be able to meet him.'

As I was turning to leave, a gleaming scabbard caught my eye. 'What's this?' I asked.

'It's a Kris—an Indonesian dagger which is supposed to hold the spirit of the owner forever inside. It has a very sharp blade which is usually steeped in poison. That little hook near the hilt is for pulling out your opponent's intestines when the blade is plunged into the belly.'

'Good God! Who on earth would want a thing like that?'

'You'd be surprised. It has already been sold for quite a large sum of money. The buyer plans to take it with him abroad. I am just keeping it safe till he can pick it up.'

173

'Where did it come from? You seem to have the most extraordinary contacts.'

'Actually I got it from an old soldier—an Anglo-Indian ex-soldier, who acquired it when his unit was operating in Indonesia in 1945. He said it was presented to him as a trophy after a successful raid on a Kampong. It had been with him ever since, but now he needed the money and had heard I was in the market for antiques and other such things. I bought it from him at once and paid him the price he asked. I sold it for four times the amount.'

This was a side of Sophie I had never seen, nor ever suspected existed. She turned off the lights and locked the room behind us. She said, 'Jurmi is invaluable in the business. He seems to have so many contacts. Of course, he gets a commission on everything I sell.'

We had just reached the bottom of the stairs when a taxi drew into the porch, and a fortyish American dressed casually in black designer jeans and blue shirt jumped out of the car and smiled. His face had been burnt by the Indian sun to the colour of brick, but his pale eyes were alert and observant. I thought he looked very attractive.

Sophie said, 'Paul, how nice to see you again. This is my daughter, Naaz. Naaz, this is Paul Davis.'

We shook hands. 'It's a real pleasure meeting you. I had no idea Mrs Jussawalla had a daughter. Are you visiting?'

'For a few days.'

As soon as he had settled into a chair he looked

enquiringly at Sophie, who smiled and nodded. 'I have managed to find exactly what you wanted but I must warn you—it is more expensive than you had reckoned.'

Davis nodded cheerfully. 'As long as it is exactly what I had asked for, I am prepared to go over my budget.'

'If you wait just a minute I will get it for you.'

Davis turned his attention to me. He had the pleasant, friendly manner common to most Americans.

'Your mother is a truly remarkable woman. Marvellous business sense. What she doesn't know about all this, you could stick on a ten cent stamp. I truly believe she is one of the most important and trustworthy dealers in the business.' He saw my expression and said, 'Does that surprise you?'

'Well yes, quite frankly it does. I thought all Sophie knew how to do was to grow roses.'

He laughed. 'Children never really seem to know or appreciate their parents. Tell me about yourself. Do you feel more Parsi than English, or the other way around? It is a very interesting combination.'

'I consider myself almost completely Parsi, although I must say, I have never given it much thought. I was raised in a home where being a Parsi and a Zoroastrian was a silent reality rather than an imperative. On the other hand I would not be at all surprised if my twin sister considered herself predominantly English.'

He was leaning forward, about to ask more questions,

when Sophie appeared, holding in her hands a small, beautifully carved wooden box. Davis jumped up eagerly and Sophie put the box into his hands. He held it carefully, as though he were handling something that might disintegrate and perhaps even disappear if handled roughly.

He lifted the hinged lid of the box and removed something wrapped in layers of creamy silk. When this was unwound, what emerged was a small statue carved in some pale, gleaming wood. Two figures were seated, wrapped in a sexual embrace, although this was so stylized and formal that it was necessary to look really closely to recognize this.

Davis said, 'Ah! Really beautiful. Vajradha and Sakti.' He turned it round and round in his long, bony hands so it could be seen from all angles. The female figure was small and delicate-looking, her arms wrapped loosely around her partner's neck, her legs crossed behind his waist, her head, with its long slanting eyes, tilted back to look into his face. Both wore elaborate head-dresses or crowns, and heavy arm and foot ornaments set with red and green precious stones. Their faces were smooth, placid, contained, as though deep in meditation.

'I love the way he is holding her,' Davis said. 'So lightly, as though she is a flower.'

He was still smiling as he wrapped the little figures in their cream shroud and put them carefully back in the box. Only then did he look enquiringly at Sophie, who named a figure which made me gasp with shock, but Davis seems totally unfazed. He took out his wallet and paid her in dollars. Sophie tucked the money away in her purse with a casual 'Thanks'.

'Before I leave, I have another request for you. A young friend of mine—an American, but a Buddhist and a disciple of the Dalai Lama, needs twenty-one small gilded statues of the Buddha for the shrine in his room, and also one larger statue of Avalokiteshvara, the Lord of Infinite Compassion and patron saint of the Tibetans. He wants this statue in bronze, and it should be a genuine one from a monastery in Tibet, not a copy made in India. Is this too much of a tall order?'

Sophie smiled. 'No, I like challenges. You may be sure that if I say it is genuine and from Tibet, it will be genuine and from Tibet.'

Davis nodded. 'I am confident of that. It is why I am so happy to deal with you. Well I must be going.' He turned to me. 'I hope to see you again. I find the Parsis absolutely fascinating. So few of them and such reluctant Indians.'

He waved as the car turned and swept out of the gate. I looked at Sophie with both admiration and surprise. 'You've certainly got a good thing going. Are they really genuine?'

'Absolutely. I wouldn't last a day in this business if I dealt in counterfeits.' She smiled at me in a surprisingly friendly manner.

'Would you like to choose something for yourself? For luck? How about this?'

From her capacious bag she produced a small bronze statue of Kartikeya, the god of war, with his peacock. I smiled my thanks, genuinely pleased at the gesture. I brought the little god back with me and set him on the table beside my bed. He was wearing a G-string and an inscrutable smile. He held the peacock gently by its long, sinuous neck. In the bird's beak was a small snake. Such statues were often used to deepen meditation and to bring one's attention to the present.

fifteen

Maxi did not like Yasmin. He avoided being in the same room with her if possible, and growled deep in his throat if she came near him. Yasmin, on her part, not only disliked but feared him as well. No amount of reassuring that he had never bitten anyone and was the mildest, most amenable of creatures made her feel any better.

When we moved to this house in Dehra, the boys were amazed and enchanted by the huge garden with its trees, bushes, hidden pools and the wildlife that lurked everywhere. Hares, civet cats, squirrels and, of course, the monkeys. Maxi had come to us in peculiar circumstances. The boys were passionately fond of animals and had been begging for a puppy for some time. I had no serious objection to dogs, and had promised that as soon as a suitable pup could be found, I would get it for them. Maxi

179

was not what I would have chosen, but sometimes there is an inevitability about what happens which seems almost preordained.

I was walking in the garden one sunny afternoon, enjoying the shade under the mango and litchi trees, making up my mind to order tea out here with the boys, when I saw them. Instead of running up to me as they usually did, they turned tail and disappeared. This in itself was very unusual; they were not afraid of me or of anyone else. Loved, indulged, even spoilt, it was disconcerting to see them disappear like this. I followed more slowly, but there was no sign of them anywhere.

Nearing the garage I saw that the doors were closed, but not locked. I called their names with no response. Opening the heavy doors with some difficulty, I peered inside. Both boys were crouched inside in the semi-gloom and sitting between them was a very large dog.

'You'd better come out,' I said mildly, retreating into the sunshine and perching on a fallen log. They emerged, still clutching protectively at the large creature. I waited without saying anything. It was Cyrus who spoke first—it was always he who took the initiative. He said, 'You see it was like this. You remember asking us whose dog we heard every day, barking and howling like a wolf? Well one day Zubin and I decided to find out. At the end of this road is a big house with a very high wall around it. The dog was inside, but we couldn't see him, and the gate was locked.

180

But there was this tree which we could climb and from the top we saw this man, his name is Captain Malik—and he had Maxi—this dog—chained up with the chain wrapped tight around his neck. No collar. And Captain Malik was beating him with a stick— beating and beating him. And then he went inside and left him all hurting and crying, and still the chain was tight round his neck. We couldn't bear to see him.'

Both boys looked at me earnestly. They spoke together. 'So we went in and rescued him.'

'It is a very high wall,' I said mildly. 'I know the house. How could you get in and out again with this large animal?'

Cyrus said, 'I got on the wall from the tree—it wasn't difficult, and then I jumped down. Zubin ran to get Sher Singh.'

Sher Singh was gardener, carpenter, electrician and sometime driver as well. He was a Nepali who had come to work for us when the house was in the process of being built. He could lay his hand to anything, and was always ready to help. When he saw the quarters we were building for the servants, he was astonished and asked hesitantly if he could bring his family and live there when they were ready. His family consisted of a young, plump wife and a fat baby with pink cheeks and slanting eyes; a girl named Pushpa. The boys spent a lot of time with Sher Singh, helping him in the garden, climbing the trees for the fruit and

181

chasing away the monkeys that came down from the hills for the litchis and mangoes.

Sher Singh himself appeared now from the shadows. He said, 'Memsahib, the children are right. They are saying what is true. I climbed over the wall from the tree. The dog did not bark when he saw us, but he was not wagging his tail either. He just stood there watching, with the chain wound tightly around his neck.'

Cyrus said, 'I went to him and he didn't move. I talked to him, telling him he was a good dog, and that I was going to rescue him. I was a little afraid because he is a very big dog, but he didn't move when I put my hands on the chain and tried to open the clasp. First I had to pull the chain tighter to get my fingers between his neck and the clasp. Still he didn't move. After three tries the clasp fell open, and Sher Singh unwound the chain. Still he didn't move. Then he discovered he was free. He stared at us and then he put his paws on my shoulder and licked my face.'

'He could have bitten you. How did you get him over the wall?'

'Sher Singh half pushed, half carried him to the top, and by his own self he jumped down the other side where Zubin was waiting. Zubin thought he might need to hold him, but he didn't want to go anywhere. He just waited quietly for us and when Sher Singh and I climbed over, Maxi was there, so we brought him home.'

For the first time I looked closely at the animal. His fur

skin deep

had come off in patches, one ear drooped at a peculiar angle, and he smelt horrid. But his eyes were beautiful—a clear golden brown.

'Is he dangerous? How do you know he doesn't have some awful disease? Those bare patches could be mange.'

Sher Singh said, 'There is nothing wrong with this dog that good food and kindness won't cure. He is starving, and see his neck—the chain was so tight that it has cut into the flesh. And he has been beaten so much that if he stays with Malik Sahib, he will die.'

The boys were looking at me with huge, pleading eyes. I stalled. 'What kind of a dog is he?'

Sher Singh smiled. 'Mostly Tibetan Bhotia, I think. Maybe some Alsatian too. But good dog. Clever dog. He knows that boys save him. Never make a sound.'

'And what if Captain Malik comes looking for him? He will surely know that the dog could not have climbed over the wall himself after unfastening the chain.'

The boys leapt up. 'We can keep him?' I nodded.

They smothered me in hugs and kisses. 'See, we will keep him inside the garden. He won't run away, he wants to be with us.'

'By the way, is his name Maxi?' They shook their heads.

'We don't know his name. But in that new book you gave us—the dog in it is called Maxi. And he likes his new name, don't you Maxi?' The dog wagged his tail. He was limping badly, and I began to feel almost as indignant as the boys about Captain Malik.

Sher Singh said, 'In one month he will be a different dog. You'll see.'

And that is how we got Maxi. Not exactly the kind of dog I might have chosen for them, but I am a great believer in coincidences. The boys were longing for a dog, and suddenly here was one, obtained certainly in a very unusual way—stolen, one might say, but the boys were right. Who would have had the heart to return him to his cruel master?

Within a short while—not much over a month, Maxi looked a different dog. Sher Singh claimed that rubbing him with neem oil would soon get rid of the unsightly red patches and grow new hair. A diet of milk, meat and cereal, as well as the love showered by the boys on this waif who had known nothing but harsh words and beatings, had its effect.

Captain Malik, we later learnt, trained dogs for a living—guard dogs and recalcitrant dogs who refused to obey their owners, either deliberately or because they simply chose to do their own thing.

I began to feel as incensed as the boys, for Maxi was turning not only into a very handsome dog, but he was also playful, gentle and showed a surprising sense of fun.

Sher Singh made the neem oil himself by covering freshly-plucked neem leaves with sesame oil and then slowly simmering them over a low fire till the leaves turned black, and the oil had a strong pungent smell. Sher Singh claimed

skin deep

that this oil was excellent for anyone who had any form of skin disease, and that it was used widely in his village with excellent results.

Maxi certainly benefited. Not only did his hair grow again, but it grew thick and glossy. I had insisted that we call in a vet right at the very beginning, and that is how we met Dr Sharma.

He recognized Maxi at once. He said, 'How did you manage to get him away from Captain Malik? What made you buy him? I have seen many dogs, but this one would have died if he had remained with the Captain. He was also very fierce; if I needed to give him an injection, or treat him in any way, he had to be held down by two men and his mouth tied with tape. Not once have I ever been able to get near him— and now look at him—I can hardly believe its the same dog, rolling on his back and letting himself be examined, even wagging his tail.'

Zubin said, 'That's because he knows we love him and will never, ever hurt him. He knows we saved him and took him away from that nasty man.'

Cyrus said, 'He hates Captain Malik. Actually he is very, very clever but he just didn't want to obey Captain Malik. That's why he wouldn't do anything he tried to teach him.'

Dr Sharma said, 'Perhaps you are right. I don't know how you got him out but it was a good thing you did. Now between us we will make him the handsomest dog in the whole town.'

He beamed at the boys. The boys loved him and they listened carefully to his instructions. He prescribed vitamins and a herbal tonic. 'But Maxi must also learn to listen to a few essential commands. Not only will he be happier, but so will everyone around him.'

We bought dog books, which the boys studied with great intensity. Every morning when they left for school, Sher Singh would brush and massage him. The neem oil seemed to be having miraculous results. In a couple of months he had put on weight and turned into a very large furry animal, whose appearance alone was enough to deter strangers from entering. He had become, to the childrens' delight, very playful and was willing to run after a ball and retrieve it, or walk around with a pink and green rubber frog in his mouth, bought for him by the boys. If he remembered Captain Malik or his past life, he showed no sign of it. When the boys were not there, he would come searching for me and lie down quietly beside me. I did not play with him but I found myself talking to him quite a lot. He would thump his tail on the carpet and often rest his head on my foot.

The boys and I pored over their dog books. We decided it was time to start teaching Maxi a few simple commands. I had read Conrad Lorenz to them and we knew that a dog only needed to learn four things—to come when called, to sit, to stay and to walk at heel. With these he would be a happy, well-behaved dog, welcome everywhere, safe and comfortable with himself and humans.

186

There was never any need to teach Maxi to come. At the first sound of his name he would come tearing up, almost knocking them down in his enthusiasm. The command to 'sit' he learnt very quickly too, but 'stay' seemed impossible for him either to understand or to obey. The boys would make him sit and then say a long, drawn-out 'S-T-A-Y'. His brow would furrow with anxiety, he would whine and then leap after them as they walked away.

I said, 'Leave it for now. It's not that he doesn't understand what you want him to do. He just can't get himself to sit while you walk away in the opposite direction. You know that I still have to hold him on the leash when you leave for school every morning. He understands, but he doesn't want to obey.'

I often took him out shopping in the car with me. He loved it, and I could leave the car unlocked even if neither Sher Singh nor I were there. Most people are wary of approaching a car with a large furry animal in it.

'*Bhalu hai*,' small boys would say, awestruck. '*Jungle ka bhalu hai*.' (It's a bear. A bear from the jungle.)

With the boys in school, he spent his time with me or with Sher Singh in the garden. There was lots for him to do in the garden. He hadn't been chained or tied up since he arrived and he enjoyed his new-found freedom. The garden was large, and apart from the monkeys' raids from time to time, they were hares to chase, birds to scare and civet cats to send shooting over the wall. His relationship with the monkeys was very interesting. He felt duty-bound to chase them, even when they kept to the trees and jumped from branch to branch. These were not the more gentle black-faced langurs, but the brown rhesus monkeys, aggressive and very destructive. They seemed to delight in plucking handfuls of litchis from the trees and flinging them down uneaten. During the litchi season in Dehra, the night is filled with the long-drawn-out calls of the men guarding the trees from fruit bats, and in the day there were monkeys, birds and bands of marauding boys.

Maxi found it hard to keep track of creatures that seemed to stay in the trees, yet do so much damage. He would leap up, sometimes catching a dangling tail which seemed to frighten him as much as it did the monkeys. By rushing around, leaping into the air and barking constantly, the monkeys had no time to settle down to pluck the fruit, and though they still came, it was less frequently.

About three months after Maxi had been rescued, Sher Singh came to tell me that there was a sahib who wished to see me. His name, he announced poker-faced, was Captain Malik.

Maxi and I were sitting in the dappled shade of the cassia tree—I with a book, trying to read with the whistling and trilling of the birds in the background, and he with one ear cocked for any interesting noises which needed investigating.

I nodded and called Maxi to sit near me. 'Let him come, and put out another chair.'

Captain Malik was a short, stout man carrying a thick walking stick in his hand. He was wearing a tweed coat with leather patches on the elbows, and cavalry twill trousers. His moustache bristled. As he approached, Maxi sat up stiffly and began a low rumbling deep in his throat.

'Good morning,' Captain Malik said. 'I believe you have recently acquired a dog—this dog. He was stolen from my compound some months ago.'

Maxi's fur was standing up on his back and his lips were drawn back from his teeth in a very menacing manner.

'Control your dog, madam. The brute looks as if he is about to attack me.'

'Maxi, SIT,' I said sternly, and to my delight he sat at once. He continued, however, to growl, deep in his throat.

'I have no idea what you are talking about,' I said. 'Maxi is the only dog I have, and he has been with me since he was a small puppy.'

Captain Malik did not appear to believe me. Suddenly raising his voice and taking a step forward he said, 'Bingo, Bingo. Come here sir. Here!'

Maxi's growling rose an octave higher and he lunged forward. I put my hand out and grasped his collar. Captain Malik retreated behind the chair. 'Your dog needs training,' he said. 'He is a vicious brute. I would be glad to train him for you. A little bit of stick is required, it doesn't do to be too soft with an animal this size.'

'Maxi is very well trained,' I said mildly. 'He just does not like you. If I let him go I feel certain he will attack.'

Captain Malik took two hasty steps back, and then turned and marched off as fast as possible to the gate and out, with Sher Singh following him to lock the gate. Maxi's growls only subsided when he had disappeared. I was laughing and Sher Singh, on returning, allowed himself a small smile.

Maxi looked very pleased with himself. The hated man had gone, and he had helped to get rid of him. He put his head on my knee and his tail never stopped wagging. Apart from the ear which still drooped, he looked splendid; very different indeed from the pathetic creature the boys had rescued.

*

When Yasmin finally came down from her room, coffee had been laid out on the rosewood table before the window. Although it is still chilly, outside the sun is dazzling and the eye travels from the hills to the flowers and back again where the Himalayas loom, mythologically large.

I had ordered lunch with great care, but Yasmin pushed her food around listlessly. The famous Parsi dish *patra-no-machi*, fillets of pomfret rolled in a bland green chutney

190

and steamed in banana leaves, was done to perfection, but she ate hardly a morsel.

She tapped the Limoges dinner plate with her fork and picked up the crystal glass into which apple juice had been poured.

'You have certainly made yourself very comfortable. It is so unfair. Here you are, fat and plain—you always were fat and nothing much to look at—and yet it is you who have everything. You married a wonderful man, you have two beautiful sons and all Grandma's money. How she hated me!'

'Nonsense. She never hated you, in spite of Sophie doing her best to make you into a good little Christian. Have you forgotten all those fabulous jewels grandma gave you when you were married? And she settled quite a bit of money on you too. You simply squandered it all.'

'It was a mere bagatelle compared to what she gave you. She gave you everything.'

After lunch we went to our separate rooms to rest. I promised to send tea to her at four. I had become accustomed to living alone and I enjoyed it. To be alone for long stretches of time is as necessary for me as food. Perhaps this visit would be even less comfortable than I had anticipated. And still she hadn't told me her reason for the visit. I supposed I would know soon enough. I called Maxi and he came with me into my room and with a sigh put his head down on the rug, but his eyes remained open.

sixteen

I got on extremely well with my in-laws. Perhaps initially Ramesh's mother was jealous of me, as I suppose she would have been of any woman who had married her only son, but she soon realized that I was in no way possessive, nor did I wish to keep him away from her. In fact, it was always I who urged him to visit, it was I who persuaded him to invite them over as often as possible, I softened and made amends for his brusqueness and lack of affection. Increasingly, she turned to me with her requests and frequent complaints.

Ramesh was right—when the twins were born she turned all her attention to them. They were her son's babies, and above all they were boys! Helpless recipients of her frustrated passion, they responded in the most gratifying manner, crowing and holding out their arms to be cuddled.

As they grew older they retained this affection for her, warm and protective, as though to make up for their father's coldness. She loved to take them out to the park in the car, and let them roll on a blanket spread out on the green grass, under the flickering shade of the casuarina trees. Often people would stop to admire the babies and ask whose children they were. She was aware that they presumed she was their ayah, and it gave her enormous pleasure to tell them that they were her grandchildren.

They were still less than a year old when she came to me and asked hesitantly if I would take Sunita and her to visit the two great pilgrimage centres of Haridwar and Rishikesh. She said, 'Before I start negotiations for Sunita's marriage, I wish to do Ganga Puja and ask for God's blessings. If I ask Ramesh, he will get angry and say it is all superstitious nonsense.' I assured her we would go whenever it was convenient for her, and we could stay overnight at one of the many guest houses and return the following morning. She was worried about leaving the twins, but I knew they would be fine with Rosie.

When I told Ramesh we were planning a trip to Haridwar and Rishikesh, he was less than enthusiastic, but when I said I had never visited these places before, he was stunned.

'But you have been in Delhi several years,' he said.

'True, but it never struck me as either important or interesting to visit these places of pilgrimage.'

It was early October, and the weather was cool and pleasant after the heat of summer. The leaves of the trees had begun to turn orange and gold, and were drifting down like multicoloured butterflies. Rosie had packed sandwiches, fruit, and flasks of tea and coffee for the journey. We could stop somewhere and have a picnic.

Sunita was bubbling over with high spirits at being out of the flat and in the car. She was really very pretty, and I smiled at her childish delight and her capacity to enjoy herself. She chattered endlessly, leaning out of the windows and letting the wind blow her hair into her eyes.

Less than halfway there, we decided to stop beside a monsoon stream for tea and sandwiches. Everything was incredibly green—the fields, the trees, even the distant hills. There was a breeze, and the clouds reflected in the stream. All along the road Sunita would lean out and stare at a passing camel, or a troop of monkeys, or even a bitch with her puppies. She wanted to stop and give them the remainder of our sandwiches, but I told her she could feed the monkeys when we arrived. Ma had already told her that once we got there we could buy peanuts for the monkeys, flour pellets for the fish and rotis for the cows.

How shall I describe Haridwar and Rishikesh, so familiar to Sunita and her mother, yet so strange and foreign to me? Sacred because of their proximity to the holy river, these towns looked even dirtier and more impoverished than the villages we had passed on the way. I looked at these places as through the eyes of a foreigner, a total stranger, an alien. The words picturesque and exotic came to mind, but it was also disturbing.

The river itself, the famous Ganga, worshipped by millions of Indians, was swollen with monsoon rains, and looked a dark and murky green. On its banks and on the steps leading down to the bathing ghats sat the lepers, stretching out mutilated hands for alms. Pilgrims threw them a few coins as they made their way down to the river, satisfied that they had gained brownie points with God. To me it all seemed like a scene out of a movie—the background hills with the Mansa Devi temple perched precariously on an impossible peak, and the sadhus or holy men, smoking their chillums, or sitting with glazed eyes staring into the distance. It was considered quite legitimate for sadhus to smoke bhang or marijuana, as though it were an essential part of spiritual life. Under huge faded umbrellas sat the men who would tell us, for a fee, what the future had in store, explain the scriptures or look up a horoscope. Everywhere palms were extended—it was the most openly mercenary place I had ever seen.

Sunita was delighted with everything. We bought little leaf boats to float down the river and she arranged the flowers and wicks inside with excessive care. She made me promise that I would guard them with my life while they indulged in the necessary dip in the sacred waters. Both of them urged me repeatedly to join them but this I firmly refused.

All around were women of all ages—teenagers to grandmothers—all casually divesting themselves of their clothes in public in order to submerge themselves in the murky waters of the sacred river. It was, I felt, something like the Catholic confessional—all sins were washed away and one emerged shorn of all wrongdoing. Nothing could be more convenient if you believed. Fanatically modest at other times, women stripped casually down to their underwear and plunged into the swiftly flowing river. It was not unknown for bathers to be swept away and drowned, and metal chains were suspended from the bridge, which could be held while plunging one's head repeatedly under the water. Sunita, ignoring the chains, splashed about in the shallows like a happy porpoise, dunking her head under and emerging again, gasping for breath.

When they came out they were drenched, their few clothes sculpted to their bodies, their hair streaming with water. The river, stirred up by dozens of bodies, became thick and opaque; the colour of glue.

I handed them the towels I had been holding and they dried themselves as best they could, wrapping saris around and slipping off their wet clothes under this fragile shield. Both had expressions of absolute bliss on their faces. I envied their complete faith, but felt they should come back to the guest house and have hot baths to wash off all the germs they had almost certainly picked up. I did not suggest this, however—germs were not important when all bad karma had been washed away. For them, the tough membrane between natural and supernatural, was only a thin, discontinuous and shifting veil.

Finally, after wandering around for some time, Ma selected one of the men sitting under coloured umbrellas for her questions about Sunita's future. He was probably a man from the hills. He had dark skin like polished wood and slanting, enigmatic eyes. It was, I thought, an interesting face.

We sat cross-legged on the mats spread before him as he looked enquiringly at us. Ma laid her hand on Sunita's head and said, 'Maharaj, tell me what is in store for this child. Will she get married? Will she be happy?'

He stared for a long moment at Sunita, who smiled happily back at him, her eyes flat and shallow, reflecting nothing. At last he said, 'Yes, she will get married very soon. But after that I can see nothing—there is only darkness.'

I repeated, 'Will she be happy? Will she be protected and safe?' For the first time, he turned his eyes to me.

'I can see darkness, only darkness.' He looked at Sunita again and repeated, 'I can see nothing more. Only darkness.' He refused the money which was put on the mat in front of him. His glance slid away into infinity, as if he had withdrawn and gone to another place.

Both of us looked anxiously at Sunita who seemed either not to have heard, or who simply did not understand what had been said. But both her mother and I were deeply affected. I was not a believer in astrology or predictions, but there was something strange in the compassionate way he had looked at Sunita.

To distract us, I suggested we visit the bazaar higher up, with the little shops full of beads and bangles, little brass lamps and statues of Ganesha, who brought good luck and prosperity. Sunita bought glass bangles and a string of Rudraksha beads, but I picked up a small brass Ganesha— small enough to fit in my handbag, where he could stay forever. Sunita suddenly gave a cry of delight. Descending from the low, surrounding hills in a series of exuberant leaps and bounds were a troop of langur monkeys, their silvery fur gleaming palely in the sun. Sunita adored all animals and seemed to have a special affinity with them. She caught my hand and looked up at me pleadingly. 'Bhabi, can we buy peanuts for the monkeys?' Ma bought several small paper cones of peanuts and Sunita began to toss them to the animals, who surrounded her so that she was knee-deep in monkeys. I was terrified that they might attack her, but they seemed friendly enough, and the girl's face was radiant with delight. One large female monkey, with a baby clutched to her breast, edged closer to Sunita and gently held her hand. Sunita had a dazzled, bemused expression on her face.

At last all the nuts were finished and the monkeys drifted away—including the female with the baby, casting longing looks behind her, till she, too, scampered out of sight.

Sunita wandered back towards us. 'Did you see them? Did you see the one with the baby who put her hand into mine? Such a soft hand, and the little baby was so sweet. I wish I had a baby monkey of my own.'

Her mother snapped at her. 'What rubbish you talk child. Here—I have bought flour pellets for the fish. You can feed them.'

We stood on the bridge and threw the pellets into the water. There were shoals of fat, sleek, twisting fish, slipping sinuously through the water, leaping high to snap up the food. But Sunita was not interested. She seemed to be afraid of the fish, and backed hastily away as one particularly large creature leapt high, as though to snatch the food from our fingers. She continued to look over her shoulder to see if the langurs might still be there.

There were other stalls selling hot puris, potato cakes and samosas. Just outside the temple walls sat men with three-feet high piles of chapatis. 'Ten for a rupee,' they were calling out. 'Ten for one rupee.'

Sunita, who had been running ahead and returning to us like a puppy released from its leash, suddenly cried out, 'Look at those poor little thin dogs—no one feeds them. Everyone feeds the cows and the fish and even the monkeys, but no one cares for the dogs.' And of course it was true; dogs are very low on the list of creatures to be fed or those that were considered sacred. Indians, on the whole, do not care for dogs. I have known people who never, at any time, set their dog free to run and play and enjoy just being a dog. I have passed scores of houses where the dog is either howling and crying incessantly or sitting wistfully with its nose stuck through the gate, looking longingly at the outside world. So it came as no surprise when no one fed the dogs.

I gave Sunita two rupees and she came back with a huge pile of chapatis. Her eyes were sparkling as she went looking for the dogs. They came slinking out from cover, tails between their legs, cringing if we so much as looked at them.

Crouching, Sunita began to break off bits of the bread and throw it to them. They were so hungry that they swallowed whole pieces, waiting for more. I had been so intent on watching Sunita that I did not notice the beggars approaching until it was too late. They had been sitting in rows, begging bowls in their hands—wild men with matted hair and beards. Among them was a blond man, as wild looking as the rest. They approached threateningly and it was obvious they were angry. One heavily built, half-naked man came right up to the girl and stretched out his hand, shaking his bowl in front of her face.

'Alms for the poor in God's name. Alms for those who beg.' Sunita was still concentrating on the dogs, and without looking up for more than a brief moment, said dismissively, 'Go away. These are not for you.'

In a single moment, before I could even take a step forward, she was surrounded like a cornered fox by a pack of hounds. They grabbed the food from her hands, and in the struggle, knocked her over, snarling and fighting like dogs. The blond one seemed especially vicious. By the time I reached her she had been knocked down, her hands covering her head to protect herself, her dupatta torn, tears pouring down her face. I picked her up and with my arm around her, edged carefully away from them. They seemed ready to pounce again, but now she had nothing left in her hands and the dogs had long since vanished.

Several pilgrims and some tourists were standing around and staring at us. Not one made any move to help us. One man, in fact, glared at us. 'Those chapatis were made by the temple specially for the beggars, not for the dogs. Do you prefer dogs to men?'

I did not reply. Sunita was trembling and shaking. Hearing all the commotion, Ma came running up. She had probably gone in search of yet another pandit to ask about Sunita. As we made for the car, she scolded Sunita. 'What made you try and feed the dogs instead of the beggars? You can really act very stupidly sometimes, child. Those chapatis are made specially to distribute to beggars—that is why they are so cheap.' She looked angrily at me.

'Why didn't you stop her? At least you should have had more sense.'

I was surprised at how angry I felt. 'Those beggars didn't deserve to be fed. Most were strong and healthy. Some were smoking bhang. They should not just sit there waiting for handouts.'

She stared at me in astonishment. 'But that is why they are there. Pilgrims need to give alms when they come here and if there are no beggars, how can they do this? In these sacred places it is necessary to give generously. If there were no beggars, to whom would we give alms?'

I did not bother to reply. The guest house was at the end of the main road and we climbed up the long stairs slowly. I had my arm around Sunita ,who was shivering and crying with shock and fright. The guest house was unpretentious but clean and inviting, and the staff, kind and helpful. When we were safely inside I made Sunita drink some tea from the flask and then tucked her up in bed. I wished I had a tranquillizer to give her; in fact I wouldn't have been averse to one myself. The sheer brutal savagery of the attack still amazed me. Ma was looking troubled, and I poured her a cup of tea as well.

I said, 'Do you really intend to get this child married? What kind of a life will she have? She is so easily frightened. Who will look after her and protect her?'

The old woman turned a troubled face to me. 'But if no marriage, then what? When I am gone who will look after her?'

I wanted to say, 'I will look after her', but the thought of Ramesh held me back. One of the reasons he had been happy to move in with me was because he couldn't stand having Sunita around.

'In our Indian society,' she continued. 'It is very difficult for a girl—any girl—to live without marriage. Marriage gives security. She will be safe with a family of her own. And now with this money you have given us, we will look for a good boy. There is no hurry. With a good dowry, the boy and his family will look after her.'

Dowry deaths, as they were called, were widely prevalent all over India. People who might have hesitated to trap a rat and kill it thought nothing of pouring kerosene over a young woman and throwing a lighted match to turn her into a living torch.

Sunita slept through the afternoon, and when she awoke she was her usual sunny self. She appeared to have forgotten the unhappy experience of the morning. We made a fuss over her, ordered hot milk and biscuits, brushed her hair and made her change her clothes. Once more we returned to the river bank. In all the turmoil of the morning, we had lost the little leaf boats which Sunita has filled so lovingly with leaves and flowers. I bought more—the largest and freshest I could find—and filled them with marigolds and pink and red rose petals. Soon it would be time for the evening *aarti*—the ritual worship of the river with lights.

The skies darkened rapidly. There was no twilight here; a bright evening turned from sunshine to darkness as though a curtain had been pulled down. Voices were muted.

Everywhere people were lighting the little wicks in their leafy boats and setting them afloat. Sunita had done this ritual before, but it did not prevent her from being very excited.

Kicking off her chappals, she waded into the shallows, and crouching down, she set the three little boats gently on the surface of the darkening river. From all around us other boats began to slip down, some setting a straight course, some veering off at a tangent, speeding up as they came under the bridge, their lights fading into the distance. I sent mine off with a prayer for Sunita, to the gods I didn't believe in. 'Keep her safe. Keep her as happy as she is now.'

I watched our little boats until they were swallowed up in the myriads of others, the river now sprinkled magically with tiny, floating lights. Cries of 'Om Jai Ganga Mata' went up all around us.

I marvelled again at the faith prevailing all around. This was not just a river—it was sacred, a holy place that cleansed and purified the believers, and freed them from the evil and sin which separated them from divine grace.

For me it was just another river, often beautiful and magnetic, but for the most part, a river that was dirty and contaminated and full of filth. I was a foreigner to this scene, but not all foreigners felt this way. In the seventh century, the Chinese traveller Hieun Tsang wrote: 'The scaly monsters, though many, do no harm to men. The taste of the water is sweet and pleasant . . . those who are weary of life, if they end their days in it, are borne to heaven and receive happiness.'

The water of this river is considered so pure that it can supposedly be preserved for years in its pristine form. Even the Mughal emperors thought this water was in some way very special, and had it carried to them over long distances.

The German philosopher Keyserling wrote: 'I feel inclined, like the pilgrims on the Ganges, to sink down every morning in fervent gratitude for it is immeasurable what it gives me. Here I feel, even today, I would receive the graces of supreme revelation.'

But as for me, I felt nothing. For me it was just a great river, now hopelessly contaminated with industrial effluent, sewage and half-burnt dead bodies.

As we waited on the banks with hundreds of devotees, the lights came on in the temples and were reflected in the dark water. I was looking forward to seeing this pagan worship of the river with lights, and seeing, for the first time, the homage and devotion and the joyous adoration of the worshippers, who felt something I did not, and could not, feel.

The pandits now began with the blowing of conches and the circling of brass trays filled with tiny oil lamps which blossomed like flowers as they waved them over the fast-moving river, making formalized patterns— sometimes blurred, sometimes sharply etched—on the screen of darkness, reflected in the water in blurry golden images. The crowds stood with folded hands and rapt faces, impervious to anything else, their attention totally focussed, as though deep in meditation.

Again, I wondered what it must feel like to have such absolute faith. Darkness filled up the river and enclosed the mountains around us. Sunita was so delighted—she laughed and clapped, and several people turned to her with indulgent smiles.

We left early the next morning, stopping only briefly for tea and samosas at a dhaba. Sunita slept all the way back, her hair falling limply across one pale cheek. Both of us were silent, preoccupied with our separate thoughts. I continued to find it strange that everything I had seen and experienced seemed totally alien and meaningless to me. Perhaps we accept everything more readily as children.

Living in Hyderabad, nothing had seemed either alien or strange—the black shrouded women on the streets, the calls to prayer from the mosques, the very distinctive and sophisticated manners, language, music and food that existed here. All this I accepted easily as part of my life. Why then had my visit to Haridwar seemed like something out of *National Geographic* magazine?

seventeen

Preparations to get Sunita married were soon well under away. Ramesh elected to stay out of everything, irritated and embarrassed by the whole business. There was nothing I could do to stop what was happening. The usual advertisement appeared in all the newspapers.

'Wanted, match for fair, pretty, homely girl, aged nineteen, well-versed in household affairs and with a good singing voice. Only those from well-to-do respectable families need apply.'

It was a masterpiece of vulgarity, but for once Ma refused to listen to me or to change a single word. It had been written for her by an elderly cousin, and not a word would she alter.

'You don't understand these things,' she said to me. 'You are like a foreigner among us. Your people live differently, think differently and behave differently. This is

the way everyone advertises. Look at the papers you get—
even the well-known English papers—they are all full of
the same details, put in by parents who want nothing but
the very best for their children. For Sunita, this is the only
way we will ever find someone to marry her. Do you expect
her to have a love marriage like yours? You see, we will
find a nice boy for her who will be happy to marry her—
specially when we are giving such a good dowry.'

For me it seemed strange and frightening that loving
parents, who had brought up their daughters with care and
affection, could hand them over to some unknown stranger
whom they did not even know.

There were more than a dozen replies, and eventually
these were narrowed down to four, and preliminary
meetings took place between the parents. Finally the choice
fell on one particular family and they were invited to 'view'
the prospective bride, a process I considered even more
vulgar and humiliating than the advertisement. My mother-
in-law assured me that this was how it was always done,
but I was absolutely appalled. It was like having an auction
in which the goods would be viewed, bid for and bought, if
the price were right.

What happened, I wondered, to the girls who were
viewed and found wanting, and were rejected? Did they go
into decline, commit suicide or refuse to see anyone else?
Or did the parents simply offer more goodies the next time?

It had been decided that it would make a better

impression if the meeting were to take place in my flat. At this time we were still in Delhi, as the house in Dehra Dun was in the process of being built.

The flat had been spruced up, and everything gleamed with polish. There were sweets, cakes and samosas ready to be served to the boy and his family. Ramesh had decided that there would be no need for him to be present, and had disappeared, much to his mother's relief. It would be simpler to make all the necessary arrangements without his silent disapproval, or even worse, his exasperated remarks.

They arrived dead on time, the whole family consisting of Mr and Mrs Kapoor, the boy, Santosh, and his elder married sister. Sunita was looking very pretty, wearing a cream silk sari printed all over with flowers. Her hair fell over her shoulders and her mouth was curved into a perpetual smile.

Mrs Kapoor was a very large woman wearing a salwar-kurta that did nothing to hide the bulging rolls of fat around her waist and stomach. Her arms were thick and solid, with skin that seemed to be made from sandpaper. She had an expression on her face that was both aggressive and intimidating—one could see at once that the others in the family were in awe of her.

She looked around the flat as if she was taking an inventory for a garage sale. It was clear that she was surprised—her meeting with Sunita's parents had not prepared her for this flat. She rubbed the curtain material between her thick fingers, felt the upholstery and stared at the carpets, trying to assess how much they cost. Far from being pleased, she appeared disgruntled and annoyed; perhaps it would have been better, after all, to have had this meeting in my mother-in-law's flat.

Sunita carried in the tray and served everyone neatly and competently. Mrs Kapoor watched her very carefully, but Santosh barely glanced at her. In his early twenties, with a round dimpled chin and eyes that seemed to be fixed on his mother with a kind of nervous intensity, he fidgeted, choked over a piece of cake, and appeared thoroughly ill at ease.

He had no job at the moment, Mrs Kapoor informed us, but he would soon be joining his father's grocery store situated in Khan market. She made it sound as if the shop was something like a department store, but in fact it turned out to be one room with stocks of oil, sugar, flour and other staples. Mrs Kapoor beckoned imperiously to Sunita to come and sit near her. Sunita went readily, smiling all the while.

I have often wondered how responsible one is for what happens, how much guilt it is necessary to assume or feel for events that might have been prevented. Human beings care ultimately only for themselves—how else can I explain that we sat around smiling and saying the usual polite nothings, when a tragedy lurked, which might have been averted.

Even at this first meeting Mrs Kapoor seemed a greedy woman, intent on getting as much as she could from this marriage. She looked at it as a business transaction from which she intended to get the best possible bargain. During the entire evening no one else said a single word. Santosh was a mama's boy and Mr Kapoor a nonentity who sat in one corner and pretended he wasn't there. The married daughter, who would soon be the same size as her mother, demanded now to see the whole flat. I took them around reluctantly.

There was no trouble at all about accepting Sunita as her son's prospective bride. Almost immediately Mrs Kapoor began to make tentative enquiries about the dowry. It had been Ramesh's fear that they would make exorbitant demands, but I was prepared to agree to everything if it made things easier for Sunita, although her mother wanted to bargain and quibble over the many demands being made. In an undertone, I persuaded her not to do any such thing. Mr Kapoor asked for a car, a colour TV, a washing machine, furniture, and in addition, all the stainless steel pots and pans considered necessary for a well-fitted kitchen. Having gained what she wanted without any fuss, Mrs Kapoor was all smiles, and chucked Sunita under the chin and pinched her cheek so hard that she winced.

Afterwards, when it was all over, I had a terrible feeling

of having betrayed Sunita, abandoned her, as it were, to the enemy.

The wedding reception was both ostentatious and elaborate. Sunita's sari, which I had chosen myself, was a beautiful, heavy Paithani in dark pink and gold. She wore bridal make-up, professionally applied, and her hair was done in elaborate coils high on her head. Her hands had been painted in floral designs with henna, so that she appeared to be wearing delicate lace gloves. She was loving every minute of it——she was the centre of attention. There were red glass bangles on her wrists and heavy gold chains around her neck. The garlands were made not from marigolds, but from white jasmine and pink, scented roses.

The most expensive caterers had been engaged for the lavish buffet, and as with all Indian weddings, the groom's side were served first. I found the whole thing extremely irritating, but Sunita was so delighted with all the attention she was getting and everyone telling her how pretty she looked, that it was impossible not to be pleased for her. She was like a child at a birthday party and it was unlikely that outsiders could tell she was not completely normal. Mrs Kapoor, however, knew. I could see that from the way she tried to shield the girl from too much conversation. I was pleased, thinking she had taken a liking to her and intended to protect her. I never dreamt that she did so only so that others would not feel that she had made an unfortunate choice for her only son. She knew exactly what she was doing.

She dominated her husband completely, and all her love and affection was for the boy. She doted on him, and perhaps even felt that in this way she would never lose him to another, younger woman. Quite rightly, she expected no competition from Sunita.

After it was all over and it was time for Sunita to drive off with her husband in the new car, she became frightened and bewildered. She did not seem to have realized that all this was a preliminary to her leaving and going away with a stranger to a unfamiliar new home. I don't know what she had been told, but now, when she was pushed into the car with Santosh, she seemed petrified, and clung to her mother and to me till she was forced into the car. Seeing her bewildered, tearful face, I wanted to pull her out of the car and take her home with me, put her to bed with a hot cup of chocolate, and assure her that she could stay with me forever. But already it was too late.

After only a few months, I noticed that Sunita had lost her smile. She had a dazed look, and no longer chattered incessantly. I assured myself that everything was all right, and that the adjustment to a new life would take time. There was really nothing more I could do.

I did indeed question her one afternoon, when I met her unexpectedly in the market. She was carrying a bulging jute bag with the strap slung over one shoulder. In her free hand she carried, with great difficulty, a can of oil. She was staggering and bowed down under the weight. I opened the car door and put her in, saying I would drop her home. I asked how things were going, and she burst into tears and flung herself into my arms. She was much thinner and her pretty hands, which had been decorated with henna at the wedding, were rough, the nails broken. I had never seen her cry before, never seen her anything but happy and singing. Her tears upset me as nothing else could, still I did nothing. I took her back and had the driver carry up her bag and the tin. Mrs Kapoor met us at the door. The bags were put down and I said, 'These are much to heavy for Sunita to carry.'

Mrs Kapoor looked coldly at me. She had small dark eyes like unripe plums. 'Sunita is spoiled,' she said. 'She thinks everyone should do things for her. She has to learn.'

I left Sunita with her, abandoned her to the hardness of those terrible eyes. I blamed myself for this forever. Why did I not bring her home with me, or find out in detail what was happening?

Exactly three weeks later, Sunita, denied even the relative mercy of sleeping pills, poured kerosene over herself and set herself on fire. There is always kerosene in the house and matches in the kitchen; no need to go searching for more esoteric, painless forms of dying. When one is desperate enough, even the flames must seem enticing.

Now, when it was too late, we heard from the neighbours about all the petty cruelties, the humiliation, the jeers and physical abuse that she had to put up with from the very first day. Always treated with tenderness, bewildered by this new world in which everything she did was wrong, she took the only way out that was open to her.

The mild scandal that followed was soon forgotten. Ramesh was summoned, but there was little we could do without filing a case against them. Deliberately, spitefully, remorselessly, Sunita had been driven to take her own life.

It was a sick game that Mrs Kapoor had played and won. Now everything was hers—the money, the jewellery, the car—everything. After some time she would answer another advertisement, and another unfortunate young woman would be drawn into the net. Meanwhile, they were a great deal richer than before—rich, smug and satisfied.

I wanted to file a case against them, go to the police, do something, but Ramesh's mother steadfastly refused. Nothing would come of it, she said; there were hundreds of cases like this every year. She could not bear to stand up in court and relate what had been done to Sunita. What good would it do now? Best forget it.

For days and weeks I went round blaming myself for what had happened, but then I too forgot and buried the memory deep inside, from where it could emerge only in dreams. I no longer saw that innocent smiling face, that childish voice raised in song, that look of happiness which

215

comes from knowing one is loved and cherished. We were all guilty, and I not the least, for her death. In my dreams I was lost, searching for paths I would never find again, a ghost wandering under dark skies, although there was sun on the hills and on the new, hesitant grass of the lawn.

Zoroastrians believe that both good and evil exist together in this world, and often evil powers, or the powers of darkness, can prevail over good and influence not only individual lives but all of humanity. 'Keep me from evil,' says the old Zoroastrian prayer, 'that I may harm no one.'

For Sunita, the dark powers had prevailed.

eighteen

We took the body to Haridwar for the final rites—
Haridwar, where, not so long ago, Sunita had fed the
monkeys and laughed at their antics, sailed her little leaf
boat down the Ganga and danced joyously as the lights of
the aarti lit up the darkening river. The fire that had
consumed her had blackened and twisted the body, but her
childishly vulnerable face had not been touched, though
some of the hair had been burnt away. There was a chill
wind and I felt cold inside and out.

There were no tears for Sunita. No wailing mourners,
no sobbing relatives, none of the usual cries of 'Why have
you left me and gone away?' Santosh stood nervously near
his mother, whose face was like stone. As the wood was
piled up and Sunita's body carried and placed on it, she
stood watching. When the flames, helped along by the
pouring of ghee, leapt up, she leaned over and hissed in my

ear, 'She has disgraced our house and brought dishonour to our family. If she wished to kill herself she should have done it somewhere else. Not inside the house which had taken her in and given her shelter.'

I was shocked into silence by these words. Could she feel nothing for that small, pathetic body, blackened and twisted in death?

Women do not normally accompany the body to the cremation ground, but with Mr Kapoor lying ill in bed, it was unthinkable that Santosh should go on his own. Mrs Kapoor was now probably planning her next move— the search for another unsuspecting victim, for more dowry. Would other families hesitate before giving their daughters in marriage to a family in whose house the first bride had burnt herself to death? And there was also the lingering suspicion that she had not set fire to herself at all. Many brides when taken to the hospital had given dying declarations, saying they had been set alight by hands other than their own. But for Sunita, the flames had killed her too quickly, or there had been a delay in summoning the ambulance.

We drove back in silence. The rich smell of rotting vegetation and the roar of the river seemed only to add to the darkness of my mood. No one said a word, and I wondered if they had spoken in the other car which had taken the Kapoors back to Delhi. Ma was pale and composed. Now and again a tear trickled down her face which she did not appear to notice. Ramesh was driving, his face grimmer than I had ever seen it.

It was already dark when we arrived back in Delhi. The city was quiet, but not asleep. There were still people astir and lights shining from open windows. A few pedestrians moved through the streets cautiously, as alert for danger as savages threading an area inhabited by alien tribes. Delhi could be a dangerous city at night.

Ramesh said, 'Naaz, I'll drop you home first and stay with Ma tonight. They need me here.'

I nodded, surprised and pleased that he wanted to do this. They were pathetically grateful to have him with them. Papaji looked as if he might collapse at any moment and though he clasped his hands tightly together, they trembled and shook without ceasing.

'Would you like me to stay?' I enquired.

'No. They need me here. You go back to the boys.' His mother put her arms around me briefly before turning and going up the steps slowly. Rosie met me at the door. The boys were long since asleep. I looked in briefly at them, lying in their cribs. Cyrus had kicked off all the covers, but Zubin lay curled quietly under his quilt. I lay my hand lightly on his round head and covered Cyrus, tucking the sheets tightly around him.

Rosie said, 'He'll throw them off again, you'll see. He likes his legs and arms free.'

I kicked off my shoes and flopped onto the sofa, leaning

my head back against the cushions and closing my eyes.
Rosie came in with a tray. I thought I was not hungry, that
food was the last thing on my mind, but hot chicken soup
and crisp buttered rolls made me realize how hungry I
actually was. I wanted to cry—for myself, for Sunita, for a
world that was so indifferent to suffering. Sunita was no
longer with us, but where was she? Did she still exist—
somewhere, in some form?

I had once seen the Dalai Lama interviewed on TV. He
had been asked whether he believed that the souls of people
were incarnated into other human beings. Tibetan
Buddhism believes in *Tulkus*, the living incarnates of great
lamas, who return to earth again and again to help people.

The Dalai Lama's reply was interesting. He said, 'No,
no. The soul is not incarnated; only the essence (and here
he held his finger and thumb together to show how small,
how fine, the essence was), only the essence is reincarnated.'

I liked the idea of the 'essence' of a person being carried
on by another. It seemed far more plausible than the whole
theory of reincarnation.

I went to my room and flung myself down on the bed,
but my mind was too restless and all I could think of was
Sunita.

Our new flat, which we had moved into after the boys
were born, was in Golf Links, and one evening I had taken
Sunita for a walk across the golf club lawns. She had never

been here before and the vast expanse of lush greenery—
two hundred acres of it in the heart of dirty, polluted
Delhi—amazed her.

'Is this still Delhi?' she enquired, looking around her in
delight. She couldn't believe it when a peacock, tail furled,
came high-stepping up to us, not at all afraid. No one
bothered the wild life that inhabited this area—four nilgai,
a few deer, flocks of parakeets, mongoose, snakes and other
small, wild creatures.

I was making for the archeological monuments which
are scattered over the grounds but just then we saw a
mongoose. It was sitting straight up on its hind legs,
surveying the area as though through binoculars. Sunita,
with her passion for animals, was enchanted.

'Is it a khargosh?' she asked.

'No, it's not a rabbit,' I said. 'It's a mongoose.'

She wanted to catch it and take it home with her, but
fortunately the creature saw us and disappeared in a flash
into the undergrowth.

We never did get to the tombs, but we did see a large
number of birds and a spectacular sunset. She was so open
to enchantment.

I lay staring into the darkness for a long time and slept
badly. Ramesh arrived early the next morning, as I was
sipping my first cup of tea. His face was drawn and his eyes

shadowed. I poured him a cup of tea as he sat on the edge of my bed.

'I feel I am to blame,' he said. 'I should have stopped the whole thing—this idea of marriage for her. I should never have allowed it to go ahead, but I did nothing.'

'We are all to blame,' I said. He shook his head.

'Ma will be all right. She is strong. But Papa has not stopped shaking, although I gave him a stiff brandy and a hot-water bottle in his bed. He won't talk, he does not cry, but the expression on his face breaks my heart.'

I put my hand out and covered his. 'You look very tired. Why don't you go and have a nap? It's still early.'

He shook his head. 'I have a meeting at ten sharp. It is important. I will have a bath and get dressed.' He looked at me.

'Naaz, will you go and sit with Ma this morning? Already people have started arriving. I don't understand this strange custom of people arriving in hordes to show their sympathy. Surely it would be better if they stayed at home and just sent flowers or cards or something, like they do abroad, in the West? All the relatives will come and howl and moan and make them feel much worse.'

But when I arrived, no one was howling or moaning. There was almost total silence, with taped bhajans playing softly in the background. I slipped off my shoes outside the door and walked in. I covered my head with my dupatta. Ma was sitting at one end of the room, leaning up against

the wall. I sat down beside her on the durrie and she put
her hand out and touched me to let me know that she knew
I had come. Her hand was cold and her head lowered so it
was impossible to see her face. It was she who had brought
Sunita up and given her more love and affection than most
normal girls get in Indian families.

There were many curious glances in my direction—a
stranger who was not a Punjabi—'not one of us', as they
would have put it. I had probably seen many of them at
Sunita's wedding. They would have liked to approach me
and ask questions about what had happened. I kept my head
down and stared at the carpet. Sitting cross-legged on the
floor was not something I was used to but it would have
been ridiculous to ask for a chair, as though I were a
foreigner. After two hours I was stiff, my back aching and
my knees locked. I wondered vaguely if I would ever be
able to straighten them again or would be forced to walk
forever in a half-crouch. Most of these women were used
to sitting comfortably on the floor for hours at a time, not
least because most attended satsangs everyday, listening to
some guru whose following could be larger than any pop
star's. Religion and puja are both very important for ninety
per cent of Indian women. I say 'women' because the men
seem to have better things to do until they retire. In the
Hindu religion they are many different gods to choose from
and puja rooms are absolutely essential in every household.
Although Ma did not have an entire room for puja, she had

converted a small alcove in her bedroom, which she decorated with pictures and statues of gods and goddesses, flowers and incense. Here she spent quiet, reflective moments each morning, praying for the peace and prosperity of her family.

Alexander David Neale, writer, explorer and spiritualist wrote:

> The energy which the Hindus project on the idol is not totally immaterial. It could be assimilated to a subtle substance which is impregnated with the thoughts and desires of the seekers. The existence, real or not, of the deity represented, has no importance; what matters is the accumulation of the psychic forces in the statue. Images of gods are fulfilling a function similar to what electricity does to a car battery. In this particular case it is the adoration of the devotees which charges the statues. Gods are created by the energy emitted by the faith in their existence.

Zoroastrians are not idol worshippers but pictures of the prophet hang on walls in temples and houses. I remember asking Grandma once whether Zoroaster really looked like the picture hanging on her bedroom wall. It was the portrait of a man with a fair skin and long brown hair, holding his right hand raised in benediction, or perhaps in warning—it could have been either.

Grandma said, 'Who knows what he looked like. The artist has his own vision. The people in Iran at that time probably had the same kind of features and colouring, but this is an idealized impression of him, just as the Christians have these idealized pictures and statues of Christ and the Virgin Mary, who were dark-skinned and dark-eyed.' She stared at the picture for a long time. 'The gods we worship are what we imagine them to be, or as they appear to us during prayer, or at quiet moments, in our hearts.'

I had been dreaming when suddenly I felt Ma fall heavily against me. I put one arm around her as she lay there, half collapsed.

'Come on,' I said. 'I'm going to take you to your room.' I managed somehow to pull her up with my arm supporting her, to get her to the door and finally into her room, where she collapsed on to the bed. I covered her with the quilt. Was she asleep, or had she fainted with all the strain and grief and guilt she had to bear? Her face, though plump, sagged and drooped. She seemed suddenly to have shrunk and shrivelled up overnight. I put my hand lightly on her forehead and she flinched and murmured something. Whatever state she was in—whether it was exhaustion or sleep—it was best to leave her. For some time at least there was peace and oblivion for her.

I wandered into the kitchen, where some cousin, perhaps an aunt, was filling glasses with a strange pink liquid to serve to the mourners. I said, 'Ma has fainted and needs

225

to rest. Is it possible to tell all these people to go home and return tomorrow? I will sit near her for now. Are you staying here?'

'If I am needed, I will stay.'

I nodded. 'Good. Ramesh will come for me later so I can get back to the children.'

I returned to sit beside the bed. My thoughts turned to Ramesh and Sunita. Having a sibling is one of the most defining experiences of childhood. To have a sibling who is not normal but 'damaged' as Sunita was, brings with it all sorts of complications. The normal sibling has the compulsion to achieve, to compensate for the parents' disappointment by trying to make as few demands as possible. There is also possibly the massive pressure to pretend that nothing is wrong. Although his parents loved and protected Sunita to the best of their ability, it was perhaps at a cost that neither they, nor even he, realized. For him, Sunita was an embarrassment and a burden, but to his parents she was the eternal child—uncomplicated, easy to control, her impairment not severe enough to cause serious problems. Ramesh had always been the quiet, self-denying brother, brilliant and steady, who would be their saviour. Now he was filled with remorse and the feeling that he could, perhaps, have averted the tragedy.

Ma began to stir, and I went again into the kitchen and asked the girl if she could make some tea for her. 'You know how she likes it,' I said. 'Very sweet and strong.'

I carried the cup into the room. I helped her to sit up and held the cup to her lips. She drank with small, tentative sips at first, and then taking the cup from my hands, gulped the liquid down.

'Have they gone?' she asked.

'I think so. You need to rest. I told the girl to tell them you had fainted.'

'Roopa,' she said.

'What?'

'Roopa. That girl in the kitchen. Her name is Roopa. She is my cousin-sister's daughter. You go back to the boys. She will stay with me till Ramesh comes. He should be with his father.' Her lips trembled. 'I worry about him— he is not strong enough to deal with this. Sunita was his darling, his little girl who would always stay the same. He did not want her married. It was I who forced it.' Tears began to trickle down her face again. I caught both her hands in mine and began to rub them, hoping it would somehow bring her some comfort. When I went into the kitchen again, Roopa was washing up.

'What about food?' I said. 'Shall I send something over or will you make something here?'

She looked at me as though I were someone entirely strange, from another planet, who didn't appear to know anything.

'For four days no food will be cooked here in this house. I should not even have lit the stove, but the old people

227

need tea all the time.' She turned her back and began to dry the cups and saucers she had just washed. She asked, 'In your community do they cook food in the house after a death?' I stared at her baffled.

'I don't know. I'll send something over.'

They boys were playing on the carpet and greeted me with open arms and chuckles. I sat down on the sofa and cuddled them, kissing their sun-warmed necks and inhaling the smell of baby soap and powder.

'It's time for their naps,' Rosie said. 'I'll take them with me and you can rest.'

Suddenly I wanted them with me; the horror of what had happened had left me drained by shock and tiredness. I wanted to forget, however briefly, with the help of these two small creatures who had not been touched by tragedy or anger or pity. I bent over them, and at once they put their arms up to be carried. I picked them up, one on each arm. They were heavy and I did not usually pick them both up at the same time, but they were delighted and wrapped their chubby arms around my neck and put sticky fingers on my face. I tumbled them down on my bed and threw myself down beside them. They were delighted with this new game and rolled around, grabbing at each other and pulling me with them. I let them play until suddenly they were asleep, their eyes closed, lashes resting on pink cheeks.

I covered them with a light quilt and lay down beside them, enclosed in the shadowed calm of the room. I slept, and dreamt of Sunita. She was wandering in a walled garden, grassy and green, but with no way out. Round and round she went in that sunlit garden, trapped and frightened, treading with fearful care, alert for small signs, as though the garden were inhabited by savages, ready to attack.

nineteen

The old people continued to mourn with a terrible, protracted intensity, as though time had done nothing to alleviate their pain and the ghost of Sunita still wandered forlornly through the dusty rooms.

I tried to go over and sit with them every few days, but apart from greeting me listlessly, they said little or nothing. We sat together in silence, until Ma would go into the kitchen and make tea which no one wanted, but which we forced ourselves to drink. Papaji's face had an ashen tinge, his eyes were glazed and his precarious composure seemed ready to collapse at any moment.

It was Sunita who had brought him his first cup of tea each morning. He would be on the verandah, reading the Bhagvad Gita and reciting the Gayatri mantra, which he had taught her with the correct pronunciation. Through repetition the wandering mind gets fixed, much as light may be focussed at one point with the aid of a lens. Sunita had soon learnt the mantra, and together they would recite it as the sun came up over the horizon, slanting its rays through the trees. Now, instead of the peace he had enjoyed, all that filled his mind was the blackened and twisted body of his beloved child.

Ma kept herself busy in the kitchen, rolling out chapatis which no one ate, and making endless cups of tea.

I sat with them, not knowing how to bring them consolation or comfort, until Ma asked about the boys and suddenly I had an idea. Perhaps bringing the children to see them would help them forget the tragedy for some time at least.

On Sundays Rosie took the morning off to go to the church of the Sacred Heart. I would bring the boys and let them play here for an hour or so. They both adored the children and it might divert their minds, even bring some comfort.

The following Sunday I put the boys in the car and Ahmed drove us to the flat. Ahmed carried Zubin up the stairs and I followed with Cyrus. They were sturdy children and weighed quite a bit. I rang the bell and Ma came to the door with her usual defeated look, which changed to astonishment and delight when she saw the boys. They stretched out their arms to her at once and she carried them both inside.

When Papaji saw them, he smiled for the first time in days. Ma put Zubin his lap, and he hugged the child, stroking his soft hair affectionately.

I spread a rug on the floor and put the children down to play. They were soon crawling vigorously all over the room and trying to pull themselves up by holding tables, chairs or even Ma's sari or Papaji's pyjamas. If they managed to stand, precariously balanced, even for one moment, they were delighted, and when they fell back with a thud, they continued to beam, as though they had done something very clever. For the first time in a while I heard the old people laugh, and I was really delighted.

I said, 'I need to do some shopping. Can I leave them with you? I won't be too long.' They were pleased. 'They can be very naughty and can't stay in one place for more than a moment,' I said.

'We are not doing anything. We will look after them until you return. They are happy with us.'

They did not glance in my direction as I left quietly. I had no qualms about them being all right, but I was worried about the strain on them. So far, as therapy, it had been more than successful.

After the first experiment I brought the boys frequently, to the evident delight of my in-laws. They looked forward to the visits and Ma had even been out shopping to buy small toys for them. They appreciated most of all the huge red ball that rolled so easily and so frustratingly when touched.

skin deep

The look of despair and remembered horror began to fade from the faces of Ramesh's parents. It would no doubt return when they were on their own again, but for some time at least, there was a reprieve.

Ramesh, on the other hand, continued to go around with a stony expression on his face, his head held rigidly, his body moving stiffly, as though unused to movement. He blamed himself for allowing the marriage, and therefore held himself responsible for Sunita's death. But what was done was done. It was time for us to get on with our lives without allowing her death to cast a permanent blight over everything.

Once the practice had been started I continued to send the boys over to spend time with the old people. Once a week they went, and all through the years in Delhi, as they grew up, they continued to visit at least once a week, right up to the time we moved to Dehra Dun. This created a strong bond between the boys and their grandparents, which was to last and improve with the years. My mother-in-law told me that it was what kept them sane and prevented Papaji from breaking down completely.

Jung claimed that most people suffer from what they consider the aimlessness and senselessness of their lives. They feel that nothing really matters, and they lose faith—both in the religious sense and in the purpose of life.

Papaji no longer read from the Bhagvad Gita each morning, and he felt as if he had been permanently set

233

apart from others. He hardly spoke at all, but once he said to me that if Sunita had died in some natural disaster, he would have mourned, but not have felt this burning rage, this desire for revenge. At night his dreams were filled with anger and despair. It was not the way he should feel, he knew, and it had destroyed his peace and his belief in the ultimate goodness of God.

When we left to settle in Dehra, Sunita had been dead for more than seven years, but still it lay like a sore that would never heal. Now he waited for death, but without any hope that he would meet his child, his little girl, in another, better life. All he wished for now was to fall gently into darkness and never wake up again.

He began to be constantly ill. There were breathing problems which caused him to gasp for air, there was constant pain in his back which prevented him from moving freely, and there was pain in his chest and arm, running up to his neck. Ma now spent all her time looking after him.

twenty

One is tempted to remember events not wholly or in their entirety, but in flashes, as though through a half-screened window. Sometimes I drift through these memories like a sleepwalker who feels that waking would be far more terrible, and that sleep is the only escape possible.

I had known almost to the exact day when their affair began. It was when I had told Yasmin to leave, that she could no longer continue to stay with us in Delhi. It was then, possibly, that that the idea lodged itself in her brain. A fitting revenge for being forced to do as I asked. After all, she was something of an expert in this and initially, for her at least, it was nothing more than a bit of extra spitefulness. Since Bobby was dead, she was all alone; we should have been feeling sorry for her and trying to help by letting her stay with us as long as she liked, or even forever. My ultimatum that she leave both angered and upset her plans. It was not that she was preparing to fall in love with Ramesh. But who can explain the curious alchemy of sex? Perhaps she had never met anyone with his shyness, his tenderness, his lack of subterfuge or his wonder at the beauty so freely offered.

She had only three days, but that was enough. Surprisingly, while seducing him, she too fell in love, although it was the last thing she had either wanted or expected. That Ramesh too fell in love, whatever those words may mean, was less surprising.

With me he had known where he was. He may not have been in love with me, but he was utterly satisfied with the way things had worked out. Our unspoken and only half-acknowledged agreement had worked well for both of us—our marriage was a success. We liked and respected each other, and if I was in love with him, my love did not in any way intrude on either his work or his life. We could always count on each other. He discussed his work with me and I helped him with contracts, legal work and anything else that was not only necessary, but absolutely vital to his success. He was aware that without my help— unobtrusive though it was—he would never have got this far so quickly. It was my money that often smoothed the way for him and gave him choices he would not have had otherwise.

The fact that they had just three days together only served to increase their passion. He never really understood what had happened. Yasmin was so beautiful. She could have had any man and it was amazing to know that, for some extraordinary reason, she had chosen him. Being a man, it did not strike him that what he was doing was disloyal, or even dishonourable.

When she left, smiling and triumphant, I knew this was only the beginning, and that they would meet again.

As soon as the house in Dehra Dun had been completed, I took the boys there and moved in. Ramesh decided that he would keep the flat in Delhi and commute every week or so. He would come and go as he pleased, and it suited me very well.

I loved the house, built especially for me—a private, secure and wholly pleasing world of my own—everything that I had ever dreamed of.

From the very beginning I had known that they were having an affair. They wrote to each other, even if they were both in Delhi. I knew, because I spied on them. I am not afraid to confess it. He seemed to have no knowledge of subterfuge—or perhaps he was so bemused, that it never occurred to him. Her letters to him were often hidden quite simply under a pile of clothes, or more often, in the inner pocket of a suit. After a few days they disappeared, probably destroyed after he had read them over and over again, the words indelibly imprinted on his heart.

When he came to Dehra to be with the boys and me, she would often ring him when she thought I was in the bath or in the garden, or with the boys. I intercepted letters, listened in on telephone conversations when possible, and was prepared to let the affair run its course. Yasmin had so far never had an affair that lasted for any length of time. I was prepared to wait and let him return to his senses and come back to me—never, for a single moment, had I anticipated that he would want to leave me and the boys to marry her. After all I had done for him. Yes, it was a well-worn cliché, but it was true. If Ramesh Verma was now well known, with an enviable reputation as an architect— if he was greatly in demand and making a lot of money— it was all because of me. I had cushioned and bought his way to the top. And yet he would rather leave me and marry Yasmin.

There were separate rooms for Rosie, who had a very special place in my life and was now in charge of everything. Absolutely devoted to me, she only tolerated Ramesh because in a sense, he, too, belonged to me. It was she who brought me the letter which was to change our lives forever. Instead of being sent to the office, it had somehow been directed to the house. I had no hesitation in opening it. I knew Yasmin's handwriting as well as my own. Although I burnt the letter, even today, after all these years, I can recall every word.

My dearest darling,
Your letter made me wildly happy. At last, after all

these months and years we will be together forever.
I can't tell you how I have longed for this moment.
I have lived only with this hope. Although it does
not really matter to me if Naaz divorces you or not,
but for you these secret meetings, these brief
clandestine moments together are hateful and
demeaning. You say you do not anticipate any
problems with Naaz, and that you have only waited
so long because of the boys. Now that they both are
in boarding school, you feel there will be no
objection to the divorce. I, however, feel very
strongly that Naaz will create problems. You don't
know her as I do, even though you have been
married for over twelve years. She is possessive,
jealous and capable of violence. I cannot see her
letting you go without a struggle. But together, we
can face anything.

I never thought I would love anyone as I love
you. It was you who pulled me out of the shadows
into a world that dazzled my eyes with its colour
and beauty. You say you plan to speak to her on your
next visit to Dehra. Be very careful, my darling. I
cannot help being fearful of what she might do.

I read the letter twice, and then folded it up tightly in
my hand. Rosie stood watching me, anxiety in her eyes.
'What does she say?' she asked.

'They want to get married. He is coming up to ask me to divorce him.'

Her voice was horrified. 'A divorce! What about the boys?'

'There will be no divorce,' I said firmly. 'But I must think about this before he comes. I must have a plan. At least now I am forewarned.'

I had already made up my mind. Over the next few hours and days, I considered my options. I was consumed by all the emotions of love, jealousy and despair. After having achieved a certain happiness—after having been so deeply involved with another that I saw much of the world through his eyes, I was now faced with being abandoned in a forest of darkness from which I must now make my escape. I reminded myself that I was fighting not only for myself, but also for the boys.

I found it difficult to sleep. Often I would wander around my room inhaling the cold night air and feel the wind that swept through the town, ruffling the feathers of night birds.

My mind spun back to my lost childhood, the years when only Grandma was there to hold my hand. If there was a divorce because of Yasmin, the bitterness, the pain, the anger and despair would be more than I could bear.

I now had to face a situation in which I would be alone once again—plunged into a world in which, once again, I was the loser.

I saw my life with horrible clarity. Slowly, carefully, brick by careful brick, I had built a life for myself and I was not going to let anyone or anything take it away from me. Certainly not Yasmin. It would have been humiliating enough to have Ramesh leave me for any woman—how much more it was when that woman was Yasmin!

Ramesh had said that this time he would be coming for a long weekend. So, obviously, this was the time he felt he could tackle me.

I thought of all the days and nights we spent together in happiness and comfort—the conversations, the slow awakening in the mornings after making love, the expectation of years stretching before us—a whole lifetime of being together. All gone—all destroyed, because he thought he was in love with Yasmin.

The wind was rising. Perhaps it would rain tonight. At other times I loved to hear the rain as I lay snug in bed. Often the rain could be heard and seen first in the forest— the thick belt of sal and pine trees under the hills. I would stand out on the terrace, still flooded in sunshine, and watch the storm approach. First the hills darkened and the trees began a slow moaning and shivering as the rain hit them. Slowly the rain came closer, across the river bed and over the house tops, before it hit the terrace, forcing me to dive inside, locking the doors and windows against the crash of thunder, the raindrops hitting the flagstones and flying up with the impact. I loved these storms, but tonight I felt threatened.

I did not want supper but Rosie brought me a tray with soup and sandwiches. She stood quietly while I ate my frugal supper. Before leaving the room she said, 'Don't worry too much. Think quietly and decide what has to be done. Whatever you decide will be best for everyone. Sleep well.'

She was right. This was not the time to panic and give way to despair. I had been through too much to have disaster strike so unexpectedly.

The next morning I visited Dr Kamal Prasad. I had found him fortuitously when Cyrus had slipped and cut himself right in front of Dr Prasad's clinic. Cyrus never cried, but the cut was deep and filled with gravel and dirt. He was limping with pain. The clinic was small but spotlessly clean, and when the young doctor appeared I took a liking to him instantly. He was a burly young man with hair that seemed to stick up around his head, and a smile that was both gentle and reassuring. Cyrus climbed up on to the table, the wound was cleaned and bandaged, and a tetanus injection administered without any fuss.

'How did you come?' he asked.

'We were out for a walk. I'll ring for the car.'

'No need, I was just closing up. I'll drop you back.' He told us that he was new to the town—he had come from Agra and had only just set up his practice. He was a GP who had specialized in heart ailments. He said, 'I was astonished to find that almost every young man in the corporate world had incipient heart problems.' He said he had as yet very few patients, but he was cheerful and confident about the situation. I felt safe and happy with him. He was professionally good, his manner comforting and gentle, and he soon became our doctor. I called him in whenever needed, and he was quite prepared to make house calls after clinic hours. I spoke of him to our friends and soon more and more people were happy to call on him for everything from children's minor ailments to more serious afflictions. When Ramesh suffered his first heart attack it was young Dr Prasad whom I called in.

Ramesh insisted that the pain in his shoulder and arm was a simple strain, and certainly not a heart attack. Ramesh, like many young men, had a long-standing distrust of all doctors and considered himself fit and healthy. 'I have never had a day's illness in my life,' he said smugly.

Dr Prasad smiled and continued with his investigations, which included an ECG. He was calm but firm. He said it was indeed a heart attack, and the tests showed he had suffered a mild attack previously. But there was nothing to worry about. Rest, medication, and most of all, a relaxed attitude would see him safely through. I promised to see that Ramesh took his pills and relaxed as much as possible.

I went to see Dr Prasad the next morning. As always, he was pleased to see me.

'It's about Ramesh,' I said. 'He is coming up this

weekend and I thought you might give him another check up. Last time he was here he was complaining of pain in his arm, vertigo and a pain at the back of his head. His blood pressure, he said, is still very high.'

He smiled at me reassuringly. 'I'll drop in and see him. Is he taking his pills? Not insisting that there is nothing wrong with him except indigestion?'

I laughed. 'When he is here I see he takes his medication, but most of the time he is in Delhi and I really don't know how conscientious he is.'

'Well, that is really the trouble. He does not want to acknowledge that there is something seriously wrong. You'd be surprised to know how many of my male patients behave in the same way. But not to worry—I'll give him a proper check up.'

Ramesh arrived by taxi just before lunch. He looked tired and uneasy. He went to his room for a wash and came out, glancing about him as though everything was new to him. I gave him a cold beer and he sat down, stretching out his legs and sighing.

'Delhi is boiling hot. You are lucky to be in Dehra, and this house is a good five or six degrees cooler than the town.' He said suddenly, 'You know, I never really realized how much you have been doing here. It is almost as though you run an additional office. So many of my papers and blueprints are still here.'

'Yes, I know. But it is much more difficult now that I am in Dehra and you are in Delhi.'

He nodded absently. 'I don't think you will need to keep the office here much longer. I am planning to shift everything to Delhi. The new secretary is very efficient. I feel she will be able to take care of everything.' He paused and looked at me. 'Have any of my letters been redirected here by mistake?'

I shook my head. 'No. Why should they be? I thought you had given clear and precise instructions about your correspondence?'

'Mistakes can happen.' He looked at me intently, but I met his gaze blandly. Outside, the warm green spaciousness of the garden stretched around the house. Suddenly Ramesh put his glass down with a clatter. 'Naaz, I must speak to you. It is very important.'

'In a minute. I'll just take my cup into the kitchen.'

'No. I must speak to you now.'

So here it was at last. The moment I had been dreading and anticipating, and still hoping would never happen. Had I survived all the pitfalls and bomb craters to have it all blow up around my ears now, in one massive explosion? And for what? For something he would no doubt call love.

'What is it?' I asked finally. 'Has something gone wrong with the new contract?'

'It is nothing to do with work,' he said impatiently. He looked at me intently, and now I returned his gaze. What do we know of the thoughts of others? What can we read that is concealed behind the shallow, reflecting eyes, the skin and bones that guard the dark jungle of a complex mind? What lies behind the sexual appetites and preferences of men that blinds them to all else? To loyalty, respect, gratitude and concern for their children?

At last he said, bringing out the words flatly, without emphasis, 'I'm in love with Yasmin. I want to marry her. I want you to divorce me.'

I removed my spectacles and rubbed my eyes. He was looking at me miserably, making no attempt at excuses. After a silence which seemed to last forever, I said, 'But you hardly know Yasmin. How can you want to marry her?'

He mumbled, 'We have been seeing each other for the last two years. I wanted to wait till the boys were in boarding school so that it would affect them less. I love her, Naaz. Oh God! This is much more difficult than I expected.'

'And what did you expect? Good old Naaz. So reasonable. So understanding. I suppose you have been having an affair, and you think it is love. Yasmin can be very persuasive. She simply can't bear to see me happy. What if I refuse to give you a divorce? And how does the fact that the boys are in boarding school make it any better for them?'

He sat with his hand half shielding his face, and I resisted a desire to pull it away and strike out at him. At last I said, 'I will never divorce you. I see no reason for it. Just because you are infatuated with Yasmin does not mean you will enjoy being married to her.'

He said, 'You don't know her as I do.' We stared at each other in silence. At last he said, 'Think it over Naaz. Let's behave in a sensible, civilized manner. We can still be friends. I know how much I owe to you—I will never forget that. But you are so clever, resourceful, independent. I am here for two more days. Please think it over. Please, I beg of you.'

I did not reply, and he rose from the chair, his hand knocking over the glass. He did not even notice as he walked out of the room.

So I had a few more days, and however hard I try to remember them, they seem blotted out of my memory. Days, hours slipped by, morning merging into night and then again into morning. We met over meals, but I remember nothing. I was too busy planning my strategy. I would make sure there was no divorce. Happiness, for me, had been the security of a two-person universe—a togetherness more important than sexual desire.

It was his last day and as usual, we had dinner together, again in total silence. Then, suddenly, he put down his knife and fork and said, 'Naaz, you haven't said a word since I asked you for the divorce. I must know what you have decided.'

I marvelled that I could keep my voice so calm and soft, so totally without any inflexion.

'I have given it a lot of thought, and yes, you can have the divorce. You can go ahead and marry Yasmin.'

His face expressed a mixture of astonishment, relief and guilt. He said warmly, 'I knew you would come around to it. I told Yasmin you would not make any difficulties—you are too generous, too sensible, and I admire you even more. If there is anything I can do for you, you must never hesitate to ask. Don't think I am not grateful for all that you have done for me. Without your help in the beginning I would never have achieved what I have in these years. I appreciate everything you have done for me, and for my family as well. Ma will be devastated when she hears the news; no daughter could have been more loving and affectionate, or done more for them.'

I said, 'Before I file for divorce, there are some things we need to settle, specially about the boys.'

He was smiling with relief. 'Of course—I have no desire to take them away from you. They can come to me in the holidays. Yasmin loves them already, and was talking about taking them to Italy or Paris in the vacations. She has lived abroad and knows these places well.'

I would have liked to scream, but I kept my voice soft, remembering how Grandma had controlled everyone and everything without ever raising her voice. I said, 'I have given the matter a lot of thought. After the divorce, neither you nor Yasmin will see, or have access to, the boys again—at least not until they are twenty-one years old. If there is to be a divorce, my first concern is for the boys. I do not want them to grow up torn between the two of us. If there is a complete break, and they never see you again, it will be easier for them to adjust and to forget. Once they are grown up, they can choose.'

His face slowly turned pale, as though the blood was draining out of his body. He did not really believe what he was hearing.

'Naaz, you can't mean what you are saying. You don't really mean this—you can't expect me never to see my boys again, or to relinquish my rights and interest in them. You can't stop me from seeing them.'

'I can, and I will. This divorce is not my idea, nor do I want it. But if it is inevitable then my first priority is to protect the boys from insecurity, conflicting emotions, and of having anything to do with Yasmin.'

He was rigid with rage. Kipling's lines ran through my mind—'But his hand was loose and weak, and the blood had left his cheek.' His skin had turned grey, drained of all colour, and the muscles of his face seemed to sag. This is how he would look perhaps, when he was old.

'Naaz, you can't do this. I will not permit it. If I were to challenge you in court, there is not a judge in the whole of India who would prevent me from having access to my sons. I absolutely refuse to even consider this.'

'You want to fight this in court? I thought the whole idea was to have this divorce by mutual consent. But if you are thinking of fighting it in court, then I must warn you that I will release to the press a long and very detailed list of Yasmin's lovers, some of them quite well known. Through the years after Bobby's death, I made it my business to keep track of her many affairs. It was not too difficult—she never tried to keep them secret, and for me it was a sort of insurance—a safeguard, in case she tried to harm me or my family. I have a detailed list of names, dates, places. It will prove how very unsuitable she is to take care of any children, and more especially, my sons.'

He was clinging to the arms of the chair as though if he let go he would fall. He stared at me as if he had never seen me before. I said, 'You know me too well to think I am making all this up. Did you really think you were the first after Bobby? Or even the second or third?'

He opened and closed his mouth, but no words came out. Although he was now a well-known, even famous architect, he was still in many ways a typical small-town Punjabi male who took it for granted that all widows led chaste, self-effacing lives, and wished only to live as quietly and unobtrusively as possible wearing plain cotton saris and no jewellery. Ramesh, if he had thought of it at all, never considered that Yasmin was a widow. She was just Yasmin incredibly beautiful and incredibly desirable.

For quite some time he continued to stare at me as though he had lost the ability to say a single word. Finally, I got up to leave. There was no point in sitting and staring at each other in silence. At last he said, 'And what about Ma? Have you thought of her? She adores the boys. They are her lifeline to sanity—if she can't see them it will break her heart. Their visits to her in the holidays make it possible for her to live. They give her so much uncritical love—if she loses all contact with them, I shudder to think what could happen.'

I repeated once again, 'It is not I who wants this divorce. I'm going to bed. Think about it and give me your decision in the morning. The taxi has been sent for at 8 o'clock.'

He was still there when I got up and left, his face ashen, his eyes staring. Rosie was waiting for me in my room, the unspoken question in her eyes.

I said, 'Now we have to wait and see, but I do not think there will be any divorce.'

Maxi, who had been waiting for me, jumped up on the bed and was told sternly by Rosie to get down. With a resigned sigh, he lay down on the rug beside my bed.

I had done all I could to save my marriage and protect the boys. I did not think there would be a divorce. Whatever noble sentiments Yasmin had proclaimed in her letter to Ramesh about her indifference to whether they could get married or not, I was absolutely certain, knowing Yasmin as I did, that her whole strategy had been to get Ramesh to the point where he was so enamoured and smitten by her charms, that she could force him to ask for a divorce. Why else had she wasted two whole years with him? Oh yes—

she was in love with him, but she had been in love many times before. Her revenge would be perfect if she could get him to marry her. He was now a very rich man in his own right, and there was no longer any need for me to subsidize or help him in any way—so she would achieve two things—getting him away from me by marrying him, and at the same time acquiring enough money to live comfortably for the rest of her life. I could imagine the sense of triumph she would have been feeling even now. But she was right to have been wary of what I might think up to foil her plans. Ramesh would never agree to a divorce on my conditions, and now that he knew about Yasmin's numerous lovers he would feel that it was neither necessary nor wise. They could continue their affair, but since Yasmin's entire ploy had been to get him to marry her, this would not work. She needed the public triumph of marrying the famous architect Ramesh Verma, who was (and this was the most important of all) her sister's husband. Thwarted of this, she would in all probability leave Ramesh for a more suitable partner.

twenty-one

I suppose I must have slept, but some types of sleep are worse than no sleep at all. I opened my eyes, and felt even more tense and physically depleted than before. Rosie was standing there with the tea tray.

'What time is it?' I asked, pushing the pillows back and sitting up.

'Just after six. I brought tea a little earlier because Sahib's taxi has been ordered for eight.' She poured tea for me and added a drop of milk. 'I'll take the tray into his room.' I nodded and continued to stare out of the window. It was a clear day, but I felt a shiver run over me. I had played my hand, and it was a strong one. Ramesh would be angry, resentful, perhaps even feel thwarted. He would be thinking not only of losing the boys, but also about Yasmin and her many lovers. He had been dealt multiple blows last night, and they had struck home. He, too, perhaps had slept badly, if at all.

At that moment Rosie came rushing in. 'Come, come quickly. Sahib is sleeping and not waking up.'

I snatched up my dressing gown and thrust my feet into my slippers. Only a very small, narrow corridor separated our rooms. He was lying very quietly in bed as though still asleep, but the very stillness made me pause at the door and look around. Everything in the room was as it always was. Ramesh was excessively neat. Clothes were never thrown around or left lying about. His wallet and keys were on the bedside table as always. The sheet was neatly turned over and tucked under his chin. Ramesh had insisted that his room be furnished with a certain amount of austerity— he did not want Persian rugs on the floor or curtains and cushions that were velvet or satin. But for all that, it was a comfortable room with expensive teak-wood tables and dressers glowing with polish, the curtains lined and pleated to fall in elegant folds. The pale walls were covered with framed photographs and pictures of buildings, most of them designed by Stein.

I put my hand lightly on his forehead and drew it away as though it had been scorched. His skin was cold, deathly cold. His eyes were closed, and he looked peaceful, and at peace with himself.

I said to Rosie, 'Call Dr Prasad. Ask him to come as soon as possible.' I pulled up a chair and sat down beside

skin deep

the bed. If it were possible to feel nothing, I felt nothing; it
was as though a vacuum existed inside me. It was the kind
of feeling one is always trying to achieve in meditation—a
blank mind, one that is not involved uselessly in thinking.

There was the sound of a car, and then Dr Prasad was
in the room, bringing with him the chill air outside and a
feeling of reassurance and competence. He wasted no time
with me but went straight to the bed, putting his hand
briefly on my shoulder as he passed. He made a slow and
thorough examination of the body. Without turning around
he said, 'Have you any idea when this happened? He has
suffered a massive heart attack. I had not really expected
this, but these things do happen.' He looked at me, but I
was incapable of uttering a single word. Rosie said, 'He
was leaving in the morning for Delhi and I took his tea in
around six. When I found him I called Memsahib.'

I listened to them without moving or saying anything.
Dr Prasad turned his attention to me. He picked up a light
shawl from the bed and wrapped it around me. He turned
to Rosie. 'Could you bring us both some really hot coffee?
She's in shock, and I could do with some coffee myself.'

I felt an enormous weariness. I should have liked nothing
better than to curl up in bed with the blankets over my
head and shut out the world. But there was too much to
do, too much to get through before the day was over and I
could make my escape. The coffee came and after the first
tentative sip, I gulped it down.

'That's better. Much better. Now we need to make some phone calls, and the first one should be to Mr Verma's parents.' Rosie brought him the number. He got through almost immediately and although I did not speak Punjabi, I understood much of what he was saying. He was telling them that their only son had died of a heart attack. There were long pauses while he listened. At last he put the receiver down.

'There are complications. Your father-in-law is in hospital with pneumonia and lung congestion. He is very sick. Your mother-in-law refused to believe that I was ringing about her son. She said he was a fine, strong young man and it was not possible that he could just die like this from a heart attack. She wants to speak to you.' I shook my head and he picked up the phone and spoke again, telling her, as far as I could make out, that I was in shock and not able to utter a word.

He said, 'She is coming up immediately by taxi and will be here as soon as possible. She will leave again soon after the funeral. Her husband cannot be left alone for any length of time. She said to tell you to get the boys out of school.' He turned to Rosie. 'Can you ring up someone—some friends of hers who could come and be with her—she needs someone with her at this time.'

'I can ring up our neighbours, the Braganzas, and the General.'

'Yes, that will do for the time being.'

I was still sitting glued to the chair when Joe and Marie

Braganza came in. They were neighbours, and good friends. Joe had retired as headmaster of a prestigious public school and Marie cultivated exotic herbs and plants in her garden. She also took care of any stray dogs and cats that been injured, or were abandoned and starving. Some were adopted, but most continued to stay with her, living happily in a large garden shed and romping all over the garden without seemingly harming the precious plants.

Sher Singh, Ahmed and Antony came into the room with flowers and candles. A Hindu, a Muslim and a Christian. And me, a Zoroastrian. I wondered what God made of this strange assortment of religions—all of them professing to believe in Him and worshipping Him in their own hugely conflicting and even opposing ways. Marie and Joe were with us very quickly, hastily dressed and full of concern.

Marie put her arms around me while Joe went to speak to the doctor. I heard Dr Prasad fill him in on what had happened.

'Mr Verma's mother is coming as soon as possible. Unfortunately her husband is seriously ill with pneumonia and other complications. But she will come nevertheless, and leave soon after the funeral.'

Joe said, 'Ramesh Verma was an important man. Word will soon get around and people will start pouring in. Perhaps even the press, though in Dehra Dun there will be less of them. We need to make all the arrangements before his mother arrives so that there will be no delay.'

Marie bent over to talk to me. 'Come, Naaz. You need to have a bath and dress before people start coming in. And what about the boys?'

Joe said, 'Naaz, shall I ring the headmaster and tell him what has happened? I can go and fetch the boys in the car. I know Peter Bailey quite well. If he calls the boys to his office and tells them what has happened, they will be better prepared. He will do it gently.' He paused and looked at me. 'Is that all right with you?' I nodded. The boys were just eleven—how would they react to this? And would it be better or worse for them to see Ramesh?

I had a quick shower and dressed. Rosie had laid out my clothes— a white and black salwar-kurta and a black shawl. I wished fervently that it was all over.

Maxi followed us into Ramesh's room. Joe said, 'I thought we could lay the body out in the drawing room and put chairs on the verandah for visitors.'

Maxi went up to the bed and began to sniff the body slowly, moving his nose carefully from the feet up to the head. Joe went to stop him, but I shook my head. 'Let him be. He is making sure that Ramesh is really dead. At Parsi funerals a dog is always brought to inspect the body and make sure there is no life still left.'

Maxi finished his careful survey of the body, lifted his head and let out a long, piercing wolf howl, which was probably heard for miles around.

Joe said, 'Good God! What was that? It sent chills up

258

my spine. He must have some wolf blood in him. I've never heard anything like it before.'

In the drawing room the body had been laid out and already there were flowers from the garden surrounding it.

I said to Marie and Joe, 'I don't want any marigolds. Anyone bringing marigolds must leave them outside the room.' Marie looked at me strangely and in some astonishment, but she nodded obediently.

I disliked marigolds which are used lavishly at Indian weddings and funerals alike, as well as at receptions, religious festivals and parties, with indiscriminate, if somewhat misguided, fervour.

All the furniture had been pushed to the sides of the room and clean white sheets spread over the carpets. Visitors would remove their shoes outside the room.

Marie said, 'Anyone who does not wish to view the body can sit outside on chairs.'

Rosie said, 'The General has arrived. Shall I bring him here?' General Firoze Nariman Sethna was six feet tall and dressed formally in an extremely well-cut dark suit. He was carrying a small bunch of white roses. I rose to greet him. Known to his friends as 'Fizz', he was one of the few Parsis who remained in Dehra. He was very fair with greying hair and light eyes that could be sharp and searching, or mild and concerned. Since his wife's death from cancer, he lived alone with four large dogs and two devoted orderlies. He held my hands in his.

'My dear, I'm so very sorry. How could this happen? Had he been ill?'

I shook my head. 'No. It was a massive heart attack.'

'What can I do to help? Do the boys know?'

'Not yet. Joe is going to fetch them from school.'

'Do you think that is a good idea? Much better leave them there till everything is over. I hope you are not planning on them lighting the pyre or anything like that— it will be much too traumatic.'

'I haven't decided. Ramesh's mother will be arriving soon from Delhi and I suppose she will decide.'

'Well I don't think it is a good idea at all. You seem to be marooned here in a sea of aliens. Not another Parsi in sight.' He looked around as if expecting to see Mongol hordes descending on us at any moment.

The General was lean as a greyhound, with a thin face dominated by a Semitic nose. Like all Parsis, he considered himself different from other Indians, if in fact he considered himself an Indian at all.

Joe came up at this moment. 'Fizz—thank goodness you have come. There is so much to do. We will need an ambulance for the body and someone to go to the cremation ground and see that everything is properly arranged. Last time I was there, the wood was all wet and we had to wait hours till more was brought. And then there was no one to prepare the pyre.'

'The ambulance and the cremation ground are easily

taken care of. What else can I do?' They left together to make whatever arrangements would be necessary. Marie was busy inside. I found myself a chair and sank into it. In India word spreads as though by jungle tom-tom, and soon the first mourners would arrive. Maxi had moved as close to my chair as possible.

Joe and the General appeared. Joe said, 'Everything is arranged and I am going now to get the boys.'

He left and the General pulled up a chair. He looked at me with both compassion and slight irritation.

'Tell me—do you believe in heaven and hell and reincarnation? Or is this the wrong time to be asking you?'

I thought of Larkin's words—'The anaesthetic from which none comes around'—but I said nothing. I have always had difficulty believing in either heaven or hell, or even in God. But if there was nothing, then why were we here at all? What was the point of this existence of ours?

'For your husband,' the General said, as though he were answering my unspoken question, 'the beautiful buildings he has created will be his immortality.' He put his hand lightly on my shoulder. 'To die in one's sleep—without pain and without inconveniencing others—is an enviable way to go. We would not fear death or dying so much, or at all, if we knew this is how the end would come.' I nodded without saying anything but I agreed with him of course. To be saved the ignominy of a life when the body has deteriorated to the point where arteries narrow and stiffen, and the heart no longer pumps blood efficiently; where there is wrinkling of the skin and loss of mobility, and worst of all, incontinence or dependence on others.

Yes, there were worse things than dying, I suppose. Marie, who had been seeing to the laying out of the body, now came and sat down beside me. 'Hello, Fizz,' she said to the General. 'Joe has gone for the boys. I've asked Rosie to bring us all tea. Or would you rather have coffee?' she said.

'No, tea will be just fine. I think the first of the mourners have arrived.'

He got up and went to greet them, and I sipped the hot tea slowly. How would this affect me and the boys? Ramesh's death would change everything. But at least I would not be worrying about how it would affect me financially. I had seen too many women whose husbands had died cry, shriek and sob, not so much with sorrow, but due to fright and anxiety about what would happen on the financial front. Soon the boys would be here and then Ma would come, bringing with her the paraphernalia for the prayers and the puja to placate the gods and to ensure safe passage into a better world.

Maxi heard the car before I did. He pricked up his ears and tore down the stairs. When the door opened he flung himself on the boys and his high yelps, interspersed with short barks mingled with the boys' laughing admonitions. At last he quietened, and all three came slowly up the stairs,

Maxi's tail wagging as though it would never stop. Joe smiled at the three of them. I stood up and put my arms around the boys, holding them close.

Zubin said, 'Is he really dead? Could the doctors have made a mistake?'

I shook my head. 'It was a heart attack. No one expected such a massive one. He died very quietly, in his sleep.'

'How can you know?' Cyrus asked. 'He might have been in pain.'

'He looked very peaceful, and the sheet was folded neatly under his chin. The doctor thinks he died immediately,' I said.

Zubin said, 'Can we see him?' I nodded. 'Take your shoes off.' We entered the room together. Someone had put on a tape, which played softly in the background. The scent of roses mingling with the incense produced a peculiarly funereal atmosphere. Zubin continued to hold my hand but Cyrus went forward, and kneeling down, kissed his father gently on his head and then on his cheek. Zubin looked at me enquiringly. I nodded encouragingly. He too knelt down, but then laid his head on Ramesh's body and sobbed quietly.

I waited without making a sound. At last they stood up and joined me. Cyrus said, 'Is Dadi coming?'

'Yes, she'll be here soon for the prayers and the funeral. She will return as soon as everything is over—Papaji is very ill.'

No one else was in the room. White sheets has been spread over the carpet for anyone who wished to sit beside the body.

Marie came in and whispered, 'Your mother-in-law has arrived with the pandit.' I turned to go out and meet her, but she came inside. Looking around, she went straight to the body. She seemed to have aged twenty years. Her normally round face was now gaunt and grey. Her hair, usually knotted sleekly, was rough and uncombed. Her eyes, sunk deep in dark sockets, saw only the body, lying so still and lifeless on the floor. Tears gathered in her eyes and trickled down her cheeks. She wiped them away with the back of her hand. Sinking to her knees she laid her head on Ramesh's chest. The boys wanted to go to her, perhaps to join her as she mourned silently, but I held them back. At last she got to her feet and looked around at us.

'I have brought everything necessary for the puja. We should start right away.'

Rosie brought her a cup of tea and we persuaded her to sit down and drink it. The pandit, a young man who seemed in his early twenties, started bringing everything in, helped by Sher Singh and Ahmed. They set it all up quickly—the deep container for the fire, the thin sticks, the incense, the water and the flowers.

The fire was quickly lit and the boys and I joined her as the pandit began his prayers. I have no clear recollection of how long the whole thing took. The fire was fed with sticks, water was poured into our palms, and from time to time we sipped it as instructed. Marie and Joe were in the room but not as part of the ceremony.

When it was over, Ma began at once to prepare for the cremation. The General confirmed that everything was ready, and they began to strap the body on to the hastily prepared bier made from bamboo poles, before sliding it into the ambulance. We would follow in cars.

Ma came over to where I was standing with the boys. She said, 'They know what has to be done?'

She looked at the boys. 'They will light the fire when everything has been made ready. Both the boys together?'

Zubin, who had been standing beside Cyrus, said firmly, 'I'm not lighting anything. I am not coming to the cremation. I will stay home with Rosie and Maxi.' He looked very small and his face was white, but I knew that once Zubin had made up his mind nothing would change it. Ma looked absolutely aghast, but the General came forward and intervened smoothly. He looked at Cyrus enquiringly, and Cyrus gave a small, almost imperceptible nod of his head.

He said firmly, 'There is no need for Zubin to come. It will only make him sick.'

We piled into cars and set off in a convoy. The traffic at this time was fairly heavy and began to hold us up, so the journey seemed interminable. It was a scruffy place—a clearing in a patch of ragged trees, with pigs rooting in the undergrowth and a tap dripping dirty water on the path. The General had been true to his word and everything was ready. The body was unloaded, removed from the bier and laid on the logs.

'Do you want his face covered or uncovered?' Joe whispered. Cyrus was standing between his grandmother and me.

'Covered,' he said firmly. Joe looked at me and I nodded. Cyrus looked very small, but he took the flaming stick, and accompanied by the pandit, thrust it into the logs. They had been primed with ghee or oil, and in seconds the whole thing was alight, the flames roaring sky-high. Everyone stepped back and Cyrus leaned up against me. I put my arm around him, holding him close.

Joe said, 'You can leave after another five minutes; your mother-in-law wants to leave as soon as possible. Fizz, the men and I will wait till the end. They will also collect the ashes tomorrow. Go home now, we will follow later.'

Ma was only too glad to get away. We found Zubin fast asleep on the carpet in his room, cuddled close to Maxi. Rosie sat beside them, sewing placidly.

The taxi was waiting, already loaded and ready to leave. Zubin woke up in time to say goodbye to Ma, who was in a hurry to get back. She took time, however, to pat Cyrus on his back and envelop him in a tight hug. 'Bahadur beta,' she said, patting him on his back.

Zubin said, 'Is it over? Is it all over?'

Cyrus said, 'Yes, it's all over. The others are still there—they will wait till the fire burns out. We came back first because Dadi had to leave.'

Zubin said, 'So where is Daddy now? Where has he gone?'

I said, 'I don't know. I don't believe he is anywhere except perhaps in our hearts, where he will stay as long as we remember him.'

Zubin said stubbornly, 'I believe in heaven, and he has gone to heaven. He was a good daddy.'

I was prevented from any further reply by the arrival of the General, Joe and Marie.

'That cremation ground is a mess. Trickling black water, pigs rooting about and all sorts of odds and ends hanging around. I must say Indians have no idea of either cleanliness or sanctity. Naaz, has your mother-in-law left?'

'Yes. I don't suppose she will get to Delhi till about midnight. It is just as well that she has that pandit with her.'

'What I need is a really stiff drink,' the General said.

I looked at Marie appealingly and she said to Joe, 'Come and help. I'll get the glasses and you get the bottles—in that cupboard there. What about the boys, Naaz?'

'They are staying the night. I'm just about to ring Mr Bailey.' The boys watched me silently. I wanted them here with me just as much as they needed to stay with me. They could return to school early tomorrow morning. I went inside and picked up the receiver. I got through straight away when I gave my name.

'Mrs Verma? I can't tell you how sorry I was to get the news of your husband's death. Is there anything I can do for you? Cyrus and Zubin took the news well, although they seemed a little stunned. Are they all right?'

'That's what I am ringing you about. It has been a terrible shock for them, and I wondered if it would be all right if I kept them overnight with me here and sent them back tomorrow?'

'It will be perfectly all right, although I promise you that when they return they will be treated with very special consideration Being with the other boys will take their minds off what has happened.'

'The work Mr Verma was doing was of immense importance to India. You must expect the press as soon as word gets around.'

'I will be closing up the house and leaving for Mussoorie as soon as the boys are back in school,' I said. 'I want some time to myself and to get away from everything. Except for a very few friends, no one will know where I am. If the boys are allowed out next weekend, I will send the car for them—will that be all right?'

'I think it is an excellent idea, and yes, the boys can join you for the weekend. If there is anything I can do to help in any way possible, please let me know.'

Both boys looked at me as I returned. I nodded reassuringly. 'It's all right. You can stay with me tonight.'

Zubin smiled brilliantly at me, and with Maxi in tow they both left to find Rosie and give her the good news.

They were all holding glasses of whisky when I sank into a chair and sighed. Marie poured me a small brandy and topped it with water. She knew how I liked it. 'I will send the boys back tomorrow before leaving for Mussoorie.' They all stared at me in astonishment.

'I need to get away for sometime before the news gets around. I need time to myself and my cottage in Mussoorie will be just ideal. Not too many people know about it and it is not easily accessible. The servants, of course, will have to be told, but they are very reliable.'

'Will you need security guards when you are away? Or is that hound of yours sufficient? I must say I had no idea you had a place in Mussoorie.'

'It was bought long before I was married and Ramesh said it was structurally very sound and didn't need much changing. We put in new electrical wiring and new bathrooms and double glazing on all the windows. I have a couple who look after the place and the garden. The hound, as you call Maxi, will come with me and so will Rosie. I'm sure Joe and Marie will keep an eye on the place for me.'

Joe said, 'Of course we will. I think it is a wonderful idea. You have our telephone number and if you need anything just give us a ring.'

Marie put her arms around me. 'What about the boys?'

'I spoke to the headmaster. They will come to me at weekends. I'll send the car for them.'

'Bailey agreed?'

'Yes, he seemed to think it was a good idea.'

'Will wonders never cease? He's actually breaking his own stringent rules. I think we should all go and leave Naaz to rest. She looks absolutely exhausted.'

The General said, 'Are you sure your staff will look after everything? If at any time you need me don't hesitate to ring. You have my telephone number? Day or night, just give me a call. Can't help feeling worried about you.'

'I'll be fine. I really just need to get away from everything for some time. It's lucky I have the cottage in Mussorie to escape to.'

After they had left, I went to find the boys. They were having supper, and Rosie had cooked their favourite food—scrambled eggs on buttered toast with fried tomatoes and sausages.

'Come and have something to eat with us, Mummy. Rosie says you haven't eaten a thing all day.' Zubin said.

I sat down with them and accepted a plate of toast fingers topped with creamy scrambled eggs. I was not hungry, but the eggs and a cup of hot coffee made me feel much better.

'We will sleep in your room tonight so you won't feel

lonely,' said Zubin, who seemed to have recovered his usual high spirits.

Cyrus said, 'Mummy needs to sleep and her bed is not big enough for all three of us. Besides, you kick.'

Zubin giggled. 'All right, we'll just come in to say goodnight.'

I was sitting on a chair, looking out of the window at the dark sky when they came in with Maxi. They had changed into pyjamas and were smelling of soap and toothpaste.

'Will you be all right in Mussoorie on your own?' Cyrus asked.

'Mummy likes being on her own, don't you Mummy?' Zubin said.

I smiled. 'Come on, lets all get into my bed and tuck up while Zubin tells us a story.'

'No. You tell us a story about when we were little,' said Zubin.

They piled into bed with me, and Maxi leapt up too and stretched himself across our legs, although he knew perfectly well that he was not allowed on beds.

I put my arms around them. I said, 'I don't feel like telling stories tonight, but I remember a time when you were both three years old and we were sitting on the terrace, looking down at the garden where Daddy had put concealed lighting, so that the flowers all looked pale or white and the leaves gleamed and shone as though polished.

And suddenly there was a power failure and as we were plunged into total darkness. Zubin's voice rang out, loud and indignant—"Where garden gone daddy? Where garden gone?"'

The boys laughed and I joined them. Cyrus said, 'That has the genuine Zubin touch.' Zubin cuffed him and they fell over me and each other while Maxi barked encouragingly.

They had somehow managed to slide right off the bed and I said, 'Bedtime. Rosie will wake you early so you can have breakfast before leaving.'

There were many hugs and 'goodnights' said before they left, Maxi in tow.

twenty-two

I fell asleep almost immediately but woke up in the middle of the night. It was dark, but not entirely so. A faint luminosity, reflected from the light on the porch, filled the room. I no longer felt fuzzy and confused as though nothing made sense. My mind was crystal clear. So Ramesh was dead, and once again I would be alone. But not completely alone—I had the boys and a whole new life—a life that might have been threatened, even destroyed, if Ramesh had gone ahead with the divorce. The boys would have been traumatized and unhappy, far more so in fact than by his death. And for me, of course, it would have meant humiliation and despair. The society pages would have had a field day—I could just see the headlines—'Famous architect marries wife's twin sister'. There would have been photographs of us both—Yasmin posing prettily in some clinging outfit, and I, plump and plain, glowering at the camera.

Father had a favourite phase which he used constantly and which often drove Sophie mad—'Everything happens for the best,' he would announce smugly after some minor disaster had caused his family to grumble or bemoan their fate.

Still lying in bed, the darkness enveloping me like a cloak, I could not but feel that there was something to be said for these words after all. Perhaps what had happened was indeed for the best. I felt suddenly at peace. There was an absence of fear or anxiety about what had happened, and what would happen. My mind, which had been going around in circles, was still and silent, and there was power in that silence. I no longer felt guilty or insecure. I had been responding predictably to what had happened, with feelings of guilt and anger, reactions automatically triggered by circumstances and people. Whatever happened now would be good for my small family, and good for Ramesh's family too. There would be no scandal, no trauma, no publicity, no blaming anyone. The situation was not of my making. I would accept things as they were, and not as I would wish them to be.

For a long time I lay awake, freed from the burden of defensiveness, resentment and fear. When, at last, I slept, it was peaceful and without dreams.

The boys were already eating an early breakfast when I

awoke. They looked at me anxiously, and whatever it was that they saw in my face, it made them feel better.

Cyrus said, 'Rosie feels we should be stoking up before going back to school, where they feed us cold porridge and soggy toast.' Both of them thought this was very funny, and I could not resist smiling back.

'Hurry up,' I said. 'I want to get away to Mussoorie before any visitors arrive. Once you have been dropped off at school I'll be able to leave.'

'You are taking Maxi with you, aren't you?' Zubin asked anxiously.

'Yes, of course. I can't do without Maxi and Rosie.' The children smiled in relief. They went off happily enough, knowing they would be visiting me in Mussoorie at the weekend.

As soon as the car returned we piled in—Rosie and I in the back seat, Maxi in the front beside Ahmed. Maxi behaved beautifully in the car, sitting up straight and looking out of the window. I had told the servants to lock the gates and to tell no one where I was.

It was early enough for the roads to be deserted and once we were clear of the town and climbing, the air smelt fresh and green, of herbs and wild flowers and greenery, instead of petrol and diesel. As we continued to climb, the valley fell away below us, spread out like a great green tapestry on which the sun made patterns.

I leaned back and closed my eyes. They were expecting us at the cottage. I would stay as long as was necessary. I felt curiously free and without responsibilities, accepting things as they were, relinquishing the need to convince or persuade others of my point of view.

The cottage stood in splendid isolation, and I would be assured of absolute privacy. From the rooms one could see an immensity of sky and hills and dark forest, and hear the ceaseless susurration of the wind.

The first sight of the cottage always had a calming, soothing effect on me. Lakshmi and Bhim Singh were there, but without the usual welcoming smiles. They had, of course, heard the news—the death of a husband or father is possibly the worst tragedy that can happen to a woman in India.

Maxi was first out of the car, sniffing the misty, pine-scented air with remembered delight. I followed more slowly, and while the car was being unloaded I wandered inside, found the old rocking chair and collapsed into it with a sigh. I closed my eyes and wished I could stay like this forever.

All fairy stories have 'happy ever after' endings and this is the biggest fairy tale of all. The concept of happiness as part of a private consciousness, independent of culture, people and surroundings, is utterly misleading. We are all shaped and moulded by the psychoculture which has formed us and which precludes any hope of being happy in isolation. The self is diminished when it seeks happiness only for itself.

Buddhism advocates achieving a state of 'awareness' in order to reach that part of the mind—what Auden called 'the centre'—which is mostly inaccessible. When I opened my eyes, I saw the garden through the open window. I sat there, staring silently, till I began to recognize distinct patterns of leaf, wood and flower. I noticed a clump of arum lilies growing wild against the trees. The sight triggered off the memory of a visit to Ootacamund with Father and Sophie when we were children. An old film, long forgotten, now played back in my memory.

Father loved Ooty, and each year the four of us went up for a month to escape the terrible heat of Hyderabad. Grandma refused to come with us, claiming that her rooms were cooled very efficiently by the khus screens which were sprayed with water from time to time.

After years in India, Sophie still found things to amaze and astonish her. Looking out of the window of the little train that took us up from the plains to the hills, the Swiss engine pushing the train from the back, she was astonished and outraged to see a herd of fat cows, chomping away happily in a field of arum lilies—lilies which she associated with church altars, candles and votive offerings. She thought it scandalous, if not blasphemous, to permit cows to chew on these sacred lilies.

Father only laughed. Arum lilies grew wild in Ooty,

and it was best to keep them down by grazing, he said. Yasmin and I loved the little toy train which chugged so bravely up the steep slope. We passed English cottages with names such as 'Alderly', 'Hillgrove', 'Runnymede' and 'Innisfree'.

We always stayed at the Savoy, where there were thick quilts on the beds and fires in the grates even in summer. In his houndstooth jacket and cavalry twill trousers, Father might easily have been taken for one of the last Englishmen to frequent these rooms. He was a member of the club, that snooty and starched core of British hill stations, created by regimental pukka sahibs, to which no Indians had been allowed. Children were only permitted in the grounds outside, and never inside the sacred precincts of the club.

I loved the look of the fluted pillars, the gabled portico and the huge brass dinner gong which gleamed like gold in the sun. '7400 feet above sea level' proclaimed a sign. The same white-jacketed bearers who scurried around with glasses of beer and whisky brought us chota hazari in the mornings—tea for Sophie and Father, cups of hot chocolate for us.

Although children were not allowed to go inside, in the early hours of the morning, when no one was around, the bearers would allow us to enter the lounge with its heavy leather sofas and leopard and tiger skins spread on the parquet floors. Because the formidable club secretary, Major Courtney, was not around, we even ventured into the dining room, where tables were being laid for lunch, the menus bearing the club's crest—a huge sambar.

Two hundred years of colonial rule had left its imprint on everything in India. For us Indians, nothing would ever be the same again. Like most Parsis of his generation, Father thoroughly approved of the British and felt, in many ways, they had been beneficial for India, providing good governance and a fair and just judiciary. It was only after Independence, he said, that we messed things up and descended into controlled chaos.

Father did not deny that the British were, on the whole, arrogant, condescending and racists of the first order. But he maintained that they did have among their officers those who loved India passionately and were absolutely fascinated by this vast and immensely diverse country. 'While the majority of British officers could say little more than "Qoi Hai" in Hindi,' he said, 'there were others who studied not only Hindi but Sanskrit and Persian as well. Do you know that William Jones translated the life of Nadir Shah from Persian and also portions of the Vedas, the *Manu Samhita* and the *Gita Govinda*? He was one of the first Englishmen to learn Sanskrit which he compared, in its construction, to European languages, thus leading to the theory of a common Indo-European language. And James Princep, an Indologist, helped to unravel India's past. He did what no Indian had ever done so far, he deciphered the Brahmi and Kharoshti scripts so that the famous Ashokan edicts could be read. These Englishmen did us a service by bringing the past of a conquered country to light.'

I was fascinated by the stories Father told us about the intrepid British explorers and surveyors in India. How thrilled he was when I chose James Princep as the subject for my PhD . . .

All this triggered off by the sight of a clump of Arum lilies! Scientists confirm that even the vaguest memory is of vital importance in forming our personalities and enriching our lives with complicated personal remembrances. Without memory we can turn into zombies, treading a world that seems to be inhabited by alien tribes.

When Nabakov wrote his autobiography, *Speak Memory*, he was confirming a truth that we take a lifetime to learn: it is memory that defines our lives.

Rosie had finished getting my room ready, and brought me a cup of coffee and a biscuit. 'Why don't you go and lie down for a while,' she said. 'It will do you good.'

I shook my head as I sipped the hot coffee. 'It's fine here—I like looking out at the garden and sniffing the air, which smells flowery—no particular scent, just an amalgam of all the flowers in the garden.'

I could hear Maxi scuffling through the leaves and rushing off with excited barks when he found something. Somewhere in the background, there was the sound of cymbals and bells and chanting. I looked at Rosie questioningly. She said, 'Bhim Singh tells me that a new ashram has been opened on the hill across the road. We can hear the sounds of singing only because everything is so quiet here.' Now, if I listened carefully I could hear 'Hare Krishna, Hare Krishna, Krishna Krishna, Hare Hare.' I wondered if it was a locally run ashram, or one of those places run by devotees from abroad—those strange blonde men and women who wore Indian clothes and danced in the streets. I have never been able to understand such dedication, such belief and such fervour expended on Krishna, the divine cowherd—or in fact on any other divinity including Zoroaster. However, unlike Rosie, who was outraged by this 'heathen' intrusion into our tranquil surroundings, I did not find the sound too obtrusive or unpleasant.

Although I was still very tired—I had been consumed for too long by all the emotions of love and jealousy—my mind and heart were now at peace. No longer did I feel that nothing was real except through the eyes of another. As I watched, the day began to relinquish some of its colour and warmth, like an artist obliterating colours from his canvas, forcing me to turn away from dreams of perfection and live only in the present.

Every night before I slept, Lakshmi would come into my room with her bowl of warmed mustard oil, and her small, surprisingly strong hands would massage the oil into my back and legs, relaxing all the tension that was held there and producing a feeling of fluid warmth, softness and peace. The oil was rubbed so deeply into the skin that only a faint sheen remained, and I could pull on a nightie and fall blissfully into a deep, undisturbed sleep.

The boys arrived at the weekend, brought up by Ahmed in the car. They entered tentatively, as though not sure what they might find, and smiled brilliantly to find me in the kitchen making cheese toasts for them instead of sitting and staring into the distance. Rosie had finished grating two cups of cheese and I was engaged in whipping up the eggs with mustard and chilli sauce, before stirring in the cheese to make a thick sauce. I allowed them to pile it on to squares of brown bread, while Rosie heated the oil. They helped to fry it, lowering the squares carefully into the oil, cheese side down and then flipping it over to brown the other side.

We took the toasts to the verandah and the boys had a contest to see how many toasts they could consume as rapidly as possible. Maxi too had his share, but he did not grab and waited politely till he was offered something.

'Mummy is not eating anything,' Cyrus said.

I smiled. 'I'm not really hungry. I'll join you for a Coke.' Rosie had just brought in the chilled glasses, and I poured some for myself.

Cyrus said, 'Have you had any news from Delhi?'

'No. Papaji is out of hospital but still feeling very low. I thought I could ask both of them to come and spend some time in Dehra, and then when you come for weekends, you could cheer them up.'

'That's a really good idea. Will they come?'

'I think they just might. Specially if they knew they would see you at weekends.'

I was really concerned about my in-laws—my father-in-law had never really got over the death of Sunita, and now the blow over Ramesh's death was almost more than he could bear.

Zubin said, 'It is too hot to go outside. Let's see what we can find in here to play with.'

I heard them rummaging around in the bookshelves. When the cottage had been restored I had brought up some books, and lots of old magazines, including *National Geographic* and some others.

It would keep them happily occupied for some time. I was considerably surprised therefore, to see them come through he door, bursting with excitement.

'Look what we have found,' Cyrus said, holding out a book to me. 'We haven't seen this in years.'

He was holding a slim book with the picture of a very large brown bear on the cover. The bear was wearing a hat, a coat and carrying a hunting rifle.

'It's Horace,' Zubin said. 'Do you remember Horace, Mummy?'

I did indeed remember Horace very well indeed. I had started reading to the boys when they were barely one year old. They would sit quietly, one on either side of me, cuddled up close as I read to them. However fractious, busy or involved with other things they were, the moment they saw a book, they staggered over to be lifted up and placed on either side of me as I sat on the sofa.

Ramesh was both amused and incredulous. 'They are too small to understand a word you are reading. They can only say two words themselves. What will they get from this?'

'They love it,' I said. 'They quieten down if they are crying, and drop whatever they are doing when they see me waiting to read to them.'

By the time they were three years old they were taking a very active part in the reading—choosing which books they wanted to read, and identifying pictures and words. Cuddled up close to me, they often could turn the pages at the correct point, although they could not read.

Ramesh would leave whatever he had been doing and come and join us. He would stretch himself out on the divan and listen with interest and often amazement to the stories I read aloud. No one, he said one day, had ever read out stories to him when he was a child.

'Horace' had full page colour pictures and very little text, but the story, though simply told and brief, was 'unusual'. I use the term for lack of anything more appropriate or suitable.

Horace was a very large brown bear with a benign

expression on his face. He lived with his family, which consisted of Grandpa, Grandma, Pa, Ma, Paul and Little Lulu.

Every day Pa put on his hat, his coat with the leather patches, picked up his gun and went out hunting. On his return, Horace informed him tearfully that he had eaten Grandpa.

'Pa was just wild and said, "I will kill you Horace", but Horace took on so, he hadn't the heart to do it—and the next day, Pa went out hunting.'

On successive days Pa goes out hunting and returns to find that Horace has eaten Grandma, Ma, Paul and Little Lulu, and each time Horace 'takes on so', rubbing furry paws into tearful eyes, that Pa hasn't the heart to kill him. Finally, Pa too disappears and Horace, wearing Pa's cap and coat and carrying the gun, goes out hunting. The ultimate bit of black humour is a picture of Horace, tearfully laying wreaths on the six graves.

The illustrations were irresistible. Ramesh, who had been listening to the story, was outraged. He sat up straight.

'For heaven's sake. Is that the kind of story to read to three year olds? It is dangerous and subversive. Naaz, what can you have been thinking about when you bought them this book?'

I did not reply, but passed him the book. He stared first at the cover, where Horace was looking very fetching in Pa's coat and cap, and then slowly opened the book and began to read. The boys and I watched intently. By the third page a glimmer of a smile appeared on Ramesh's face. He read slowly, and as he reached the last page he burst out laughing. The boys started to laugh too. They patted the picture of Horace, cooing over it.

'Nice Horace,' Zubin said. 'I wish we had Horace.'

Ramesh shuddered. 'Thank heaven for small mercies. Where did the book come from?'

'I really can't remember whether I bought it, or whether someone gave it to the boys.'

The boys were delighted with their find. They pored over the book, which had somehow reappeared in their lives at just the right time. They turned the pages, smiling and often laughing aloud.

'Can we take it back to school with us?' Cyrus said.

I was seriously alarmed. 'Good heavens, no. I think Horace should stay safely here. You can always read it when you come home from school.'

Reluctantly, they agreed. But at regular intervals through the day and when they were resting after lunch, they returned to Horace. Death, dying and loss were very far from their thoughts.

twenty-three

A day before I returned to Dehra, I sent Rosie down in the bus to open up the house and have it cleaned, aired and dusted. It was raining when we left—a thin, silent rain, blown by the wind into flurries which spattered against the rolled-up car windows. From time to time a gust of wind flattened a wet leaf against a window pane, rousing Maxi to give a startled growl. Bushes and roadside trees bent and swayed in the wind. The road was often narrow and steep, with sharp curves which turned on themselves, making driving risky for a careless driver. But with Ahmed driving I had no qualms, and felt confident enough to close my eyes and relax my head against the back of the seat.

One of my favourite quotes has always been, 'Traveller, there is no road. The road is made when you walk on it.' We carve out our own destinies, although luck, and the lack of it, do have an influence. I have never believed, however, that our lives have been preordained and that everything depends on karma or the stars. We make our own road, travelling through complex avenues and surrounded on all sides by trials and tribulation. There is no help from the gods, which we ourselves have created, and which have no reality beyond the reality that pure, unquestioning belief provides.

The belief that man is free to plot his own destiny is part myth, part reality. Things can happen over which we have no control— we only have control over how we deal with these events.

I could acknowledge now that Ramesh's death was perhaps not as huge a tragedy as I had first thought. It was, on the whole, better for me, better for the children and better for Ramesh's own family. The divorce would have torn our worlds apart.

As we arrived in Dehra the rain stopped, and the sun began to dry everything up rapidly, like a very efficient hair dryer. They were all there, waiting for me with welcoming smiles—Rosie, Sher Singh with his wife and fat poker-faced baby, and Antony. I was surprised at how pleased I was to see them all.

Maxi, as usual, was first out of the car, and greeted everyone exuberantly before dashing off to look for monkeys or other exciting entertainment.

The first thing to catch my eye as I entered the house

was the pile of mail lying on the table. 'So many letters,' Rosie said. 'But first come and sit down and rest, and I will get you a cold drink. These flowers are from the General, and there is something also from the Braganzas. They said they will come after you have rested.'

It was good—very good—to be home. I did not miss Ramesh or expect him to be around, because his visits from Delhi had not been too frequent, and I was accustomed to being on my own.

All the apprehension and depression was gone. I had come through a very trying, even tragic period, with not too much damage to either the boys or to me.

By the time Yasmin appeared, I had settled down to a new, quieter, more private life, but one which suited me perfectly. Yasmin's visit, only half expected, was a disruption, nothing more.

Looking at her now, strolling aimlessly in the garden or sitting and staring into her cup of coffee, as though trying to read the future from the dregs while lighting yet another of her interminable cigarettes, I wondered what she could have found to do when she married Bobby. They could not, surely, have partied from morn to night. For her, reading was not an option—it bored her—and she was not interested in cooking or sewing, or any of the other numerous activities with which women were traditionally supposed to occupy themselves.

I had known that Yasmin would arrive eventually in

Dehra, to confront me, and to learn what had happened .
How had all her well-laid plans simply dissolve into
nothing? She would not rest until she discovered what had
happened, even though it was now too late.

From the very beginning I had planned my response to
her questions. Yasmin would want to know how and why
Ramesh died, and what had ensued before his death. She
would not rest until she had dug up every little detail. But
for my part, I had absolutely no intention of even admitting
that he had asked for a divorce, or that I had known of
their affair. My plan was to deny everything.

Now she turned to me and said explosively, 'How could
they have married me off to Bobby without knowing
anything about him?'

'They knew he was heir to all that money,' I said drily.
She crushed her cigarette out in the painted, blue ashtray,
stabbing it down repeatedly, as though she was trying to
kill an insect.

'It was all Sophie's fault. It was she who arranged the
whole thing. She persuaded me that Bobby was the ideal
choice for me.'

'Sophie knew absolutely nothing about either Bobby
or his father. How could she? It was Grandma who made
all the arrangements. Sophie and Father approved, of
course. How could they not? He was very, very rich, young
and handsome. And he had khandan! What more could they
possibly ask for for you?'

'They could have found out if he was a man! He was absolutely impotent. That beautiful face and body. It meant nothing—he didn't want a wife, what he wanted was a mother. His mother! He simply adored that fat mother of his, and she doted on him. On our honeymoon, even I, young and innocent as I was, realized there was something wrong. Every night at precisely nine, he rang his mother and they would talk for ages. He was never so animated with me. At the end of the call he would hand me the receiver and say, "Ma wants a word with you", and then her voice, raspy and somehow threatening, would whisper, "You take good care of my boy, understand?" It sounded to me like some Mafia threat.'

I couldn't help laughing. 'Was he gay?'

Yasmin shook her head impatiently. 'How would I know? At that time I didn't even know such things existed. All I knew was that he was a Mama's boy, and sex with me, or with any other woman for that matter, was difficult, if not impossible.'

'The marriage could have been annulled,' I said.

'Yes, I went back to Sophie, expecting support and help. All she said was "everyone has their own cross to bear, and this could be yours. You must learn to make the best of it. After all there are other compensations."'

'But what about Father? Didn't you talk to him?'

'Oh, Father! When did he ever concern himself with us, except to read us those extraordinary stories of wars

291

and invasions which glorified the British? And he was having recurrent heart attacks, and Sophie guarded and protected him as though he were made from the most fragile glass. My news, unwelcome as it was, would probably have brought on another heart attack. I found my own solution——what Bobby couldn't give me, I found with other men.'

She looked at me defiantly but I said nothing. I was well aware of Yasmin's need to attract. I had often watched her, even when she was a child, open up in the presence of an attractive male, like those Japanese paper flowers that bloom miraculously when dropped into water. Her skin, her hair and her eyes seemed to take on a luminescence, her mouth a deeper, more seductive curve. She plunged into a series of blatant and highly publicized affairs. She made not even the slightest attempt at camouflage. She wanted the world to know.

I said, 'I thought that all those lovers of yours would have showered you with jewellery, even given you some blue chip shares which would have lasted you a lifetime.'

She turned on me furiously. 'I only slept with those men with whom I was in love. I suppose that sounds very strange to someone like you——so cold, so calculating. You simply would not understand what it means to be romantically in love with a man.'

I smiled. 'No, I confess, I know absolutely nothing about what you refer to as "romantic" love. Like something out of a Mills and Boon novel. How you devoured those paperbacks when were in school. You can hardly expect a reasonably intelligent human being to behave as though love is the only, or even the chief interest in life. Even you cannot possibly believe that the glow of passion lasts for ever.'

To my surprise, she laughed instead of being annoyed.

'Oh, you! How did Ramesh ever stand you for more than a few minutes at a time. You are always so right. The luckiest thing that ever happened to you was finding someone like Ramesh. He was so kind.'

She paused, and a shadow seemed to flit across her face. Her eyes darkened, as though the grey had somehow turned to black, and it was obvious to me that she was maintaining a precarious self control. She pulled up her chair close to mine and sat staring into my face.

'After Ramesh died,' she said slowly. 'They told you, didn't they, that I came up here, but the house was locked and there was no one here except the servants. Even Rosie wasn't here. The servants seemed to know nothing, and when I questioned that lawyer chap of yours, he merely said you had gone away for an unspecified time, and that no letters were to be forwarded. I told him I was your sister and that the matter was urgent, but he just said he was sorry, there was no way he could help. What happened to you? Where did you go?'

'I had gone to Mussoorie, to my summer cottage, to

get away from everything and everyone. I needed some time to myself. Of course my lawyer knew where I had gone, and so did the servants. Rosie was with me and so was Maxi. I suppose you saw all the write-ups in the press. I had no idea you would come tearing up here—why should I? Sophie had been informed, but she didn't come. Why should I have expected you? Why on earth did you come without informing me? You were the last person I expected.'

She glared at me. 'I had every right to come up. Oh, not because of you.' She paused, as though trying to make up her mind. Finally, she got up and stood by the window, her back to me, staring out at the Mussoorie hills, now as pale and insubstantial as a mirage. Without turning around she said in a flat voice, 'I was in love with Ramesh.'

'One of those romantic loves that you seem to experience so easily.'

At last she was angry. 'There's no need to be so damned smug. Ramesh was in love with me too.' She broke off abruptly, afraid that she had said too much, but all I did was to continue to smile, infuriating her even more.

I said, 'What nonsense you talk, Yasmin. I suppose it gives you some kind of perverse pleasure. Just because you couldn't bear to see how happy we were together. All your life you have had everything your way. You were not brought up to compromise or to take anything but centre stage. Few things could have been more irritating or demoralizing for you than to see yourself sidelined and ignored.'

'Oh God! You are so smug. I tell you, Ramesh was in love with me—desperately in love. He wanted us to go away together, but he felt the boys were still too young. He said he also had obligations towards you. I could never understand why he was so fond of you and grateful for what you done for him. He said that without your help and constant support he would never have got where he had. But for all that, he still wanted to marry me. He didn't like those secret meetings we were forced to resort to, or the clandestine affair that lasted so long. He wanted everything out in the open, and he was planning to ask you for a divorce so that we could get married. For some reason he wanted your consent. He said he knew you well, and that if things were properly presented to you and explained, you would be reasonable. And then—when he had come to Dehra Dun to ask for the divorce, he died. Just like that—he died.'

I looked up at her, no longer smiling. 'So what is it that you are trying to say, Yasmin? I knew Ramesh as well as I knew myself. He may not have been passionately in love with me, or I with him, but for all that we had a very good, solid relationship based on something far more enduring than romantic love. He was simply not interested in other women, even when they ambushed him at parties. His work and his family were all that mattered to him. He would never have done anything to endanger that.'

'I don't expect you to believe me, but he wrote many letters to me.'

I became very still——a deathly, preternatural stillness, in which I wondered if Ramesh had really been so stupid as to write letters to her. Was he even capable of writing love letters?

I said, as calmly as possible, 'I should like to see them.'

She flushed. 'As it happens, I destroyed them. Ramesh asked me to destroy them, and I always did as he asked.'

'How very touching. And what about your letters to him? I presume you wrote to him as well?'

'I don't know. I have no idea what happened to my letters. I wasn't here when he died. I had no access to his belongings.'

She stared at me as though trying to gather the courage to say something more. At last she said, 'In his last letter to me he said he was now in a position to ask you for a divorce—— the boys were in school and he felt certain you would understand, and that everything would be all right. And then, before he could return to Delhi and to me——he died.'

I was no longer smiling. 'Yasmin, are you perhaps suggesting that Ramesh did not die of a heart attack? That in fact there is something suspicious about his death?'

She was frightened now, but she stuck to her point. She said, 'It was certainly very convenient for you, and knowing you as well as I do, I could believe anything. You were only six when you tried to kill me.'

I sighed ostentatiously. 'I knew that when your marriage with Bobby ended so disastrously, you envied and resented my happiness and the stability of my marriage. But even I never thought that your frustrations and distorted imagination would come up with something like this. There is no mystery about Ramesh's death. He had already suffered one heart attack—you obviously didn't know about it, and he didn't tell you. He was on medication with instructions to take things easy and relax. The doctor's certificate said that Ramesh had suffered a massive anterior myocardial infarct. Perhaps you need to see a psychiatrist.'

She was very pale as she turned again to face me. She said, 'There was something else. Ramesh was aware of my financial condition and he wanted to help. He said he would transfer a sum of money which would free me, for some time at least, of any financial difficulties.'

This time my astonishment was genuine. 'You can't be serious. Are you asking me if Ramesh has left you some money?'

'That is exactly what I am saying. Have you been through his papers? I asked in the Delhi office and they knew nothing, so it must be here.'

'There is nothing here. How could there be when you have made up this whole business?'

Yasmin continued to stare at me. She said at last, 'When Ramesh arrived here to ask you for a divorce, what happened? What did you both do?'

I had a fair idea of what was going on in her mind. Having fallen in love (as she would put it), she had tried to

297

use Ramesh's infatuation for her, to the utmost advantage. She knew how enamoured Ramesh was with her, enamoured enough to break up our marriage and ask for a divorce. She had felt confident of the outcome. Death had not entered her mind. It had never occurred to her that I was not the only obstacle.

I had planned to give Ramesh conditions for the divorce which he could not, and would not, accept. It had shocked him to the point where he was incapable of speech. First, losing the boys, and then the knowledge of Yasmin's multiple lovers. It was a terrible shock. He had no doubt that it was true—he knew me better than that—and he would never get over it, or even adjust to it.

When I was plotting my strategy, I had considered that although he would not press for a divorce under my conditions, he might still continue his affair with Yasmin. But for Yasmin this was not an option; her whole objective was to get a divorce. It was essential—the ultimate public triumph over me, which she could flaunt to the world.

She had planned and schemed so cleverly, and she could not understand what had gone wrong now. She refused to believe that Ramesh had come up for the fateful weekend and not mentioned the divorce. It infuriated her that I continued to deny any knowledge of the proposed divorce.

'When Ramesh came here on Friday, did he say anything about me?'

'No, why should he? He was tired after the journey, and after a cold beer, I took him to see the new greenhouse which he had designed, with automatic sprinklers that operated at regular intervals depending on the ambient temperatures outside. I was charmed with the whole idea. The garden is my passion and Ramesh was aware of this.

'I really can't remember what else we did. He was scheduled to have a check-up with his doctor, but somehow that didn't happen. A few friends dropped in, we had a quiet lunch and since the taxi had been ordered for eight in the morning, we had an early night. Much the same sort of weekend that we usually spent together.'

'And he said nothing about asking you for a divorce? Nothing?'

'I'm getting a little tired of this. I have no idea what you think you can gain from this nonsensical fabrication. If you thought it was one way of getting a little extra money, forget it. Ramesh never had the slightest intention of ending our marriage. After all, the boys meant so much to him, and he valued the stability of our relationship. Is this why you came up to see me? To tell me a cock and bull story about Ramesh wanting to marry you? Yasmin, I really feel sorry for you. What will you do now? Go back to picking up men on every street corner?'

'I was in love with Ramesh,' she said.

'Love? Everyone means different things when they use

the word. I have no doubt you thought you were in love with him, but he was committed to me.'

I will never forget the look of defeat on her face when she turned away. Against the finality of death, there is not much that can be done. She turned around and slowly walked away.

It won't be long now before she leaves—tomorrow, perhaps, and I can resume my quiet days of seclusion and study. Yes, study. I have decided to research and perhaps write a book on Father's great British heroes.

Yasmin will no doubt return to her life with a succession of men who give her what she most wants—comfort and freedom from financial troubles. As she grows older, this will become increasingly difficult, and for the first time I have discovered that I no longer envy her and her spectacular looks. Learning this has taken a long time.

There was a storm at night, thunder crashing in deafening bursts and lightning flashing and streaking across the sky. Yasmin did not come down from her room for supper, and I sent up soup and sandwiches with Rosie. She had always been afraid of storms, cowering under the blankets while Sophie told her there was nothing to be afraid of. Maxi too does not like storms, and I let him jump up on my bed and huddle against me.

Tomorrow it would be fine, the air washed clear of pollution, the leaves glistening in the pale sunshine. Staring out of the window, I wonder, did I intentionally create the confrontation which brought on Ramesh's fatal heart attack? Was I unconsciously, or even consciously, hoping it would happen?

It is a question I prefer not to answer.